THE *FOLKS*
THAT LIVE
ON THE HILL

KINGSLEY AMIS

THE *FOLKS* THAT LIVE ON THE HILL

Kingsley Amis

HUTCHINSON

London   Sydney   Auckland   Johannesburg

© Kingsley Amis 1990

All rights reserved
The right of Kingsley Amis to be identified as Author of this work
has been asserted by Kingsley Amis in accordance with the
Copyright, Designs and Patent Act, 1988

This edition first published in 1990 by
Hutchinson

Century Hutchinson Ltd, 20 Vauxhall Bridge Road,
London SW1V 2SA

Century Hutchinson Australia Ltd, 20 Alfred Street,
Milsons Point, Sydney, NSW 2061, Australia

Century Hutchinson New Zealand Limited
PO Box 40–086, Glenfield, Auckland 10, New Zealand

Century Hutchinson South Africa (Pty) Ltd
PO Box 337, Bergvlei, 2012 South Africa

British Library Cataloguing in Publication Data

Amis, Kingsley, *1922–*
 The folks that live on the hill.
 I. Title
 823'.914 [F]
 ISBN 0–09–174137–8

Set in Linotron Sabon by Deltatype Ltd, Ellesmere Port, S. Wirral
Printed and Bound in Great Britain by
Mackays of Chatham PLC, Chatham, Kent

To
Peter Quennell

ONE

Bunty Streatfield poured boiling water from the electric kettle on to the bowl of dried apricots destined for tomorrow's breakfast. The water left unpoured made a fierce whooshing noise on the element when she set the kettle down. Overhead the strip lighting went on with its giant-mosquito whine, and just then the dishwasher entered the throbbing, growling part of its cycle. Even tiny kitchens in quite small flats were no longer the quiet places they must once have been.

Shutting the door on this one with the necessary bang, Bunty came out into the eating part where Piers Caldecote sat at the scrubbed pine table, at least it looked like pine. He was smoking a cigarette and reading the evening paper in a tolerant, uncommitted sort of way. At Bunty's approach he plopped his half-finished cigarette into the mug of tea he had taken half a dozen sips from.

'Ah, you're off then, are you?' For reasons best known to yourself, he seemed to imply, as often when others' activities were in question, but still tolerantly.

'You'll be going out yourself, will you?'

Piers inclined his head inch by inch towards the telephone. 'I may. I may. Then again I may not.' Suddenly he beamed at her.

Bunty hesitated. 'If you don't, there's some of those soused herrings and some tongue and stuff in the fridge. And . . .' She hesitated again.

'And, put them back when I've taken what I want and jolly well clear up after me a bit. But of course. Say no more. Stand on me. Now you run along, little thing. Have a good time.'

'I don't suppose we'll be late.'

'*And* . . .' He extended his neck and cocked a half-shut eye at her in a way she had once thought must mean he was drunk, but which she now knew meant he was pretending to be caring.

'. . . you're not to let that silly girl walk all over you. It's not good for her character for one thing. Nor for you my dear. The more you let her have her head, the more trouble you're laying up for yourself. You mark my words now.'

'I'll rule her with a rod of iron.'

'She might quite like that.'

'Sorry, how do you mean?'

'Forget it. Failed joke.' Then, 'You look very nice,' he called after her.

The flat had a reinforced hardboard front door which Bunty shut behind her with no bang at all. It opened directly on to a staircase with donkey-coloured carpeting, so directly that she had to hang on to the flimsy knob while she peered down into the hall and listened, not liking herself much for doing so. For the moment there was no sign of Mrs Brookes, the little old lady, in fact the not so very old but still stooped-over and awful old lady who lived on the ground floor and who was liable to start talking to Bunty on sight and at extreme range. A no-sign situation at this stage could not allow for Mrs Brookes's speed off the mark from the middle room where she mostly lurked, and a frightening number of times, like three in the year, she had been discovered crouching on the front step just as Bunty opened the house door. But this evening the way was clear, and the *Psycho*-type creaking of the middle-room door resounded too late.

The bright May sunshine in the street suffered from what Bunty had half-supposed to be a rock concert in the nearer middle distance but now turned out to be merely the output of some sort of radio playing to no visible audience from the scaffolding on the house opposite. Further along, a burglar-alarm pealed steadily and somewhere else what was perhaps another form of alarm sounded a continuous fluctuating whistle like an automaton pronouncing sorry-sorry-sorry-sorry without end. Somewhere else again a loud male voice blurted unformed syllables. And this was supposed to be a quiet suburb, handy for the centre, but still quiet. It had only recently begun to dawn on Bunty how she longed to spend even an hour or two a day somewhere that really was quiet: how older people coped with it all she could not imagine. But she knew there were other things besides, harder to define than noise, that she wanted to get away from.

She hurried down to the corner with Shepherd's Hill itself on her left, the half-dozen sloping acres of parkland that gave the district its name. Children and dogs ran to and fro on it, in and out of the lengthening shadows, and couples strolled or sat on benches. Bunty turned her eyes away and her thoughts to what sort of state the flat would be in when she saw it again. Although Piers must be getting on for forty he was no nearer being housetrained than ever, what with taps, lights, even gas, cigarette-ends, scattered newspapers, used crocks, unsoaked pans, nothing very much really but bothersome for finicky people coming in to find. He was not too bad, would often tidy away after a fashion unless something came up, as he put it, and something was always coming up in Piers's life, though he kept very quiet about what. Her guess was that it was a succession of little things, no great mystery there, just this and that, probably near the edge of the law. There seemed to be no women in his life but, in that sense, no men either. And how long did he propose to stay, or go on lodging with them, or sharing, or whatever he called it?

Actually if it had been left to her he could have stayed as long as he liked within reason. After all he was one of her only bits of family, not very close, true, being no more than Harry Caldecote's son by his first marriage, and Harry being what to this day it took her a couple of seconds to work out in her head, her stepmother's divorced husband, but still. And she had been known to be glad of Piers's company, and she would have had to admit she liked having a man round the house, even a man of a questionable sort. And there was no getting away from it, he could be very charming, for instance always ready to tell her she looked nice, and usually with better timing than just now.

She thought anyway she probably looked about as nice this evening as she ever would, going to be thirty-two in the autumn, a little tall for her own liking, a little ruddy-cheeked, but with abundant browny-red hair a few people seemed to think was quite attractive, trimmed rather short as it was nowadays and scraped back behind not-too-bad ears. The navy corduroy suit had mostly gone down all right in the past and nobody could have quarrelled with the new plain cellular shirt. Obviously a nice type of young woman, in the words of a testimonial she had once sneaked a look at.

3

Too much so? Not in a good way? She was turning right into Shepherd's Hill Road when a man of her own age began to cross towards the King's public house, a personable enough young man in collar and tie, even perhaps a nice type himself, and he eyed Bunty pretty thoroughly until they were about five yards apart, when he suddenly seemed to get very interested in the stained glass in the pub windows and doors and faded away. She was used to just that sort of double take, she ought to have been by now, but had not altogether stopped wondering about it, wondering if it could have anything to do with the look she had once or twice surprised in photographs of herself, coming upon them unexpectedly, but had never managed to catch in the mirror: a kind of joyless look, a worried and worrying look, the look of someone who without being in any way aggressive was always going to need a bit of handling, a bit of careful watching. At such times she came near guessing that her school nickname had been attached to her by way of irony, to point up her lack of easy dependable warmth and whatever other attractions might once have been expected in a girl called Bunty.

Now she was among the shops, including the bistro where the man shouted at the customers and the art place where the pictures on display really made you wonder why the artist had bothered until you noticed the price-tags on them, and reached the post office, or rather the post-office-cum-stationer's-cum-newsagent's-cum-tobacconist's-confectioner's-delicatessen-cum-video-library-cum(from next week)-dry-cleaning-establishment it had progressively but swiftly turned into. The two Asian (Indian or Pakistani) brothers who were the proprietors greeted her in their impressively informal English. 'Nice to see a bit of sun for a change, eh?' said the elder, and the younger said, 'You wait, we'll be paying for it later on.' Bunty nodded and smiled but could not think of the required next conversational move, try as she might.

Each of the brothers had a full moustache shaped like a square bracket and wore a thick dark pullover and expensive shoes; the younger's came into view when he darted round the front of the counter to put his hand on a special anniversary card called for by a fuchsia-faced old girl who carried a stick and got a 'How are you keeping?' and a 'Mind how you go now' thrown in. Bunty picked up her *Standard* and the new *Private Eye* and had her change in her hand in about four seconds. With a pleasant but slightly bland smile the older said, 'Have a nice weekend.' His brother said, 'Be seeing you soon.' She knew or hoped she knew that it was not being a misery or defeatist of her to imagine the 'What that one needs is a good screw' and the 'Sooner you than me, chum' that could follow her exit – but, she guessed, not if it could be overheard.

Off she went again, past Beautiful Dreamers now that sold nothing but beds, not even quilts, etc., past Potandum that sold wine but only a case at a time, past the house on the other side of the road where Harry Caldecote lived with his widowed sister, a rather pretty house, or rather half of a substantial Early Victorian house in white-painted stone on four floors, a lot of space for two even with a mostly-absent lodger on the top floor and a room or so in the basement that in some sense belonged to Piers. Well, Harry had done for her more than many stepfathers would have done and had gone on trying to help her after she had become no more than his ex-stepdaughter. He had been on her side when she took up with what the rest of the family had considered a thoroughly unsuitable boy-friend, and had still not stopped trying to repair what had turned out to be her less and less workable marriage to him. Anyway, they had stayed in touch one way and another until a year ago Harry had marvellously, providentially, got her into the flat she now occupied, and so they had become neighbours. It was all a little odd, though no odder, probably, than her relations with any man would have had to be. Harry had remained somehow a distant figure, book on lap in his first-floor study, seeming to hold back as instinctively as she did from the affectionate embrace that might have seemed natural to two people in their position and with their history. He was a shy man anyway, she guessed, and after all what of it? It had its good side, too; she had never managed to feel it quite natural to be close to a man in any sense, and this one had a trick of hesitating sometimes before he spoke to her, as if wondering whether she was quite up to what he contemplated saying, that helped to keep them at a distance. But from across that distance she was full of gratitude, respect, esteem, loyalty.

Anyway, it was thanks to Harry that she was here on Shepherd's Hill, and it was a nice part, a comparatively clean

5

part, even – workmen's radios and burglar alarms excepted – a quiet part, having its streets so choked with parked cars and vans that nothing on four wheels could hurry and heavier vehicles tried to by-pass it. But across the garishly painted railway bridge, where all traffic was now prohibited, the tube station promised infallible noise, noise enough and to spare. Although Bunty more or less had to use the Underground for work, she never went into its booming, battering depths without a moment or two of acute dislike. Years ago she had once seen that fear as the fear of a greater fear, but had gone no further with her analysis after that; in her experience it was very far from true that a fear was lessened by being better understood. Tonight as it happened was easier than many, with plenty of people about, no wait on the platform and something to look forward to at the far end.

That something was to be found in Chelsea, in an older and prettier house than Harry's, in Stokes Row. A blue plaque by the open front door said that Johann Christian Bach had lived there for a short time in the 1760s, and many of the paintings and drawings on view inside referred to that period. They thoroughly covered the walls of the passage that ran through the house to the garden doorway, which showed like a bright yellow-green oblong at the end of a gloomy tunnel. The sound of voices from the open air had a flat, insubstantial quality. Bunty squared her shoulders, then rounded them again to appear less tall and stepped out into the late sunshine. She hoped she had not come too soon.

There were not really so many people as all that standing and sitting about drinking out there, perhaps fewer than twenty. When they realised she had turned up, which took a few seconds, some of them stared at her briefly while others welcomed her at top speed, delighted at her arrival, not far from astounded she had been able to make it. '*Bunty* how are you?' they said. '*Bunty* you're looking well! Here's *Bunty*! *Bunty* it's good to see you!'

Of course good old Bunty was not in the least put out by any of that. It was standard, what she had heard a man call par for the course. Alternatively it was how people behaved when they were embarrassed by her and trying to be nice, which was much better than unembarrassed people not trying to be nice, but unfortunately not as good as any sort of people not trying to be anything. That had sometimes happened in the King's on a

Saturday morning. All her life she seemed to have been longing to be taken no notice of. Now she exchanged a fast hug with the hostess, who was American and the most delighted and the nearest to being astounded of all, as well as having the deepest voice and the heaviest bags under her eyes. Bunty wondered if they had met before. She looked away, noticed at the end of the small garden a sculptured and much-eroded head and half-torso almost smothered in garden ivy, concentrated on it rather than look round for anybody. 'You'll have a *drink* won't you? You must have a *drink*. Have a *drink* for goodness' sake,' they said, and generally did their utmost to talk her out of dashing off again.

Bunty soon got her drink, a moderately full glass of some fruit mixture topped with thawing fragments of ice. After another pause she started answering insistent questions about what was happening on the legal front while some of those near by told others that she was a solicitor, pretty high-powered one gathered. She had just started to feel hollow inside in a kind of provisional way when suddenly it was all right.

Much better, in fact. What happened was that Popsy simply came up and kissed her without the slightest hesitation and with exactly the right emphasis, as if she had been reading her mind. Then she said in the slightly hoarse voice and the slightly bothered or complaining tone that Bunty could never get enough of, 'Right on time as usual, darling, I don't know how you do it. And now I'm going to get you to take me away from all these lovely chaps and chapesses.'

'Oh, you can't do that,' some of them said. 'Come on, have another *drink*. Bunty's only just got here. Have another *drink*, Popsy. Oh and *Bunty*, you have another drink.'

But Popsy was quite firm. She kept smiling and pushing at the air like somebody trying to shush applause and saying it had been a marvellous party but she absolutely had to go. Not once did she give the slightest hint that she in any sense had to, or that she might have preferred to stay even a couple of minutes longer or that going was anybody's idea but hers. That kind of thing was kept for when there was trouble or competition in the offing. None of that now. Bunty felt a glow.

Not that the struggle was quite over yet. 'What about eating? Yes, what arrangements have you made about eating?'

'Oh, Bunty's seen to all that, haven't you, darling?'

'If you let us know where you're going we'll join you.'

'Oh, sweet of you but honestly we just want to sneak away somewhere quiet, don't we, Bunty?'

'Oh I see, there we are. Bit mean, breaking up the party. Well, that's it, then.'

Not long after the hostess was finally convinced that Bunty and Popsy were sure they wanted to leave, she moved attentively off with them. The three were about halfway to the garden door when a considerable silence fell over the scene they had just left, followed after a couple of seconds by an excited gabbling as though everybody had started to speak at once. Popsy squeezed Bunty's hand for a moment.

'Good-bye, darlings,' called the hostess from her time-eroded doorstep, where someone else had polished the brass boot-scrapers to great effect. 'Talk to me soon.' From the way she waved alone it was easy to see how perfectly normal she thought it was that two women should go off like that so very much on their own. But then she looked as if she thought that most things that were conceivable were also perfectly normal.

'I've booked at a new Italian place just round the corner supposed to be quite good and reasonably quiet,' said Bunty to Popsy in one breath. 'Unless of course you'd sooner — ' She would not have dared to sound so concerned in front of another.

'No. That sounds perfect.'

They turned along the river where, on the sunlit further bank, a huge building out of a 1930s science-fiction film promulgated on its tower an extinct brand-name. A few battered gulls, too stupid to have taken off downstream in the good weather, sailed peevishly about. Popsy said, 'Actually that was a pretty ghastly party. You'd have hated it, darling.'

'I'm sure I should. Was it as bad as the last one?'

'The last what?'

'The last party I picked you up at the end of.'

Bunty was very sure she would have hated the party they had just left, and the one before that too, but yet she was rather thinking to herself she would not much have minded the chance of being allowed in for an hour or so instead of five minutes to make up her own mind. She would have sworn she had done no more than think that, not let it show, but Popsy at once stopped blinking.

8

'Are you complaining about something?'

'No, honestly, I was only – '

'Because if it's a big drag for you to come from like Shepherd's Hill to Chelsea then don't bother and next time I'll go out to dinner with the others, okay?'

'I didn't mean anything like that.'

'Because everything's been so nice up to now, don't let's spoil it, eh? I had to go to that do to meet some ghastly Canadian who might be interested in the gallery then I wanted dinner alone with you. Selfish of me, but what would you? Satisfied, baby?'

Bunty nodded vigorously. She was afraid her voice might tremble if she spoke.

Popsy looked round the restaurant, which was full of little flights of stairs and entirely made of identical white-painted strips of perforated cast iron. By her expression it seemed to please her and so did the people sitting about, though Bunty had no idea of even the sort of people they were. Ten seconds with the ornate menu were enough for Popsy. She liked eating out but ate hardly anything, got through a lot of chocolate between times without it showing. 'It's nice here,' she said. 'Did you check it out yourself?'

'No, I just asked jolly carefully around.'

'Well I think it's jolly clever of you to have found it. Full marks, darling. And, by the way, it was mean of me to have dragged you across town, I realise that now. I just hope I can get you to think it was worth it.'

It went on in the same blissful style till Popsy's attention was caught by two well-dressed but berkish young men at the next table nudging each other and saying things about them to each other. She noticed at once and leaned over and said not very loudly, and in just an interested tone, 'What line of work are you in, Sammy? Sewage disposal, would it be?'

The two sat for the barest instant taking in what had been said.

'I get it, right, well if you ever feel you need a really good punch up the bracket you come right over and see me and I'll fix you up with a couple right away. Super. Sorry, my love,' she apologised to Bunty, 'but you have to make your point fast if you're going to make it at all. Now where exactly had we got to?'

The young men had not yet ordered, or at least had had no

food set in front of them. With a speed of thought and reaction that augured well for their careers in most lines of work they sprang to their feet as one and were clear away before Popsy was well into her next sentence, which went on from about where they had got to.

It was a good job she did not ask Bunty for help in remembering where wildly approximately, let alone exactly, they had got to, because she would have received none. She, Popsy, had started earlier by talking about something to do with the gallery, the Alder Street gallery where she supposedly worked, though Bunty had perforce a very poor idea of that gallery except that it was of some size and a going concern trafficking in contemporary works, never having had more to do with it than walk past it a couple of times. Popsy had forbidden her to visit her there in any capacity and though a colleague did appear from time to time it always seemed a matter of inadvertence. It was the same with other connections of hers – the occasional old schoolmate, a colleague from a former job, what might have been an ex-neighbour, once an undoubtedly genuine dull married cousin with husband and children in the background, but no part of any circle Bunty might have been invited to join. She sometimes wondered what she was to Popsy and decided she offered a handy pad and no questions asked and unlimited devotion. She hoped it would go on being enough.

What made it all much better than enough to Bunty was times like now, with Popsy on about the gallery and who knew what else and her halfway into a trance, bowled over by her continuing presence, by having her so long and so closely on view as she talked. She looked like an ethereal soccer hooligan, with a thin mouth habitually open and square separated teeth, arched eyebrows, bright wide-open brown eyes surrounded by skin of a delicate fawn, a pallid complexion, unluxuriant hair, a small frame, and was to Bunty altogether irresistible as she stood. Her accent, fitfully moderated, came from Birmingham or possibly Leicester and Bunty guessed she was about forty.

They had been sort of together for nearly two years, ever since their first meeting at a house in Hampstead after the Saturday lunchtime session at the Flask. It transpired that Popsy had been invited along only because of somebody's mistaken impression that she had been drinking with Bunty in the pub, and she had so to speak gone on from there, never saying anything much about her previous life.

But Bunty was content, in a contentment flecked with tiny moments of shame and fear. But there was no call for any of either at the moment. When they got home they found that some miracle of forbearance or industry on Piers's part had put everything in order, everything bar the extinct butt of a filter cigarette left standing upright, a great hate of Popsy's snatched out of sight just in time. The two women smiled at each other lingeringly. All was well, everything.

Later Bunty said in the dark, 'I wish we could just go away somewhere lovely and peaceful where no one would bother us.'

'But you must realise that's out of the question, darling. I've got the gallery and all my friends here in London. And you've got your being a solicitor.'

Popsy had spoken with affectionate exasperation, thought Bunty, and that was pretty restrained after having such an awful gooey remark made to her, a nine-year-old's remark. 'Oh, I didn't mean it wasn't out of the question,' she said hurriedly. 'It was just a thought like everyone gets. You know.' Not exasperation – impatience. Impatient tenderness.

TWO

'I feel responsible for him,' said Harry Caldecote rather peevishly. 'I don't like feeling it, because it means among other things I have to keep seeing him, but I do. I don't know, I keep feeling responsible for people and there doesn't seem to be anything I can do about it, I'm sorry to say. It must be the hand of Dad at work. Through early training or through the genes.'

'The way he carried on, it's certainly not through example. But which bit of Freddie's life do you feel responsible for?'

'Well, there he is married to Désirée. Isn't that enough?'

'It would be enough to drive most men mad, even men who had started off perfectly sane, but it's hardly your responsibility, I should have thought. You didn't put any pressure on him as I remember.'

'I brought them together. That's to say she was a pal of Gillian's.'

'And of yours,' said Clare Morrison, Harry's and Freddie's sister.

'We won't go into that just now if you don't mind. And then there's the poet thing.'

'Harry, I've heard you say something like this before but I've never taken it in. Are you telling me you encouraged Désirée to pursue Freddie by telling her he was a great or something poet?'

'No, what happened was I didn't do my utmost to put her off him by telling her what a lousy poet he was and how certain to be an abject failure as the writer he seemed set on being just then. A man can't just shrug off a thing like that.'

'I'd have a good try with this one if I were you. All you can sensibly say is that you may have helped to draw Désirée into Gillian's arty set that included Freddie whom she then proceeded to mark down. That was her business, and the fact that Freddie hadn't the sense or the backbone to get away from her, that was

12

his business. Not yours. Oh, before you go off, why do you keep bringing up those poems? Just how bad were they really? And remember poetry's not my strong point.'

'Well now, put it this way, if they were ballet dancers you'd have to cover up your eyes until you were quite sure they'd all finished and gone off.'

'But is there – this is just idle curiosity – could you see anything of Freddie in them? Do they sort of remind you of him at all?'

'Well, you couldn't make head or tail of large bits of them, of course, and they didn't seem to get anywhere much, you thought, and by the end he seemed to be on about something quite different from what he'd started on. And you couldn't imagine why he'd bothered to write it in the first place. But here and there there were just a few interesting little oddities. There wouldn't have been more than two or three dozen of them all told.'

'Very like Freddie, in fact. But if they were as terrible as you say – '

'Yes. Well, plenty of stuff that was just as terrible was being published then, or come to that at any other time since about 1620, but Freddie's was just right for the late Fifties. The worrying thing is that it's coming up again.'

'What? How can it?'

'Well, he was yammering something about taking up the struggle again or renewing his attempt to forge a personal diction or . . . Very worrying.'

'I'm sorry, I don't understand the point about forging a personal diction.'

'No, well, it was rather the sort of thing that poets said they were going to do in those days to show what sound chaps they were. Like . . . like giving the Hun a taste of his own medicine.'

'Oh. But I still don't see what you're worried about. If there's as much lousy poetry about as you say, a bit more can't do any harm.'

'Don't you believe it. I don't like the sound of it.'

'Well, perhaps you'll find out a bit more about it today.'

'What? How?'

'I take it you haven't forgotten they're coming to lunch.'

'Oh Christ Almighty.'

'Harry, I do wish you wouldn't blaspheme like that. For one thing, it makes you sound so old.'

'What on earth are you talking about?'

'The young don't go in for it any more, or have you stopped noticing? It's not considered cool.'

'Fuck the young, and I mean that very seriously. All right, all right. And stop sounding like a . . .'

'Like a wife. Thank your lucky stars I'm not. Not your wife.'

'Oh, I do. Frequently. And fervently.'

After two divorces (one from Gillian in the long-ago, a second from Daisy finally made absolute as recently as 1988) Harry considered he had had enough of the married state to last him indefinitely. At the same time he would have had to admit that that state had certain positive advantages for a fellow if properly handled. Many or even most of them, he would inform his circle at the Irving, seemed to be at least adequately supplied by having one's widowed sister housekeep for one. He would tell a rather smaller audience at the club that the new arrangement had certain negative advantages too. Both sets had got under way those four years ago, when within a period of six weeks Daisy had finally buggered off and poor old Arnold Morrison had finally and quite independently breathed his last. Clare had moved into the Shepherd's Hill Road house in the first place temporarily, while she looked around for a place of her own, but had found on doing so that all she could afford was a Moscow-sized room-and-a-bit in a part of Holloway where the only white people were Irish. For poor old Arnold had been feckless old Arnold too, perhaps even mildly shitty old Arnold, though admittedly expensively-nursed old Arnold must have come into it towards the end. Anyway, her parental legacy, what there had been of it, had been silently swallowed up, and most of the value of the Arnold–Clare residence had gone too. The two sons were very ready to be visited, but she was not going to impose herself on them; neither had amassed a personal fortune sufficient to set his mother up in the London of 1990, and she had never shown interest in anything like a mansion in Manchester.

'About that poetry of Freddie's,' she said now. 'It might be a way of, you know, what we've always said he needs, a way of escaping from Désirée. I mean presumably he'd have to go off on his own to write his sonnets or epics or whatever they are.'

'And have her make him go over them with her afterwards line by line. Could you read that bit again, dear. Could you explain that bit, dear. I think you could put it better like that, dear. Can't you just hear her?'

Clare shuddered. 'All too clearly. Well, we'll just have to hope for the best. Have a think about it. So: united front, try to be nice to Désirée . . .'

'. . . without making her think we want to see more of her . . .'

'. . . resign ourselves to being told all about the bit of trouble . . .'

'But we've already been told all about the bit of trouble.'

'Only a couple of times or so. And, Harry, try to cheer yourself up by telling yourself that whatever else you may be responsible for about Freddie, the bit of trouble is not part of it.'

'Just one stipulation if I may – no sneaking off to the kitchen for a kip as soon as you've brought in the coffee.'

Clare seemed not to hear that. Picking up his breakfast cup and saucer, she said, 'Piers rang while you were in the shower.'

'Oh dear. What did he want?'

'Just to establish the lie of the land as usual. No news. You know, Harry, if you're on the look-out for somebody to feel responsible for you could make a start with young Piers.'

'A start? That's a good one. I've never stopped.' Then he gave up trying to be funny and said, 'I know. I just can't get near him. Do you know, Clare, if this doesn't sound too much like somebody's auntie talking, I can remember holding out some toy to him when he was really small, two or three, and he just looked straight past it and past me too. He didn't want that toy or any other toy from me. It's been the same ever since. We just move in different universes.'

'Was he all right with Gillian?'

'I think so. It looked all right. She never said anything. I'll never find out what he really wanted today. He won't answer messages or make dates. It takes two to keep in touch, you know.'

'Well, he has just rung, and you told me yourself he was putting up with that pair of lesbians you found a flat for.'

'Clare, dear, let us be quite straightforward on one thing, I did not find a flat for those lesbians, a fellow in the King's mentioned someone was clearing out of it just that day I heard Bunty – yes, rightly or wrongly another of my supposed responsibilities – was looking for somewhere. Piers had been looking for a room at the same time.'

'He's got a perfectly good room in this house.'

'Which doesn't suit him for some reason. I don't know why. Please don't ask me.'

'All right, you're let off.'

They stared at each other for a moment and then went into the silent laugh with eyes nearly shut that they had inherited from their father. Just then the bark of a dog was heard from the garden at the back of the house, a bark and a half, a woof if there ever was one, complete with opening and closing consonants, of a pitch a good couple of octaves below middle C, accurately declaring the woofer to be of excessive size. Brother and sister looked at each other differently. Clare blinked for a space, opened and shut her mouth and said, 'Couldn't you take him to the pub with you just this once, not as a regular thing or anything, just today and perhaps once every couple of weeks? He would love it so.'

'So he well might.' At times like this Harry came about as close as he ever came to missing his second wife, though not in a tender sense. In this situation Daisy would have blinked at him much faster and told him that if he cared for anyone or anything besides himself he would have been taking poor bloody old Towser as a matter of course when he sneaked out to the pub. In their later years together at least, this would have ensured immediately that Towser stayed at home and Daisy could complain to her mates and handmaidens to her heart's content that the bloody man kept that great dog cooped up in the house and the backyard twenty-four hours a day rather than run the risk of being seen with it in public. After much practice Harry had managed to condition his mental digestive system to throw a protective film round stuff like that. Clare's stuff took more dealing with. She was good at catching him on a weak point of his, dislike of seeming a shit. Unfortunately for her in this case she had also come up against one of his strong points, resistance to having any of his pleasures taken away, spoilt or even much diminished, and one try had been enough to show that Towser did that to his trips to the King's. 'He won't settle down in there,' he told Clare now, reminded her rather. 'He keeps wandering about.'

'Don't let him. Keep him on his lead.'

'And be dragged the length of the bar. He's not a bloody sausage-dog, you know.'

'All right then, what's wrong with letting him wander a bit? He's completely harmless and gentle and he always comes when you call him.'

'I've told you, he can't keep his nose to himself. And I don't just mean he sticks it into plates of cheese, I mean he –'

'I know what you mean, thank you.'

'The most unsuitable dog in the world to keep in London.'

'You've told me that, too.' Briskly, to forestall any charges of piling on the pathos, Clare said, 'He'll just have to wait till this afternoon,' when as every afternoon since he came to live here, she would take bloody old Towser along to charge about Shepherd's Hill like a monstrous puppy, knocking down small children, making pensioners reel and clutch at their sticks, cocking his leg as near to as many people as possible, fleeing in stark terror before a savage toy poodle or feral King Charles cavalier spaniel. Far from drawing off his energy the exercise seemed to charge him up, so that on his return he was at least as ready as ever to spill things and lick things and more besides.

'I told Désirée a quarter to one,' said Clare, dropping the subject and Towser seemingly for ever and turning away.

The readiness, even cheerfulness, with which she had finally yielded on the dog question made its impact on Harry. Before he could change his mind he said, 'I'll ring them and tell them to come to the King's at half-twelve. Take the edge off Désirée a bit. And Freddie loves pubs. A pub's like an Aladdin's cave to him. I mean full of mystery and wonder as well as intoxication and such states.'

'Oh Harry that is sweet of you.'

'I'm not taking Towser, mind.'

'I'm relieved you've said that, otherwise I might have thought you were going off your head.'

He followed her out of the breakfast room with his eyes and grinned slightly. On current form he would never be in danger of imagining that her merely being his sister somehow made Clare less effectively a woman than the rest of her sex, or what was nowadays called her gender, as if like all the others she had become a noun or adjectival form in an inflected language.

17

With a sigh of pleasure and a sense of some relief – why the relief? Did he always feel some, just a tiny bit, that an encounter with a member of the opposite gender had gone off all right? – Harry moved to the large bay window on the first floor of the house, where his study was. Before reaching it he dislodged with his hip a puce-bound volume of nineteenth-century commercial memoirs that lay on an intervening table. As he stooped for it, swearing in the antique fashion noted by Clare, his glasses fell off. They did that all the time now he had bent their frames so that they no longer hurt his ears where the side-pieces went over them. Half a lifetime as a librarian had no more made him handy in such respects than it had taught him patience or exactitude. Harry Caldecote's face and figure were entirely in keeping with his trade: soft, self-indulgent, languid, but alert against any threat of exertion or inconvenience. He had been saved from overall unsightliness, indeed made quite a personable, neat-looking man by inheriting from his mother the fair colouring and slight physique to be seen to rather better advantage in Clare.

The library that Harry had long worked in and not briefly been in charge of was that of the National Historical Institute at Rokewood House in Duke's Gate. (It was characteristic of him that he must have been one of the last men alive to go on trying to call it 'Rookwood'.) He had taken an early retirement deal just ahead of the new technology, clutching what had soon enough been revealed as a barely adequate lump sum. The fate in store for him had seemed to be mild, relative penury relieved by idleness. Neither seemed to be coming to pass. He had always had much correspondence with other libraries and librarians far and near, academic, public, private, institutional like his own case, even with booksellers and auctioneers, for he stood out from his profession by being quite interested in libraries, books and associated matters. And there was the reputation, perhaps the bare name, of the Institute itself. Anyway, Harry had started to get requests for his services from all over the place.

Three such happened to have turned up that very morning. Admittedly, the first he picked up had come his way, as he soon saw, from somebody who thought he was still in the saddle in the Institute, and in any case required a demeaning chore of him like looking up a book in a catalogue. He tore that letter across with a practised movement. The second invited him to what sounded like a large public dinner in Indianapolis without any explanation, without any offer of travelling costs or accommodation expenses either. But the third, from a solicitor in Norfolk, asked him to come and advise on the scholarly importance of the considerable library of a recently deceased local bigwig. Harry could tell from here that that importance would turn out to fall somewhere between almost zero and zero, but in this instance an overnight stay was offered. Also a small fee.

Harry's imagination ranged over land and ocean to the sultanate of Brunei, which he had never visited in the flesh nor as much as seen pictured on television. Nevertheless he found he could visualise with perfect ease his generous, cultivated host there, the very considerable library of which the latter was master and its inexhaustible, truly unheard-of scholarly importance. Speeding up a trifle now, his imagination moved to his own luxurious apartments, first the well-appointed reading-room, dining-room and bar and then the even-better-appointed bedroom. And everything paid for – no fee, no annuity, no lump sum, just no bills ever. And as regards what happened in that bedroom, a unique and rigidly applied ordinance of the sultan himself forbade any contact elsewhere – no co-habitation, no form of marriage, no obligations to anybody, just . . .

At this point the dusky limbs, night-black hair fragrant with sandalwood, etc., exquisite tiny hands and so on that Harry had been fuzzily dreaming about became superseded in his mind. Again in unlibrarianly style, this time showing ability to think and move at a speed if anything above normal, he reached for the telephone on his desk, which weighed about an ounce and a half, and punched a local number, a novelty affording him some moments to himself before the ringing tone started.

A woman's voice answered quite soon. 'Maureen?' said Harry. 'Darling, would it be all right if I brought a bottle of Gordon's round at about – Who? I'm sorry, I'm afraid I didn't quite – Oh. *Who?* I see. All right darling, be in touch. I said be in *touch*.'

Wondering how he could ever have thought they had a place in his life he stared at a vertical pile of Irish annals (1852–1905) that rose knee-high from the floor. Just when Maureen might have immediately called him back the telephone rang, or gurgled metallically in the way it now had.

As one whom long years at the Institute had trained to conceal his identity whenever possible, Harry made a blurred noise into the speaking part of the telephone. He made it sound no more than broadly human.

'Harry, it's Desmond here. Is this a good time to talk?' – rather as if Harry might have been in the midst of playing the international money market.

'Yes, absolutely.'

Here is as good a place as any to remark that the voice that now went on to converse with Harry, or rather its accent, came from somewhere a rung or two down the social ladder from his, and without the least ostentation made no bones about the fact. It belonged to a certain Desmond Streatfield, Bunty's estranged husband. Harry had found him quite unlike the berkish hulk represented to him by Daisy and others, to be got rid of, pushed out of the picture and out of Bunty's life. Since encountering the real Desmond he had found him more than possible to converse with, though it was hard to imagine how he had come into Bunty's life and stayed there even the short time he had. He had never explained this, but he had managed to recruit Harry in his campaign to recover Bunty, adding one more to Harry's tenuous and unpromising quasi-responsibilities. Why and how he wanted her back God knew, but he did.

'Look, Harry, this dinner next Tuesday, I'm afraid you'll have to let me off.'

'It's not a dinner, for Christ's sake, just me and Clare and a – '

'I've got nothing against Clare at all but it makes the thing a dinner and I'm sure that's the wrong approach. You and me in the pub trying to sort Bunty out is fine but not this. She'd close up like a clam. So would I, quite frankly. Not my scene at the best of times. So I'll give you a ring probably tomorrow and we might fix to have a beer at the King's. Sorry, Harry.'

The King's. That was the sort of social bull-ring where those two would have first bumped into each other and got slung and stuck into their incongruous, absurd – what the hell could you call it? – not a relationship as anybody ever normally thought of such a thing, a mere collocation, splicing, yoke, syzygy? Perhaps he would come up with a word on his way to the place (minus Towser) later that morning. Perigee?

THREE

Chris Markou stepped smartly out of the Shepherd's Hill Wine Centre and had to wait while a silver-painted Belgian truck the size of a railway carriage passed majestically across his front between the rows of parked cars and vans, moving like a liner among supply boats for the moment but destined for a fearful traffic-blocking struggle when it tried to turn in front of the footbridge. The sort of thing that was ruining the area, thought Chris as he bounded up the couple of steps to the post office.

It was the slack time before the lunch-hour rush. A young mother in bright squalid clothes dragged and shoved her two children towards the door, cursing in a preoccupied way, and Chris had the elder Asian brother's undivided attention from behind the counter. The glass top of this bore a pile of magazines offering the true facts behind a Royal pregnancy and another of copies of a pornographic short-story collection by a local feminist writer, signed by her on the title-page too.

'Well, squire, what can I do you for?'

'Could you be a real sport and slip me a couple of hundred quid?'

'Now you just tell me why I want to go and do a stupid thing like that.'

'It'll only be for a couple of ticks till I've sold a few bottles of hooch. Old Caldecote just came in to cash a cheque. Seems to think he can use me like his bloody bank, you know, and he's the local lord or something. I suppose I should be flattered, should I, is that his idea? With the pub his next port of call and loaded with currency and only too willing to oblige.'

The younger brother was rearranging the video stand to give the horror and crime greater prominence. 'Are you saying old man Caldecote cashed a cheque with you for two hundred?'

'Well, I was low on cash to start with and then he came along and bloody near cleaned me out.'

After a pause and a sort of sideways shrug of the head the elder caused his till to glide open. 'I've always had this silly, trusting, gullible nature, right from a small child.' The tens and twenties crossed over at top speed. 'Count them, count them. And take care of them. Don't get mugged while you're crossing the street. There's some nasty foreign types have moved into the district lately. Be warned, now. Oh, two-thirty will do, okay?'

'Thanks very much, Howard.'

The name was not a jest, on Chris's side at any rate. None of their customers had once heard the brothers' original names to their knowledge. Even between themselves they used them only in exasperation or to pass off a racial slur. Except at such moments, and sometimes when their wives were present, they likewise spoke English to each other, though neither had ever read a book in the language. Quite a few column-inches of newspaper, though, and a great deal of various pamphlets.

The younger, called Charles, said when they were alone, '*Mutts* indeed.'

'I beg your pardon?'

'Thank you very mutts. A dead give-away. None of them can pronounce words like that properly.'

'By *them* I presume you mean gentlemen from Cyprus.'

'I mean Greeks. Are we supposed to believe old man Caldecote took anything like two hundred pounds off him this morning? Fifty it might be, at the outside.'

'What are you getting at, Charles? I don't care for the look of that nasty gleam in your eye.'

'Tell me, think, why does he want all that cash suddenly? To pay for something, not to put on a horse. And what's an office manager paying for that only cash will do? And the answer's not cocktail-sticks.'

'Your trouble, *one* of your troubles is you think everybody is as bad as you.'

'A short-notice delivery of what shall we say, three cases, four cases? Going for a song to clear in a hurry, before the Old Bill come round.'

'I think you've got a horrible mind. I'm surprised at you.'

'By Gad, sir, nobly spoken, I do declare.'

'Now Charles, don't you fool around, you're the one who's going all British. You're even starting to look British, you know that? Soon your eyes will be turning blue and your ears sticking out.'

'I know you mean it kindly, Howard, but I don't appreciate your saying *British* like that. Chris is British. Hardly the same thing.'

'All right, English, and where would you prefer to have come from, my lord? Kent? East Anglia?'

'They do nothing but manufacture turkeys in East Anglia. Preferably the West of England. Devon, perhaps. Cornwall. Somewhere I can get the tang of the sea in my nostrils. This way, please,' Charles called to a new arrival, a bushy-faced old gent with a literary look who was asking about typewriter ribbons at the counter. 'Do you know what group? All black or black and red?'

The shop was beginning to fill up. Quite soon Howard and Charles were hard at work behind the counter, moving like dancers or boxers as they dealt with two or three ranks of shoppers at once, thrusting articles into paper bags – white for eatables, brown for general goods – cashing up, scribbling in the ledger, clicking with the credit-card imprinter, darting round the front every other minute to put their hand on a particular pot-holing journal or crock of honey. A short queue formed in the post-office section proper, where a middle-aged woman who really had come from a place like Kent reduced the tempo of activity to something nearer the authentic British (or English) level. Howard's wife strolled out of the room at the back of the shop, where it was Charles's wife's turn to stay with the two younger children, and lent a hand with fetching some of the easier items off the shelves. This addition to the team speeded things up hardly at all, because male customers up to quite an advanced age tended to linger in sight of her flawless creamy skin and great dark eyes. But the brothers were well satisfied with her overall contribution to trade.

In a momentary lull Howard murmured to Charles, 'You see that one just going out now? – yes, there, in the blue.'

'Took the *Tatler*. What about her?'

'Fine pair of bristols, didn't you think? Small but, you know, solid.'

'I suppose so, I hardly noticed. You're vulgar, it's the only word for you. Anyway she's forty-five if she's a day.'

'You know who it is? That's old man Caldecote's bit of stuff. Not bad, eh?'

Charles said nothing to that. His attention had been caught by something outside over the road. 'Do you see what I see?'

They hesitated briefly before, calling 'Bear with us a second, would you?' and 'Don't go away now' to the two or three within range of the counter, they moved along to the broad pavement window beside the door and, as if rehearsed, started fiddling with an elaborate display structure intended to attract people to performances of an anti-nuclear drama at a small suburban theatre near by. Meanwhile they peered across to the Shepherd's Hill Wine Centre. Parked next to it, in the little side-road that ran down to the branch library, stood a square grey van without markings, its rear doors standing open. As they watched, a tee-shirted youth picked up an equally unidentified cardboard carton from the inside and carried it with unnatural speed towards the shop entrance.

Howard and Charles looked at each other, nodded slowly in unison and burst into loud laughter. As always, this last bothered slightly some of those within hearing who wondered whether the brothers might be enjoying a typical Asian joke at some of the stupid Brits they served and made a good living out of. But this was rare.

FOUR

At about the time Chris Markou was counting out the tens and twenties for three unexpectedly available cases of Stolypin vodka, Désirée Caldecote was saying to her brother-in-law, 'Yes, Freddie's been altogether different since he had his prostatectomy.'

'I'm glad to hear it,' said Harry.

Glad or not, hear it he most certainly and clearly did, and so did a dozen or more other people sitting about on the powder-blue upholstery at the lower end of the King's downstairs bar. Those who had tried to define the purely sonic quality of her voice, a company that included many she had never directly spoken to, had been more or less stuck with calling it not so much loud, not what you usually thought of as loud, but penetrating, none the less, quite penetrating, with a touch of a hectoring Tannoy-like quality. However it was to be described, she went on in it now, in about her fourth or fifth remark since settling herself on the horseshoe-shaped banquette, 'Actually they didn't take the whole thing out, the whole prostate gland. These days they often don't, you know.'

'No, they don't. I mean don't they?'

'They just cut away as much of it as they have to, just from round the neck of the bladder, enough to relieve the pressure on the urethra. Anyway, it's certainly been effective, he used to be up in the night I needn't go into how many times. To urinate,' Désirée elucidated, though by now those in range were bawling things about wallpaper and breakfast cereal and the Pope at one another. 'Of course there are these other effects which perhaps I needn't go into for the moment.'

Most people getting a sound-only version of this scene would have assumed that Freddie was not present at it. Even a visual three-shot might have had him there merely for documentary

26

filling-out. He sat placidly next to his wife as if he had not been mentioned at all in any context, blinking and showing his teeth in the way he always did with the look of somebody who had recently had a bright light shone in his face. He also looked vaguely aristocratic, understanding the term to include, indeed stress, things like effeteness and ineffectuality. This went along with a kind of outlandish touch as in some bygone portrait, suggesting the past existence of pioneering vegetarians and other dietetic enthusiasts, minor noblemen who had founded forest communities where women were rumoured to be held in common, or simply fellows who had played billiards all day every day for fifty years. All in all he made a much posher impression than Harry, who said now, merely to forestall Désirée, 'How's that Indian woman of yours getting on next door?'

Freddie's face showed no change. 'Oh yes,' he said. He had never liked committing himself, not even to having failed to understand what had been said to him immediately before. When he spoke he sounded posher than Harry too, just over those two syllables. Again he always had.

'The one next door to you who plays her television set too loud. How's she – '

'Oh the *Indian* woman.'

'Yes. How's she getting on, I mean does she still play her – '

'We had a talk with her, or Désirée did, didn't you darling? She's quite old. She goes to that day centre place between nine and three.'

After a pause, Harry asked, 'I suppose she talks to a lot of other Indian women there, does she?'

'Yes, come to think of it I suppose she does, yes.'

'And what does she do when she comes home from doing that?'

'Oh. Oh, she plays her television set,' said Freddie, knitting his brows.

'But not as loud as she used to.'

'No no no, no. No. She plays it just as loud as she ever did. Every bit. She's a widow, name of Patel I fancy. She just has the two rooms on the ground floor, you know, Mrs Patel.'

Harry could not quite bring himself to make the remark about the current relative numbers of Patels and Smiths that everybody

27

else in the King's would inexorably have made at that point, not even for the sake of annoying Désirée. For one thing, she had apparently been listening for nearly a minute, and it was not often enough that she did that for anyone to pass up the chance of watching her at it. In relative repose, blinking behind her perfectly circular tan-tinted glasses but with nothing like Freddie's speed or commitment, the middle of her lips a fraction apart, she could quite easily have been mistaken for an attractive woman. Certainly, though in fact a couple of years older, she looked more than a couple younger than her husband, and the apparent gap had widened since their marriage. That had been in what felt to Harry like about the year 1909, but was really more like 1959. As many times before, he wished now that a merciful Providence had kept her firmly and for ever in the ranks of the great unfucked, a phrase redolent of that era and one he remembered having shocked Clare with just about then. But, as many would have agreed, it was not only speech habits that had changed in the meantime.

The lull was soon over. Freddie had gone on to mention Mrs Patel's visiting son and would have been more than likely, given time, to infer that he too was of Indian race. First releasing his hand, which she had been clasping at arm's length since starting about his prostate, Désirée gave some of her lecture on the necessity of adapting to Britain in the 1990s, with special attention to the entailed multi-racialism. It was much, much better than Freddie's prostate, but Harry had still not got used to crap from that angle. Arms cuts, State education and the Arts Council were the sort of thing he thought he was equal to seeing off, and he sensed irritably that Désirée had no time for them either. Asking the two of them to meet him here had been a gross error, a silly old sod's refusal to be done out of his hour in the pub disguising itself as a bit of niceness to Clare. When would he learn to be selfish only to his own advantage?

Désirée cut short the bit about privatising the armed services (could it have been?) to send Freddie to the bar for more drinks. Explaining to him what that involved usually took so long that men had been known to give up and go themselves, but she had him on his feet in seconds and gave him a middle-grade shove in the back. '*Off* you go darling,' she said.

Freddie now looked as if somebody had exploded a small

flash-bulb under his nose. 'I haven't any money,' he said, so he understood part at any rate of what was required of you when you went to the bar for more drinks. But he was everlastingly one of those who never have any money to hand at others' call, any more than a light or a cigarette or a stamp or a comb or a pen or an envelope or an aspirin or the least clue when asked about anyone's telephone number or address or recent movements or name or where anything from a drawing-pin to the city of Birmingham might be found. When on this occasion he had at last been persuaded to find his pocket and find his wallet in it and find some money in the wallet – not that under the rules of his household there would ever be much there – had got some sort of fix on the bar, and had moved circuitously off, Désirée said to Harry, 'There were just a couple of things I wanted to talk to you about, you know, with just the two of us.'

Just the two of them it indeed was now, close, intimate, that kind of thing. What the change boded made him rather hanker after the twenty-two of them it had been a few minutes before.

'I wouldn't tell anyone else this,' she said, lowering her voice in pitch as well as volume, 'but then . . .' She gave him a look that spoke volumes, volumes he would very deeply prefer should remain forever unopened. 'After all, you and I have had rather a . . . special relationship – silly old word – for quite a few years now . . .'

Désirée might well think she had had and still had a special unilateral relationship with Harry, but that was as much as he would have acknowledged. What she was alluding to had happened the year he met Daisy, or perhaps the year before. None of the rest of it rose above the level of probability, conjecture, impression, assertion. There was supposed to have been a sexual encounter of uncertain duration between the two of them in and around a smallish car in some woods or on some waste ground somewhere. Whether it had amounted to an act of intercourse even God might have been a little bit uncertain. Neither Désirée nor Harry had said more than a couple of words about it at the time. Then gradually it had dawned on him that she was treating the whole thing (what whole thing?) as unmistakably special, specially intense to a degree that transcended its brevity and elevated it to some undefined area of the great-loves-of-our-time category. He had long given up hope of finding a way out of any of it. Now and for years, usually when she thought no one else was looking but not always, she had reminded him of it with a semi-amorous glance, a mouthed kiss, a squeeze of arm or knee, a caress near the edge of a sensitive area, a not very cryptic spoken hint, or, most alarmingly and awfully, in direct reference, as now. Were there perhaps others in his position, a troupe of special-relationship-sharers all over London and all unknown to one another? Just occasionally Harry wondered what Freddie had been told, or thought, or noticed, or remembered, or cared. Once, no more, it had flashed across Harry's mind that perhaps Désirée pretended to be his bit of stuff, or to have been his bit of stuff, simply because he was so terrifically attractive, but when he mentioned this theory to Clare, late one night over a small nightcap, she had told him she thought it could safely be ruled out.

Now Harry nodded, silently, bracing himself for what was to come.

'It's made much more of a man of him again,' she began. 'If you know what I mean.'

'Yes. Oh yes.'

'The surgeon said it wouldn't affect his performance one way or the other, but he was wrong this time. Freddie's whole attitude seems to have changed. As I say, he's definitely more of a man.'

'Oh, good.'

'After all, the psychology of the thing is very important.'

'Undoubtedly.'

'Not just a matter of the old block and tackle.' She squeezed his thigh, perhaps to make sure he understood her drift. 'But I don't want to go into anything that might cause embarrassment. What I really wanted to say, I know he's a silly old thing, I know he's all wrapped up in himself, I know he can't stand the thought of responsibility, I know he's utterly hopeless . . .'

'Yes,' said Harry readily.

She looked at him very briefly through the circular lenses. '. . . but I'm sorry, there's nothing I can do about it, I just happen to love him.'

Although she laid no special stress on the last word, Désirée pronounced it with a full initial aspirate. To Harry Caldecote, this on its own stamped her not only as an irremediable third-

30

rate genteelist bullshitter, along with those who talked of tissyou paper and yesterdae and one's fawhed, but in the present context as one who could only be pretending to feel the emotion she alleged. But he came no closer to confiding this to her than to bawling at her that nobody *just happened* to love anybody. These objections of his, however, were linguistic rather than emotional or philosophical. 'Well, that's nice,' he said even so, and he had to admit it was probably a good thing on the whole that she had said something like what she had said rather than that she would have liked to send her husband's head spinning from his shoulders, however impeccably she might have articulated the sentiment.

Désirée smiled. 'You're not such a crusty old codger as you make yourself out to be,' she said, looking at him over the tops of her glasses, 'I think you're quite fond of idiotic past-praying-for brother Fred and me in your funny old way.'

Harry dared not trust himself to speak or move.

'Actually you've done something quite important for him recently.'

'Done something?'

'You've probably forgotten. Concerning poetry.'

This would have to be taken an inch at a time. 'What exactly?'

'I suppose not many people remember now that old poet of the Fifties, Frederick Caldecote.'

It was safe enough to agree with that. Freddie really had been a poet of the Fifties in the sense that his career was almost totally confined to the years 1958–59. In the former year he had published a volume hailed as a handful of masterpieces by a leading cultural pundit of the day, a man way out in front with Eliot and Edith Sitwell. Unlike either of these, however, he was known or thought to be interested in personable young men, such as Freddie might possibly have been considered at that time. Anyway, Freddie had proved immune to any such blandishments and the pundit had withdrawn his support, so thoroughly and influentially that the second of Freddie's volumes had not only fallen flat but, by a mysterious retrospective process, shown up as worthless the contents of the first. The story was incomplete and probably untrue in parts but the fact remained that by 1960 Frederick Caldecote was an ex-poet, scorned by even the littlest of magazines. So there was nothing to be gained or lost now by a couple of muttered comments about students of the period and the passing of poetic fashions like others.

'Well, Frederick Caldecote with your encouragement is contemplating a return to the art of poetry.'

'With my encouragement?'

'I knew you'd have forgotten. But Freddie hasn't. And this will be something quite new for him. A long poem. His life, what he has seen, what he has heard. A poet's autobiography on the lines of would it be Wordsworth he was mentioning?'

'Has he started it yet?'

'Still planning, still dreaming.' Désirée moved her hands about. 'I think it's a wonderful idea.'

Harry took a moment off to consider the odd fact that those totally insensitive to an art so often think it more wonderful, etc., than those who are not, then seized the point. 'A poem of that order,' he began firmly, 'is a uniquely serious and responsible – '

'Oh well done darling.'

That was for Freddie, beating his personal record back from the bar with a glass of white wine for Désirée and what would have been a small Scotch and Canada Dry for himself. When he showed signs of sitting down again if left undisturbed, even for a moment of handing his wife some change, Harry said, 'You haven't forgotten mine, have you?'

'What . . . what . . .'

'A bottle of Holder's Super Lager. Lager out of the bottle.' Harry specified it hard because it offered the best hope of getting a full-sized drink off Freddie, ever an instinctive provider of, if anything at all, halves and singles and the cheapest brews available.

'He is hopeless,' said Désirée, gazing fondly after her husband as he veered away again. 'Head in the clouds.'

'Now Désirée I have something very serious to say to you,' said Harry in a grave tone, and watched her face, shoulders and more overdo their reaction. 'I want Freddie to hear it too so we'll wait till he comes back. Naturally I'm delighted by this news. But I want to ask your help – I'm counting on your moral support. This may turn out to be one of the most important poetical efforts of the last part of the century and it would be a crime if it were to be in any way neglected or mishandled or prevented from taking anything but its most perfect form.'

'Anything I can do, of course.'

For Christ's sake get a move on, Freddie, thought Harry, racking his brains for more of the right sort of bullshit. If he had been at any sort of library meeting there would have been no problem. As it was he had to fall back on looking seriously at everything while he thought about the dusky limbs of Brunei, hoped he was reducing Désirée's morale by effectively for-bidding her to speak, a grave deprivation in her case, and tried to rehearse the next bit.

Eventually Freddie was back, and bringing with him the right drink too. Now that he had them both in front of him with Freddie, taking his time from Désirée, also ready to hang on his words he felt more confident, also more determined. Here was a real chance to do something for his brother and he must not muff it.

After some initial solemnities, he said, 'When you were a young man, Freddie, a young poet, you were the most unsystematic worker I've ever met. I can remember,' lied Harry, 'how you used to scribble your poems on odd pieces of paper and often leave them lying about for other people to rescue. Several of them must have got lost.' Not enough. 'You also talked about your work, read bits of it to whoever might be listening, asked for suggestions and made changes.' Harry got this to sound positively ignoble. 'Those two things must cease. A poem of the kind you're contemplating could be one of the literary land-marks of this part of the century. You owe it to all of us not to fritter it away. So I am going to urge you, *require* you, to do two things. You must get hold of a large manuscript book and write your poem in there and nowhere else, and you must show what you write to nobody, not to any fellow-poet, not to me, not even' – dramatic pause – 'to *Désirée* until it's complete. It must be *you* and no one else. Your work, untouched by any other, *unseen* by any other until the last word is written. And of course it must be written in complete solitude and complete seclusion. Do you understand?'

It was questionable how much Freddie understood or even believed of the earlier parts of this guff, but as soon as he realised that here was something he could do on his own, an escape-route from Désirée, he was on to it like a knife. He moved parts of his face about and said, 'Keep it all in one book. Not show it to anyone. Got it.' Thinking faster than Harry had, he went on, 'Can I discuss it with anyone even?'

'Certainly not. Fatal.'

'Right. You understand these things. I'll stick to that.'

And Désirée, rather touchingly making the best of things, said, 'I'll see he follows your advice. Thank you, Harry.'

Well, he had done his best, and it might work, for a time, he said to himself as he went to fetch a last round before the three of them went off to lunch. It was twenty past one.

'Morning, Harry,' said everyone in earshot when he approached the bar. They included the glamorous female fishmonger in for a quickie from her stall opposite, the very serious black man from the picture-framer's further along, two of the three ear-ringed, bare-armed yobbos from the antiquarian bookshop, the chain-smoking old lady with the snappy little Yorkshire terrier, another of the American couples who must have read that piece in the *New York Times* and contemptibly chimed in with the rest, the old boy who looked like a retired schoolmaster with his (adopted) Asian son, and others. Not the least was the landlord, another figure of distinction with something of the air of a First Division football manager about him. On an early visit of Harry's he had taken him on a tour of the upstairs bar, where hot snacks and one of the less unbearable kinds of popular music were on offer and original crayon drawings hung, their subjects including Francis Bacon, Dylan Thomas, Anton Chekhov and other roisterers from round about. Now he said anxiously, taking another not very cold Super Lager off the cold shelf, 'I've been going to ask you, Harry, you do quite like those new pictures in the little snug where you go, don't you? I wasn't sure.'

They were old pictures as well as new, being heightened reproductions of orgies, crucifixions and gladiatorial combats from films of sixty years before. 'Very nice atmosphere, Kenneth,' said Harry.

'Freddie's looking well after that little bit of trouble he had.' Nobody knew how they could know these things, especially about somebody who could hardly have been in here more than a couple of times before. 'Oh, and that lady he brings with him

34

and you've been talking to, his wife I take it, she's an actress I presume?'

Harry resisted the temptation to say anything more than 'No.'

'Oh, we all thought she must be an actress, didn't we?'

Several of them evidently had.

'Not even years ago? I suppose it must just be the way she looks and talks. Oh well.' Disquiet returned to the landlord's manner. 'That new carpet up there, Harry, I've kept meaning to ask you, you don't think the pattern's too busy, do you, you know, for in here?'

'What? No, fine. Just right.'

'You see, I care about these things, but then I am an old-fashioned pub landlord from way back. And you know what? We're on the way out. We're a dime breed.'

'Sorry, you're a what?'

'A dime breed. Dine out like the dinosaurs.'

Just then, to Harry's momentary relief, the stale-cheese-coloured telephone made a jolly trilling noise and Kenneth picked it up, wincing as he lifted it to his ear. Almost at once his eyes moved to and stayed on Harry, who put down again the drinks he had started to gather together.

'Yes, he's here now.' Kenneth's eyes stayed where they were when he passed the handset over.

At Harry's first words an unnatural voice spoke, amplified and also given a fuzzy, buzzy quality like something in a tank or submarine. 'Mr Harry Cowldycoats?' it seemed to him to say.

'Who? Oh, Caldecote here.' His own voice sounded to him thin by comparison, a tremulous pipe.

'Sorry – Mr, Mr Cawldycoats.'

'Caldecote actually.'

'Christ – Cawldycotts. Anyway, er, it's the licensee of the Rifle Volunteer, Blackheath speaking, and I've got your daughter spread out on my kitchen floor.'

'Your kitchen floor?' echoed Harry in a very echo-like way considering.

'That's right, my kitchen floor, and she's on the floor because she can't get up or won't get up, I don't know which and to be quite honest I don't care, and it's the kitchen floor she's on because I'm not having her anywhere I can't hose down, all right?' Distortion robbed the words equally of relish and regret.

'Now are you going to come and take her away, because there's nobody here's going to touch her, right?'

'Well, I don't see how I can just – '

'Or I can call the police, no problem, I have an excellent relationship with the local force, it's a matter of complete indifference as far as I'm concerned. Do you understand me?'

'Well, I'll obviously have to – '

'Listen, in point of fact I wouldn't have bothered you, I'd have got on to the police straight away only I don't like to see people in more trouble than they need be. Your daughter's in a state, you know.'

'Yes, I do know.'

'I'm not talking about in general, Mr . . . bugger in general, I mean right now. So my advice to you is get moving.'

'Who shall I ask for?'

'Just walk straight in the front bar and say the governor's expecting you.'

'Couldn't I come and meet you in your – '

'And don't try and find a way in round the side or the back or you're liable to run into my Dobermanns, right?'

The voice was quenched.

Harry felt as if he had been thrust out of a great door on to a desolate hillside. For a moment he could not believe that anybody in the building had missed a word of what had been said to him. Perhaps none had. The landlord, the chain-smoking old lady, even the ear-ringed yobbos were all finding him invisible. But by the time Harry had mechanically picked up his drinks again Kenneth's eyes had moved back to him.

'Not bad news, Harry?'

'Just, you know, a family upset.' He tried to work a rueful-confidential expression on to his face.

'Anything I can do?'

'Oh, well if you could possibly order me a minicab. To go to Blackheath.'

'Blackheath.' Kenneth nodded in medium tempo and picked up the telephone again. 'Right away.'

'Really most kind.'

Not the right note. Not the way to treat an audience who must have picked up intriguing scraps at least about someone's kitchen floor and the police and Dobermann pinschers. Harry was as invisible as before but in a different way, being offendedly looked through. Never mind. He had no time to worry about conciliating the locals with Désirée already getting into position to demand a full bulletin.

'It isn't as if she's your daughter,' she said at a fairly early stage.

'Oh yes it is,' he said at once. 'In every disagreeable and pestiferous way it's exactly as if she's my daughter.'

'Harry, she's your niece by marriage,' said Désirée as one reasoning with a madman.

'You pay for her, do you, Harry?' asked Freddie with interest.

'Well, no, well, yes, well . . .'

'Oh I see.'

'Fiona is your first ex-wife's sister's child,' Désirée was going on. 'Gillian's niece. It's sad that she's the child of a broken marriage and that her father and her father's people were evidently a rotten lot, but it's not your fault. There's absolutely no reason – '

'There's no one else. Believe me.' Harry wondered why it was that people always let Désirée go on as long as she did. 'I can assure you I dislike putting myself out at least as much as any man of principle and good will. The point is, her stepfather just won't – '

'But she's got to learn to stand on her own two feet.'

'You don't know how true that is, my dear. I'll drop you at the house and have a word with Clare, it won't come as any great surprise to her.'

Désirée sat up indignantly, thereby demonstrating her long neck. 'But surely you're not going off to where did you say, Blackheath *now*? It's twenty miles.'

'In a few minutes,' said Harry. 'I'm terribly sorry but – '

'But what's her own father doing?'

'He's in New York like everyone else. She thinks of me as her father. Or she says she does. There's nothing to be done. Believe me nobody could be sorrier than me to break up the party' – Harry's biggest lie of the morning.

'But what about your lunch?'

'I'll get a sandwich here.'

Only now did it begin to dawn on Freddie that his own lunch might have been thrown in some jeopardy by recent events and decisions, and this at the gravely late hour of half-past one. His face shifted as he seemed to envisage possibilities of further delay, inconvenience, even hardship, though perhaps not of actually having to do anything himself. But then he found that only Harry's immediate future was to be disrupted while his own remained intact, and his expression cleared and he blinked contentedly round the pub till the minicab came and took them all away.

FIVE

'Can I get you another glass of sherry, sir, while you're waiting?'

'No, I'll just nurse this, thanks,' said Desmond Streatfield.

'Of course. Your friend is definitely coming, sir, is he?'

'She. Well, she said she was, but you know what women are.'

The proprietor of the Shepherd's Crook Bistro seemed to think this was an undue familiarity. 'The point being, sir, the reason I ask, I'm a wee bit short-handed in the kitchen there tonight and I shan't be able to keep the situation going there as late as I would wish and as I would in fact if things were a hundred per cent up to scratch, you see, sir. That's why I'm just a little concerned at the way the minutes are ticking by.'

This was delivered in tones of forbearing explanation, at a volume that might well have been audible in the kitchen, at least when no traffic happened to be passing, and in the kind of officer-class accents that recalled a black-and-white RAF movie. A spreading moustache and a scarlet brass-buttoned waistcoat went with them a treat. Earlier there had been a tremendous clashing of carving-knife and steel as the fellow strode up and down the narrow aisle between the tables and a great hollow clopping noise of spoon in jug while he mixed a dressing or a sauce. It must have been he who had painted the bottom third of the front window dark green, furniture-van green, and had covered the walls with light framed photographs of unidentifiable scenes of town and country, a kind of boat-race with the crews in shirt-sleeves, two glum middle-aged women by a sundial in a formal garden, a crowd of people, some on bicycles, leaving a factory, a toothy buffoon wearing a battered tweed hat and brandishing what might have been an authentic shepherd's crook. They might all, especially the last, have been chosen in the first instance in a spirit of jest or mockery, like the name of the bistro itself, but anything like that had long since evaporated.

Desmond tried to ignore it all. From where he sat he could see through the clear glass that Potandum, the wine retailer's, was still open at well past eight o'clock, indeed a gigantic fork-lift truck was even now gliding towards it under an unsteady column of white cartons, enough in collective content to keep the immediate neighbourhood, at any rate, happy for the next twenty-four hours.

'I mean I wouldn't bother normally, sir, but just pro tem I do have this unfortunate staffing difficulty. I'm afraid it's turned out a wee bit awkward.'

Desmond had never been inside the place before, and it would have taken someone far thicker than him to see that its owner had never expected to see him there. Perhaps he was hoping that if he went on about short-handedness and staff difficulties hard enough he might induce Desmond to withdraw. If so he was positively squandering his time. Or perhaps he was always like this. More likely he was just going on showing his disapproval of Desmond's turquoise rally-squad sweatshirt, on-the-forehead hairdo and non-RAF way of talking, having opened the proceedings with a brilliant display of doubt whether the chappie in the doorway had been offering himself as a customer or was just a passing street ruffian. But then the whole charade was forgotten when another party came in, a couple in their forties and a teenage boy all dressed up as if for a school prizegiving. The man peered about for a bit before he caught sight of his objective.

'Ah!' he then said at what seemed the customary local volume, but with relief and satisfaction too. 'I wonder if I could prevail on your good nature to the extent of providing three hungry and thirsty wayfarers with a few items of refreshment, my good sir?'

To Desmond's ears this was a dangerously offensive and accurate caricature of the governor's own speech, perhaps undertaken for a bet, but far from offering violence the latter said that would be positively and assuredly and so on all right. As he stood near by in the aisle, menus under arm, and waited for the three to get into their seats, Desmond said to him, 'Well, now there's a stroke of luck, I seem to have acquired a few minutes' grace, don't I, my friend? Oh, and could I change my mind and order another small dry sherry from you? When you've got time.'

The sherry had barely arrived when another lot turned up, a group of four steered by a fat old josser who definitely worried Desmond by providing more of the same noise in everything from volume to off-posh back-of-the-throat enunciation. And this one was a stranger too. How was it done, how could they tell just by looking at the outside of the Shepherd's Crook Bistro that it was a home for reproduction squadron-leaders? But before any light could be thrown on the problem Bunty had shown up at last.

She was looking for him before he had seen the door open and started apologising with her expression and movements as soon as she saw him. Her face was half a shade pinker than usual. 'Sorry,' she said, 'I am sorry. I couldn't be any quicker – ' In the way he had always noticed she bent her knees a fraction as they kissed, dipping just enough to cancel out their couple of inches' difference in height. ' – because Popsy didn't get back till less than five minutes ago. Her telephone wasn't answering . . .'

'You're here now. Sit down and have a drink.'

Rather noisily she did sit but went on talking. 'No, I mean please let me tell you, I would have rung here, but I couldn't remember the name of the restaurant though we come here quite often now. I had one or two things to tell her and she doesn't like being left notes . . .'

'She did know you were coming out with me, did she?'

'Yes, she didn't mean to be late but she missed the time.'

'Forgot all about it, you mean.'

'No, she remembered all along but when she looked at her watch she found it was later than she'd thought, a good half-hour later than she'd meant to be. She couldn't help it, not really.'

This sort of thing was so familiar to Desmond from other contexts that he nearly went on to tell Bunty that she knew what women were. Instead he said, 'And I bet she was full of apologies, right?'

'Oh yes,' said Bunty, nodding vigorously and in general making a heartfelt effort to tell a convincing lie, except by looking him in the face. 'She couldn't think how she'd been so stupid.'

'M'm.' He was not going to press it but he was buggered if he was going to let her think he was letting that Popsy off. 'There we are. I see. Well now love, what about a nice Campari soda, eh?'

'Oh that would be super.'

Desmond had been prepared to witness a stiff dose of proprietorial gallantry in the meeting of Bunty's wants, but he had not reckoned that she, and no doubt Popsy too, would already be known to the management. There was of course no sign of greeting. Instead, rather less assertively than having the message up in coloured lights, the scarlet-waistcoated one intimated that, while he might decently agree to serve certain people, he reserved the right to feel jolly bloody old-fashioned about what he understood they got up to. Or so it struck Desmond. He fancied too he got a couple of looks himself that wondered what kind of man it might be who would engage in a tête-à-tête with that kind of woman, but that was probably just him being sensitive. Bunty seemed to notice nothing, and after all it seemed she kept coming here. But then again she sort of had to keep coming somewhere.

He let it go, sending off a look or two of his own to be on the safe side. No more at any rate was said of lateness or short-handedness. When the roast beef appeared, even before he tasted it, he decided that the reason for all the fuss with the carving-knife was to make sure that it was in tip-top condition to slice through the Hyperfresh bag in which the meat had travelled from wherever whoever it was had cooked it. The Yorkshire puddings, little cup-cakes of pale spongy batter, were more authentic. Again Bunty found nothing out of the way, eating as she ate everything, in intense bulk-shifting bursts with sudden dreamy pauses. During one of these she said, with a little preliminary gulp or grunt to show a special question was coming, 'How's Philippa? She well?'

'She's fine,' he said rather shortly, but soon relented and went on, 'Still the same old lazy cow. She thinks she's a cut above lending a hand in the bar.' The bar was not primarily a drinking-place but a wine-bar in Muswell Hill of which Desmond was co-owner. 'There are some evenings I see what she means, but, er . . . Well, that wouldn't stop you, Bun. You've never been too grand to wash a floor.'

In the next minute a middle-aged couple entered the bistro, decelerating sharply as they passed Desmond and Bunty to indicate in dumb-show, but with the greatest clarity, that these then were the kind of people among whom one was expected to dine these days, real gracious stuff from way back. Bunty might have seen. All she did was say, this time in the manner of an old pal, 'Are you going to marry her?'

'Foof. Hooh.' He made other noises showing doubt or resignation and shook his head a good deal.

'I'd love to meet her some day.'

'Actually I doubt that.'

'Anyway, it seems she doesn't object to your coming out to meet your ex-wife.'

'She does and she doesn't. She says she doesn't but she says it in a way that makes you rather she'd say she did a bit, but of course she never would whatever you said. But then . . .'

For the second time in under an hour, and creepily, he found himself on the point of telling Bunty that she knew what women were. He managed to go on quite smoothly to say, '. . . we don't want to spend the rest of the evening discussing her,' and filled in with some good yawning stuff about the thieving of the kitchenware in his wine-bar so Bunty could see he was coming to the point. It was the same point as he always came to. Of course it was.

'Got time for a sweet, have you? Or a bit of cheese?'

'Oh yes, absolutely,' she said with some fervour, as if she had been waiting all along for this stage to be reached.

'Haven't got to rush back, then.'

'No. Actually I think I'll have some cheese, the puddings here are a bit blowy-out. Unless there's some fresh fruit.'

'We'll have a look,' he promised. 'It's lovely seeing you, Bun, but this isn't a patch on having a proper chat, you know, out like this, and old Popsy sitting there at home with her eye on the clock. Doesn't she ever leave you on your own, go away for a night or anything like that?'

'Well yes, she does, occasionally, but . . .'

'But she wouldn't like the idea of you coming up to my luxurious flat and us letting our hair down and Philippa out of the way somewhere. That kind of thing makes Popsy nervous.'

'Darling, you know I'd love to do that but you know what would happen, that's why I made us come here.' Bunty spoke gently. 'It wouldn't just be us letting our hair down, you'd start telling me how much you missed me and why couldn't we slip away somewhere nice and quiet for a weekend or just overnight, of course separate rooms, no hanky-panky, just to have a real talk without either of us having to rush away. And by then, you'd be saying it with your arms round me or trying to and saying what about a little kiss, just one, no obligation, and then I'd have to . . . It would only make it worse.'

Being Bunty she had refrained from saying that they had been through it all before a dozen times in talk and fact, and being Desmond he denied none of it. But he did say, 'If you've got it so clear in your mind you might have done better not meeting me at all.'

'Would you have preferred that?'

'Well, it would have been a bit more . . .'

'Straightforward? Honest? That's not very fair of you, Dezzie. Or very straightforward either.'

'No, I suppose it isn't. Sorry, Bun.'

'You see, I love seeing you, I don't want us to stop doing that for anything.'

'If I could get you to get to know me again, I have grown up a bit in the last three years. Anyway I don't think you really knew me before.'

'It isn't that I don't know you.'

'I was only a kid myself. Inexperienced. I realise now I must have seemed a bit of a brute to you.'

'And it isn't that I don't like you. Obviously. But it's hopeless. I wish there were some way I could convince you of that.'

'Nothing's ever hopeless. We could move in under the same roof, I mean just share a place and go our separate ways, I mean lead our own lives. Say for a fortnight to see how we got on. We could – '

She gave one big shake of the head. 'Look how quickly it's come up, in this minute. It always would, all the time. If – ' Now very abruptly she stopped speaking and at once looked down and started steering a torn lump of Yorkshire pudding with her fork round the imperfectly homogenised and now cold gravy on her plate. 'You couldn't ever not try to make love to me and I couldn't ever want you to. It's a damn shame. If there was ever going to be a man for me in the whole world it would be you. But there isn't.' A tear fell on to the back of Bunty's circling hand and she hastily wiped it away. 'I can't tell you how sorry I am.'

Desmond had been going to ask her about children and all

that, then. He had noticed she had seemed to get on not too badly with other people's and had several times come to the conclusion, as objective a one as he could have managed in the circumstances, that she would make a pretty fair mum herself, being affectionate with animals and so on. But it would have been mean to bring that up now, and no good either, and also he knew really that being her she would have been through that side of it in her mind already, like most other sides of it. The problem now was to cut off the waterworks without letting her think he had not paid proper attention to any bits of what she had said. To deal with it he let her know several times he understood and looked respectfully shaken. Then he made some end-of-subject faces and she responded straight off, smiling, getting ready to listen.

'At least there won't be darling Philippa to explain to,' he said. 'You know there are some people who don't understand what an explanation is, never have, never will. Funnily enough they all seem to be women, which I'm sure will have come as no surprise to you.'

So now at the third attempt he had managed to tell her that she knew what women were, and the two were soon chatting away in a style he would have enjoyed but for jealously, gloomily, bloodily stupidly wondering all the time if she was the same with Popsy. But he had no real reason to suppose anything of the kind, having only met the creature on about one and a half occasions, for a prearranged unenjoyable threesome drink at a pub in Kilburn, and for an impromptu no-better moment just the other week when he had been delivering Bunty back to the Shepherd's Hill flat. Both times Popsy had kept him under observation out of the corners of her eyes as if it had been him who was the funny one, or as if he might have been going to suddenly spring at her throat, which he had felt rather like doing in the pub as a matter of fact at the sight of her leather-clad arm draping itself unconsciously round Bunty's shoulders.

Cheese came, a rather sweaty piece of cheddar with cracks in it like those on dried mud, coffee that had been through the filter-paper and to be fair was not that bad, and the bill, steepish on the food but reasonable on the booze. At the paying stage Desmond decided to give the head man a bit of the cheek-ache, in plainer language to ruffle him by an uncalled-for show of good will.

'Most enjoyable, and here's a wee bit extra for the lads, okay?'

Instantly the air marshal swung aside to exchange ringing farewells and thanks with a departing group of his close relatives. When he swung back again it was more slowly and with a face emptied of expression. 'Lads?' He seemed puzzled.

'That's right, signifying the work-force as a whole.'

'Thank you, but I assure you the recommended service charge is quite sufficient, sir.'

Desmond smiled. 'French bloke, are you?' he asked. He would not be coming here again. Bunty looked at him and began to make for the door.

'I mean you don't seem to be very handy with the English language, do you, or you might have come up with something a little more suitable just then. Worth working at, you know, your English, if you want to make a real success of this place. Mind, anyone'll tell you the same.'

Some high-pitched inarticulate noises were the only response.

Outside, Bunty said, 'Did you take the money back?'

'Oh no. I went on as if I was seriously considering it and then left it. I'm sorry, Bun. That fellow got me down. I haven't exactly smoothed your path in there in future, have I? I'm really sorry.'

'Don't worry about that. Next time we go in, that's Popsy and me, we don't go very often, I don't care for that man either, I'll make sure I get there a few minutes after her so she can chat him up.'

'Popsy chat that joker up?'

'Yes, I realise it's rather a lot for you to take in, dear Dezzie, but she gets on rather well with men. Some kinds of men. She's sort of companionable with men in a way most women aren't, not with men. I'm no good at all there. Well, she knows quite a lot about cricket.'

'Oh yeah.'

'Of course I realise I can't expect you to see the point of her, any of her.'

Bunty had spoken almost wistfully, anyhow with none at all of the brisk resentment some women, some kinds of women, would have got into that kind of remark. Nevertheless Desmond failed to stop himself from saying, 'How a woman like you, how any woman, can . . .' before shutting up and at once wishing it unsaid.

46

'Darling, it doesn't do any good to – '

'I know, I'm a pig, I'm sorry. But when there's a man available, not a terrific man, just me, but . . .'

He shut up again. His trouble was his unshaken disbelief, unreinforced by conceit or jealousy, that somebody who was in all senses a woman could prefer the sexual company of another woman unless in some way deluded, deceived, in one sense or another led astray, or ignorant, or damaged by earlier experience, or *something*. In fact in his system the whole notion of actual preference was wrong and only some variety of imaginary preference could exist.

'It's not particularly easy for either of us,' said Bunty into a silence.

'But we're not going to stop seeing each other.'

'Not if you don't want to.'

They had reached the bend in Shepherd's Hill Road where the grassy slope ran uphill in the direction of where Bunty lived. Opposite stood the bookshop that sold progressive children's books and works by black Africans and Latin-American communists, and next to it Chez Odile, in whose basement wine-bar there hung, so Desmond had heard, a large and vivid painting of a lady's genitalia. A tremendous voice, matched by an acoustic like a subterranean cathedral's, still sang or roared from the Duke of Wellington back the way they had come. Just as they stopped on the corner a miniature traffic-block began to build up hand over fist near them, no easier to account for than many another in the capital and accompanied in this case by drunken hooting and a few shouts.

Bunty had always disliked noise, Desmond knew. The present burst of it had perhaps intensified the troubled expression that seldom seemed to leave her even in her most affectionate and trusting moods. For the moment he could see her face well enough in some light or other. The way she smiled and blinked at him reminded him of his first sight of her eight years before – gentle, vulnerable, nervous, ready with affection, the unmistakable face of a person, of the person he must from then on devote himself to protecting. That he had seen at once, and after everything that had come later it was still there.

SIX

The dog Towser stood at the front window of Harry Caldecote's house with his front paws on the tops of the turn-off radiators that came up to within a couple of inches of the sill. He was quite big enough to see through the bottom pane from a natural sitting position, but something in the street below – a man, a child, a car, a bird, a sweet-wrapper stirred by the wind, a movement of part of the large and verdurous plane tree to his right front – had seemed to call for his special attention. The frequency with which this happened was testified by the network of scratches his nails had left in the white paint of sill and radiator and by considerable traces of mud, hair, saliva, etc. At the moment his panting mouth was close enough to mist up and smudge the glass that the window-cleaner had left crystal-clear that morning.

Clare Morrison wished Towser no harm in the world, but she ardently and continually longed for his death. He had been Arnold's dog, which in the way of married men's dogs meant that the man concerned had chosen, paid for and named him, always spoken of him as 'his' dog, often addressed him in a hearty tone of voice, seldom taken him out and never done a blessed hand's turn about his bed, coat, messes, food, water. Conscience and pity had been enough to make her bring him here (where else?) after his master's death and see to it since then that he had as good a life as was reasonably possible in a crowded suburb for a creature who ought to have been running about on a chilly mountainside. That much took quite enough out of her, but could largely be done on automatic; what really got her down was the strain of pretending to Harry that she liked the bloody animal. Her brother would never have taken the lead in anything as vulgar, or as likely to be unpopular at his club, as having an able-bodied dog put down, but he would certainly not have been above going on at her to do so a dozen times a day

48

given a hint, tormenting her with the idea as a way of working off his irritation at having his hand suddenly slobbered over or a belt of grey-white hairs rubbed off on the leg of his trousers, horrific things like that. So it was just to keep in practice that now when she called to Towser to move she spoke gently.

His great head swung round at the sound of her voice as if he had never heard it before and fine chains of spittle swayed from his jaws. With an air of crucial decision he flopped down from the front window and bounded off to the one at the other end of the room, his energy undiminished by his half-hour's all-out gallop over Shepherd's Hill and ten minutes or so on the way there and back doing his best to dislocate Clare's shoulder at the end of the lead. On automatic as usual for the next thing she took a Towser-cloth out of a dresser cupboard and wiped his most recent leavings from the sill. Doing so she was in time to see somebody moving out of her view towards the front door but not to identify that person. When the bell rang Towser changed direction again and, vindicated at last, let off a metrical series of the great booming barks that came about third on the list of what Clare hated most about him.

The visitor was Piers, Harry's son and to her knowledge no one's favourite man. The dog however calmed down as usual at the sight of him and, after no more than a token attempt to smear him and his clothing with moisture, retreated to a distant, written-off rug where he cast himself down with a sigh that would have racked the frame of a Homeric warrior. Clare wondered as usual if Piers could once have given him an unrecorded kicking or other form of discouragement from physical contact. No: Piers's iniquities, grave as some of them possibly were, did not lie that way.

He gave her one of his shrewd glances and said, 'You're looking a tiny bit tired, dear Clare.' At this stage it was either that or she was looking marvellous, the picture of health, he had no idea how she did it. 'I think that boring old bow-wow gets you down.'

'Well . . .' She dallied for a wild moment with the thought of telling him, telling anyone, how she really felt about Towser before stoutly putting it away. 'He's not so bad when you get to know him.' Behind her she heard the dog make a loud sticky noise she thought best left uninvestigated. 'He's a good-natured old thing,' which she reflected was just as well given the size of the creature.

'You're the one who's that,' said Piers, on her side now against the world. 'To your own detriment. To a quite foolish and ridiculous extent. If it were me I'd have taken to drink years ago.'

'No dog's as bad as that to look after.'

'I was thinking rather of Daddy. Coping with him, running this place.'

'I get plenty of help. Mrs Osborne comes in Tuesday to Friday and her son's marvellous at fixing anything. He's a plumber who knows about lights.'

'Nobody can *help* with *Daddy*. Er, I suppose he isn't in by any chance, is he?'

'He's at his club,' said Clare, who had given up wondering what form of surveillance or parapsychology her nephew had mastered. Harry's comings and goings were as unpredictable as those of most men without fixed occupation and not insane, but Piers invariably managed to miss him whenever he wanted to get her on her own. Just what service might be required of her remained obscure, or at least unspoken, for some minutes. Having learnt with faint distaste of his father's whereabouts he seemed in no hurry to come to the point. Perhaps he had none to come to, perhaps he had simply dropped in for a chat like a normal person, a normal irregularly employed person, rather. If it went on long enough she might even find out how he lived, in the sense of how he got hold of enough money for things like laundry and cigarettes. He had had time to smoke a couple of the latter, letting fall little scraps of ash round the pretty gold-rimmed coffee-saucer she had put out for him as an ashtray, before he said, 'Any news of poor Fiona?' He spoke with compassion already firmly in place.

'Well, after she collapsed in that pub your father got her into Queen Alexandra's but she discharged herself the next afternoon. You know how they can.'

'Yes, I had heard that.'

'Now she says she'll go into a place in Surrey one of his friends at the club has to do with, but she'll have to wait until there's a bed.'

'So where is she at the moment?'

Clare shrugged her shoulders. 'In the flat in Buckland Village for all one knows. With the Irish boy-friend perhaps, or perhaps not. I think he's in and out.'

'Who pays for it? The flat, I mean. Just remind me, dear Clare.'

'Nobody, I mean it's a council flat.'

'Well, that's something,' said Piers, somewhat mollified.

'After she got out of Queen Alexandra's she went to a place in Chelsea that cost a hundred and fifty quid a day and it took three days for your father to find her and take her out of it. The Irish boy-friend – '

'But that's . . .' Piers did mental arithmetic. He looked shocked, morally outraged. 'How often does this sort of thing happen?'

'Eight days altogether since – '

'But he can't afford to splash out that kind of money in his position.'

'When there isn't a National Health bed – '

'People like Fiona have got to help themselves, you know, Clare. Nobody can do anything for them until they do. They have to start by hating what they are and wanting to be different.'

'I think Fiona already – '

'All the love and all the expert attention in the world is wasted without that.'

In his earnestness he was blinking forcefully, which drew attention to the somehow anachronistic bright blue of his eyes. His dark curly hair, though deeply recessed at the temples, had the same effect. In the jacket he wore, a kind of mauve blazer with heavy nickel buttons, and the well-chosen shirt and pink tie, he looked to Clare quite like someone to be reckoned with, almost of some consequence, with actual opinions and beliefs. But from all she knew of him from Harry and her own observation, he was of about as little standing as was possible for a sane adult in a democracy. He had been an art student for some years, also supposedly in and out of public relations (of course), industrial hygiene, hospital administration, the hotel business. The last of these was the best established, in that a friend of Clare's was nearly sure she had seen him not so long ago wheeling a trolley of dirty bed-linen along a corridor in a hotel in South Kensington. Nobody knew how high or low he had been placed in other spheres or geographically where, particularly because he could somehow never be telephoned at any place of work. Or nobody was saying; Harry presumably knew that and more, and no doubt worse, but Clare was more than content to let it go. When it came down to it, she knew rather less about Piers's activities than about those of pixies and a little more than about the man in the moon's.

'I can't imagine what these girls think they're up to these days,' said Piers, still in his responsible vein. 'It's not just a matter of bad behaviour, it's more like losing the whole concept of good behaviour, if that doesn't sound too pompous.'

'Oh no,' said Clare. This might be it coming up now, she thought, or perhaps just signalled the end of the beginning.

He lit another cigarette and threw the match into the swept fireplace. 'I'm not sure how much longer I'll be able to put up with life up on the hill.'

'The hill?'

'That quite peachy little flat looking on to the park that silly old Daddy put Bunty Streatfield and her mate into. *I* don't know why he feels he has to give all these helping hands to hopeless people who are *really* no responsibility of his. You get no thanks in this life from helping lame bitches over stiles.' When this drew no response from Clare, for instance a question about how many lame anythings he had helped over anything, he went on through a defiant cloud of smoke, 'Those two have never been what you might call couched side by side in peace and tranquillity, but these last weeks things have sunk to a level of sheer lack of taste that I find quite shocking, to be perfectly open with you.'

Piers's stock of synonyms for 'frankly' or 'honestly' could only be compared in size with his ways of giving you a pretty poor idea of just what it was that he was being so open, frank, etc., about. 'I refuse to descend into the sordid details,' he added, holding up a hand and turning his face away as though someone like Clare had been offering to wring one or two of those details from him. 'Oh, what time do you expect Daddy back?'

'I don't know. I mean it could be any time between now and about five or even later. It depends who he runs into in his club.'

'And who might he run into?'

'Well, there's a judge he drinks port with, and a funny old publisher, and a man on the *Independent*. Oh, and, er, what's he called, Neville Chamberlain.'

'You can't be serious, darling Clare.'

'I mean Neal Chamberlain. Of course I mean Neal Chamberlain.'

'Still not registering, I'm afraid.'

'The tall one in *Friendly Relations*. You know,' said Clare, beginning to quail as Piers went on shaking his head. 'Where they're all in the house in the country where all the things keep breaking down. Oh, God, the . . . The man who acts the old cousin in the television programme where they're all in the – '

'*Oh*,' said Piers with a kind of sneering laugh in it and looking like somebody's mother-in-law, Clare thought. '*Television. Of course.*'

'He's meant to be very good fun. Your father thinks so anyway.'

'*Damn*,' said Piers now, looking at his watch. 'I can't afford to go on just . . . Well. Put it this way, my dear – not to beat about the bush, the end is at hand.'

'Oh, I see. You mean, do you mean you want to come back and live here? Because since that South African chap moved out – '

'Oh, no. No, no. No no no. Sweet of you to think of it, but not. I have to be somewhere where I feel I can come and go as I please.'

'But there's that garden door – '

'I know *you*'d leave me completely to my own devices, darling Clare, and thank you, but no. I'm sorry, but it just . . . wouldn't do.'

'If you ever change your mind . . .' She wondered what would do and whether he was about to describe it.

He started shaking his head again, evidently deep in reflection. Now and then his expression changed, from dismay to resignation and points between. At last he half extinguished his cigarette in the coffee-saucer and said,

'I'm afraid I'm getting a wee bit desperate. I'm afraid I may find myself doing something very ill-advised and rather outré. And rather awful.'

This time he failed to remark that he would be absolutely candid with her. Much more important and comforting, he showed no signs of actually being it. For the moment, Clare could think of nothing she would have hated half as much as hearing even a hint of the very ill-advised, rather outré and rather awful thing Piers was afraid he might find himself doing. She shied away from identifying to herself the area where it, the thing, might have lain, but it must be somehow connected with the secretiveness of his life and the apparent absence from it of female companions, she could dare to go that far in her mind. Clare decided she must be a very conventional person and saw clearly but briefly that that was the hold her nephew had over her, and doubtless others too. Not to have to know about him seemed worth any amount to her. She said hesitantly, 'I suppose there's nothing I could do to help?'

Oh, no, there was nothing at all, nothing in the world. It was sweet of her to have thought of it, but . . . At this point Piers went rigid all over. If he had been eating at the time his jaws would have frozen in mid-munch. As it was he sat canted over slightly to one side in his chair, one hand suspended near his middle where he had perhaps been about to plunge it into his jacket pocket for a further cigarette. In due course his eyes, which had been bent on vacancy, came back to life as he began to consider the idea that had reached his consciousness from outer space. 'Actually there is something,' he said.

In her bedroom to pick up her cheque-book, Clare tried to think of her nephew's forbearance and her own good luck in that he called for these subventions fairly seldom, or at least not as often as he might have done considering – well, considering him and her. She hoped she was not being set up to deflect some titanically ill-advised, colossally outré and vastly awful thing he might one day find himself on the brink of doing. And no kind of near-certainty, that it had all always been a bluff, was ever going to be near enough for her. That was his strongest point.

'Could you be an angel incarnate and make it two hundred?' he asked her as she filled in the date.

She nodded without looking up. In a moment there would come a bit about wishing there had been some other way, and she could have dealt with that as it deserved if it had come from Harry instead of Piers. So always.

'If there'd been anybody else I could have gone to,' he said.

'Yes, I know.'

He scanned the completed cheque for an instant of time before reverently folding it and installing it in a large, expensive-looking wallet. 'Bless you, dearest aunt,' he said, and gave her a really attractive smile for once, full of innocent relief, or maybe undisguised triumph. 'It wouldn't actually make Daddy any *happier* to hear about this, would it?'

'I shouldn't think so,' she said, no less aware than he was that all Harry would ever do if he did hear was tick her off for being soft and encouraging sloppy ways.

'*Such* a wonderful reprieve, I'm quite weak. Could I beg a cup of tea?' When she got up to get it he closed his eyes in mute gratitude.

Towser left the room and came along to the kitchen with her and should have considered himself lucky not to incur some grievous thump on the way. After taking up water from his bowl with an amount of noise befitting a creature several times his size he stood with his nose against the crack of the kitchen door and squealed like a much smaller and, had such a thing been possible, even sillier one. Out on to the little lawn he bounded as soon as released, squandering energy by the kiloerg as he saw off the ravening pigeons and wild-state sparrows that infested it.

As she had meanly hoped to do, Clare on her return caught Piers on the telephone. 'No problem,' he was saying and then, when he saw her, 'you silly old thing, you,' and disconnected, only to pick up the handset again and reselect, glancing at her the while. He also glanced briefly at his watch again. 'Hallo, international operator? I want a transferred-charge call to Christchurch, New Zealand, please. Priority.' He read out the number on the telephone before him. 'I don't know the code for New Zealand but the area code there is . . .'

While he recited more numbers she put the teatray down on a low tiled table more heavily than she had intended and took a jerky step or two towards him. She felt ridiculous and drearily inadequate. 'Can't you . . . Wouldn't it be better . . . I'm afraid Harry . . .'

He laughed and passed her the earpiece, where a man's recorded voice proved to be confidently pronouncing the time of day. 'They're in the small hours now down under,' Piers told her.

'I didn't know that, obviously.'

'I'm sorry, I just couldn't resist it. It's that little Caldecote imp. Freddie has it.'

'No doubt, but I still think it was only pretty moderately

funny,' she said in spite of feeling a hundred and twenty as she said it.

'I said I'm sorry, it was only a joke.'

He was all hurt small boy now, closely recalling how he had looked in that role as a boy in years and now as then asking to be given enough of a clip to make him really sorry. But then he lost no time in repairing the damage, going on about the precise nature and worth of her generosity, regretting more bitterly than ever the iron impossibility of his having approached anyone else in the matter. As always, through her impatience she felt herself falling for it, unable not to, finding him a bit of a winsome rogue while knowing she was supposed to, more than half won over like a fool by his sheer audacity, as he forced you to think of it. By the time he left she was a little less clear than before that the whole purpose of his visit had been to take two hundred quid off her, and after all he had amazingly been known to pay back some of the money he had raised in this kind of way.

With a look of profound gratitude and a cheery wave of the hand, Piers had stepped into the sunny outdoors and was gone. On her return to the sitting-room Clare wondered what had ever led her to assume that she would come to understand people better as she grew older. On the contrary, they were more of a mystery to her than ever. Her feelings about them, too, were on the whole less clear-cut than they had been in earlier years. All manner of things made her think of Arnold, but nothing more surely than finding herself alone after being with someone, as now. Even if she had really wanted to she would have been incapable of deciding what sort of man Arnold had been, really been, in any of the ways that were supposed to be important – calculating by nature or thoughtless: companionable or wrapped up in himself, happy inside or unhappy – and more than one without any either/or to it, such as how he had felt about their making love. She was as sure as she was of anything that he had loved their sons, not so sure that he had loved her, but she never went into that, nor into how much she had loved him or even liked him. Mostly, most continuously, she just remembered the general feel of how much he had had to do with her life every day, and yet what she missed above all was not him actually being there but herself expecting him back from work or anywhere, him coming in and the two of them starting to talk.

There was a little rounded alcove by the sitting-room fireplace lined with starred dark-blue wallpaper and fitted with a couple of oak shelves above Towser's reach. Arnold had gone in for playing the flute at one stage and although he had given it up years before, he had hung on to the half-dozen instruments he had collected at different times. Kept polished and grouped on these shelves under a small diffused light, they made what Clare considered a pleasing decoration here, whereas in her bedroom they would have had a silly shrine-like look about them.

The collection included what she had been told was an eighteenth-century baroque flute from Germany, a flageolet in a pretty light-brown wood and a bamboo object that might have come from the Far East, and all together were quite likely worth a few quid. Behind them she had arranged a few photographs: Arnold holding a flute, Arnold not holding a flute but talking to an unknown wild-eyed man holding a violin, Arnold actually playing a flute while someone else played a harpsichord, Arnold aged about thirty-five just smiling at the camera. Also on view were two or three sheets of his music and the dainty porcelain box he had kept his cuff-links in, placed so as to show its lid, on which was painted a boy with a pan-pipe, not a flute admittedly but the closest he had been able to find. His copy of *A Shropshire Lad* was there too, nothing at all to do with flutes as far as she knew but a nice leather-bound pocket edition and a favourite book of his when a young man.

Clare would have said she was fond of music but knew almost nothing about it. Even so an organist friend of Arnold's had once told her she had a very good ear 'for pitch' as he had put it. Arnold would never have called himself more than a very moderately talented amateur musician, but he had played quite a lot when they were first married and with some quite good people, and yet just now and then he would produce an amazingly flat or, more often, sharp note without seeming to notice. When, carrying the teatray, she paused now at the alcove, she remembered taking a cup of tea out to him in the little summer-house at the end of their garden in Hertfordshire and he had been practising something by Bach, and just as she was leaving he had blown a real stinker, halfway between the right note and the one next to it, and she had looked quickly over her shoulder and caught his eye, and he had scowled at her for a second and then begun to shake with laughter. How long was it since she had thought of that? About then Towser started woofing to be let in and she hurried out to the kitchen.

SEVEN

'Are you all right, Fiona? All right, are you dear?'

'Yes thank you Roger. I'm absolutely fine, really I am.'

'Let me give you a hand with those things,' he said, meaning the bulging black plastic sacks she was hauling out on to the concrete walkway in front of the block. 'Awkward great things they are. I'll take 'em down for you now. Here, go on, let me, only take a second.'

'No, honestly, it's all right, I can manage easily, thanks.'

Roger Greenhough came up and looked carefully at her and she turned her face away. 'Ffhh,' he said, wincing at the sight. 'You know, you don't look at all well. Have you seen yourself today? You look rough, I'm sorry but you do.'

He was about seventy, Fiona supposed, a widower living alone, thin and rather tall with a neat grey moustache and a flat brown tweed cap always in place, originally there perhaps to conceal baldness. Although over more than a year he had shown her nothing but good will, however unskilfully applied, she considered she had no reason to trust him. At the moment she wanted to tell him to at least go to hell, but she never quite got so that she said it. She might not trust him but she depended on him, not all that often but when she did she really did.

'I couldn't sleep.' She tugged at one of the sacks and a loud clink sounded from inside it. 'It's okay, I can manage.'

'I hope you can, dear. Will you let me ring the doc?'

'Honestly . . . please . . . I'm all right.'

'Ring Sean then.'

'What for? Anyway he'll be out on the site still.'

'When he gets in.'

'I'm all *right*,' she said, starting to let some of her real feelings show.

He stared at her. 'You're the boss,' he said.

59

Conscious of the old boy watching her with hands on hips, Fiona dragged the sacks down the short concrete stairway and, with many a clink and clack from them and grunt and wheeze from herself, heaved them into one of the bins in the sort of communal bunker at the edge of the pavement. Although she had hoped to, she had had no real chance of sneaking out unseen by the old man, who spent hours on the brickwork balcony outside his next-door flat. Like its duplicates along the whole front of the block it was the sort of balcony meant to look good on the architect's drawings and impress favourably any planners or developers who might be passing, not to be used, but Roger had found he could get something about the size of a camp-stool on to it and keep an eye on the neighbours from it. However he was nowhere to be seen when Fiona dropped the lid on the bunker and clumped back up the steps.

In the hall of her section she passed the two little Pakistani girls from up top, incredibly old-style English with their red-ribboned plaits, pinafore dresses and spotless white socks, and quite English enough too in the way they looked at her in round-eyed silence and whispered and giggled together as they went out. The glass door boomed shut behind them like that of a squash court. Fiona stopped when she got to her landing, blinking in the sunlight through the deep window and swallowing as fast as she could so as not to start retching. She must have come up those stairs in too much of a rush – for what?

Going into her flat she remembered for once to keep her mouth open for a bit so as not to come fresh from the outdoors to how it smelt. Actually when she got to it she found it less bad than it might have been, nothing much more than stale clothes. The flat itself was looking fairly all right too. The great thing about it was that it was very simple and had very few large objects in it: bed, sink, TV, stove, fridge, table for eating TV dinner off, two chairs for watching TV from. The bed was of course supposed to be turned into a sofa by day, but Fiona only bothered with that when she was expecting someone round and sometimes not even then. At the moment it was parking a few dirty clothes for the launderette and clean ones from it and, quite carefully segregated by a sheet of plastic, a few bits and pieces that would not go into the bin.

Fiona never put bottles on the bed/sofa, full or empty. Full ones tended to go down between the side of the bed and the wall and empty ones under the bed or anywhere handy – there were not that many places to look when she did a clear-out, like just now. At the moment there were two full ones on the table and a clean glass. Before she sat down she looked round the flat and was glad she had managed to tidy it, the sink, draining-board and stove clear, food shelves squared up, clothes on hangers and hooks in what was called a corner wardrobe but was actually a wooden triangle nailed to the ceiling with a plastic curtain hanging from it. She had even wiped the bath round and thrown some Domestos down the toilet. In fact it had been a good day so far, with not only her fortnightly Giro cheque in but her able to get to the post office with it and so treat herself to a couple of litres of White Nun instead of the Jugland Niersteiner with the car-acid in it. And she had dropped off unusually early the night before, so that at this stage she only felt miserable and ashamed and no use to anyone instead of absolutely awful.

Thinking she had better have something to eat if she was going to, she cut herself a small piece of Emmenthal cheese but soon found it was not small enough. Not long after that, the question of what difference it would make to her physical state was overtaken by whether it would stay down. The effort of persuading it to do so make her whole body feel hollow and also light, kept from floating off sideways only by the weight of her clothes and boots. How rough did she really look? She went and peered into the mirror over the sink.

Rough, was the answer. The light there was poor, but she could see well enough that, for instance, the skin of her face, once comparable in hue to cream or ivory like her glamorous mother's, seemed to have moved another fraction towards milk-top cream and the ivory of an old snooker ball. With her black hair, which admittedly was still very largely as black as ever, though fuzzier, more Jewish, she had been supposed to have dramatic looks, like Mum again. Yeah, well, still dramatic, only more in the style of your House of Horrors. Definitely late-night viewing.

Now she opened the first bottle and poured out the first glass, but left it at that while she went to the balcony window and fetched in some tights that were drying, not because she thought it might rain, but because she thought she should before it got to be too hard to do so. Then she realised it must be coming round to ringing-up time and sat down at the table with the classy new push-button phone and, after some search, the coverless Stephen King paperback that had her numbers written on the blank pages and parts of pages. She would have been helpless without it because she never tried to remember anybody's number and often mislaid it for hours as it was. Since she never remembered whereabouts in the book anybody's number was either, telephoning took up a lot of her time, but that was no problem.

One telephone number was different from the rest. It had been dashed down on the inside of the bathroom cupboard in magic marker by Sean and he had done a lot of explaining about it at the time. She had forgotten most of this but not all of it. He had been very angry about something or somebody, not her, she did remember that, and had told her that if she ever wanted anybody done, or anything really serious taken care of, or if there was anything some bastard had done to her, then she was to ring this number and it would get done fast and sure, but it would cost her. But supposing nobody paid up, she had said just to be pointless, and Sean had said, 'They'll pay up. And don't ask for anyone, just say you're speaking for Stephen.'

Naturally she thought of none of this while she decided it would be all right to get off, drained her glass, refilled it, lit another Marlboro and tried Marilyn. There was no reply after about ten rings so she hung up. Then she tried Baz and got him straight away, but he was rather short with her, saying he was going to spend the evening watching TV with his mum. Of course it was early days yet for him. What about that mate of his, the one who worked at the what was it? Fiona had laboured through a column of numbers before it dawned on her that she had not yet thought of the bloke's name. Not that more than about half the names she had just read over meant anything to her. She tried to think about it while she swallowed a bit more White Nun. Then the doorbell rang, making her jump, as it always did until she had a couple of glasses down her.

'Just a minute,' she called, already pushing herself to her feet. For the next twenty seconds she moved at top speed, her top speed, almost silently and without thinking, emptying her glass into a tea-mug which she topped up before putting both the bottles round the end of the bed, rinsing her mouth out at the sink with mint-flavour Corsodyl and smoothing her hair back. She started to feel much better.

A short stocky man in his late twenties stood outside. He had a dark moustache and the rest of his face was not closely shaven. He sniffed cautiously and looked at her for a moment before saying, 'Fiona Carr-Stewart?'

'That's me. What can I do for you?'

He made an eyebrow-raising face, perhaps at her accent. 'Well, it's probably more, er, what I can do for you. I'm from the Gas Board.'

'Oh yes.'

'Well, I mean you or someone rung up and said there's a burner on the stove isn't working.'

'Oh yes,' she said, heartily this time, as if she knew what he was talking about. 'Do come in.'

'Cheers.' There were stains on his bomber jacket but his tee-shirt and jeans were fairly clean and his hair was not too bad.

She had no sooner shut the door behind him than the telephone made its swanky noise. A strange man wanted to know if Keith was there and of course she was going to say no when whoever it was went on to mention the Gas Board. 'Are you Keith?' she asked.

'Yeah, cheers.'

At this point Fiona could have done with being able to stroll into the library or out on to the croquet lawn, but not having anywhere like that to go she dropped the muck off the end of the bed into the bin, found places for the washing, sipped at her mug and listened to Keith's conversation.

'Well, I don't know, do I?' he was saying. 'Well, I know, but you never know. I only arrived here, er, just, well, now. Well, I haven't looked at it yet, have I?' He had been keeping Fiona in sight out of the corner of his eye and as he said the last part he gave her a fuller glance, catching her in the middle of a stiff pull at the mug. 'Well, I won't know till I've looked at it. What? All right, cheers.' He ended the call.

'You can't really be called Keith. Not seriously.'

'Yeah, horrible, isn't it, but there's not a thing I can do about it. Like you're called Fiona.' He separated the syllables of the name in an unnatural way. 'Now where's the defective burner that has caused all this excitement?'

Fiona had switched back to feeling so nervous that she had forgotten for the moment why precisely he had come. Fortunately there was no question of his not being able to find his way to the stove unaided. But any moment he was going to ask her which of the burners was the one, and as far as she knew she had only ever used the left-hand one nearest her. She watched helplessly while he put up on top of the fridge a black plastic holdall she had not noticed till then and unzipped it. Then, causing her more relief than she could remember ever feeling before, the telephone rang again.

It was Rob and he was well away. He said he was hoping they would have a chance to meet before he went off to Spain as planned to start filming with Michael Caine and Joan Collins. There had been a slight hitch over one or two details in the contracts, but that was all cleared up now and any moment he might be up to his ears. Meanwhile he had cooked up what he called rather a jolly little scheme for getting her uncle, by whom he meant Harry Caldecote, to make what he called a small contribution, by which he meant shelling out cash destined to make its way to him. He went on about premiums and percentages in a way that would never at any time have been comprehensible to Fiona, but that might have mattered less if she had not heard it all so often before, or something sufficiently like it – sometimes it was Robert Redford and Elizabeth Taylor. Very little response was required of Fiona, but by now she had cooked up a rather jolly little scheme of her own and said a few things back like oh and no in a gloomy kind of tone, which came easily enough. When she hung up she saw that Keith had finished with the stove.

'Everything working okay now,' he said.

'Oh, fine.'

'In fact everything was working okay when I tested it.'

'Oh.'

'What, what seemed to be the trouble?'

Fiona started to cry.

'What's the matter? You're never going to tell me you're crying about a bloody gas-stove, are you?'

She shook her head and went on crying. She had been afraid she would find it an effort, but once she had started it too seemed to come easily enough. 'My boy-friend says he doesn't want to see me any more,' she sobbed.

'*Oh*,' said Keith, sounding like a man who has suddenly understood the rule of some game. 'Anything I can do to help?'

Blinking back her tears she reached out and took the telephone off its rest.

What seemed like five minutes later, but was probably nearer twice that, Keith started preparing to leave. Despite some dissimilarities, Fiona was reminded of a night a couple of years ago when two young officers had very quickly and efficiently smuggled her into Chelsea Barracks, and not long afterwards, *without either of them having laid a finger on her in the meantime*, which she had considered a bit fucking insulting, had smuggled her out again even quicker and with no less efficiency at all. She still had no more than the remotest idea of what they had noticed about her in the interval, but in the present case she thought it might have had something to do with the three-quarters-full bottle of red Cinzano down at the side of the bed. Whatever it was, she was a little afraid of crying not on purpose should Keith show her some affection on his departure. As it very soon turned out, though, she need not have worried her head about that.

After a good mouthful of the Cinzano she went and had a bath, a real one with hair-washing included, and put the telephone on again just in time to take a call from Baz. Without referring to his previous intention to read and watch TV with his mum, he said he would see her at Linda's about half-six. When Fiona heard that she felt better again, and sat down in her dressing-gown in front of the TV with a Marlboro and, not bothering to go back to the Jacobean tumbler she had been drinking out of, punished the White Nun out of her tea-mug until it was time to dress.

By then she was feeling more or less up to things and found it almost fun to assemble the fairly new black Dorothy Perkins suit (Harry's Christmas present), diamond pattern tights, white shirt and suede stilettos. The shirt, however, though clean had been lying in a ball on the bed and elsewhere and would need an iron, and the stilettos would make for dodgy walking by the end of her sort of evening. Pleased with her own forethought she re-grouped, putting on the old Spanish-style jersey skirt, grey-and-white-flecked mohair sweater and, as before, low-heeled, limited-damage boots. Having got so far she rang for a minicab.

She used the first number she came to on her list because she had long ago used up all the firms in the area, meaning there were none left whose drivers had never heard about her. Then she prepared her real-leather shoulder-bag, a birthday present from Harry still amazingly not left behind or simply dropped or stolen off her long ago. The essential items went in, cigarettes, household matches, plastic bottle that had held Head & Shoulders shampoo but now held red Cinzano in case of an emergency, and fresh box of tissues not just for wiping her nose. Oh, and a couple of Night Nurse capsules in a Band-Aid tin should she need a downer quick.

The minicab was driven by a black West Indian of about thirty. As far as Fiona could tell she had never seen him before, but she had been quite wrong in similar circumstances in the past. After a bit she said, 'Do you ever go in any of the pubs round here?'

'I'm sorry, do I ever do what exactly?'

'Sorry, I only just asked you if you ever happened to go into any of the pubs in this neighbourhood.'

'The answer is no.' Then, evidently feeling he had been a little ungracious with her, the driver added, 'I'm afraid the kind of company one comes across in such places doesn't appeal to me, that's all.'

'Fair enough, I was only trying to make conversation.'

'If you don't mind I prefer to concentrate on my driving.' After another pause, he said, 'A man needs all his wits about him in today's traffic conditions.'

'I know, a friend of mine knocked a bloke off his motor-bike only the other day.'

After the driver had nodded his head several times at this stroke of fate, he sent the car round a sharp corner at speed and Fiona was sent sprawling from one side of the back seat to the other. Obviously he could not have arranged for there to have been a corner just at that point, but she felt that the way he had taken them round it must really mean he really had no wish to talk to her and perhaps even hated her, so after that she just showed how normal she could be and feel.

Arriving at Linda's always made Fiona feel good. It was on the other side of Shepherd's Hill from where Harry lived but still in quite a nice part, with things like pricey food shops and a travel

66

agency. The flat was at the top of a proper house, full of furniture and ornaments and magazines and stuff and yet all tidy, like a room in a film or in her own life until really quite recently. Fiona sometimes wondered who paid for it, and had guessed a husband or ex of Linda's or possibly her father, because Mike was ruled out. He almost certainly lived there but he worked at a meat-packer's and seemed rather the type of person who would have had that sort of job. If Linda was paying for the flat and everything herself she had to be a very unusual girl from the point of view of Fiona, in whose world it had always been men who paid for things.

Anyway she quickly poured herself a glass of wine and started chatting to Mike, Baz, Marilyn and a couple of the others. After a few minutes Dave the Rave appeared and as usual the party began to warm up straight away. By this time Fiona was feeling completely relaxed, which meant she stopped thinking at all before she spoke. Now and then Baz or Linda or one of them seemed a bit thrown when she said something, but that was probably her imagination and they all went on being very jolly. Presently Mike turned up the music and everybody danced. As a rule the mere thought of dancing gave her butterflies but tonight it was the easiest thing in the world, like all the other nights.

Later they were in the Duke of York, or it might have been the Paviours' Arms, anyway it was the pub or one of the pubs Dave the Rave arranged about the strippers for. There they were under the circuiting lights with their chairs and bananas, sometimes rubbing themselves against the fellows by the bar, who were mainly Irish builders and waste-disposers. Once Fiona thought she saw Sean among them but she made no move towards him. About then she started feeling rather disgusted with what was going on and also bothered by the lights, which were going on and off very fast now, and the stereo going full blast. About then too she got rather a shock when she took a fresh packet of Marlboro out of her shoulder-bag and found when she checked the other stuff in it that the Head & Shoulders plastic bottle was empty, and she was sure it had been full of red Cinzano when she came out. The other thing she noticed around that time was that she could not see Marilyn or Mike or Dave or any of them anywhere.

The man sitting behind the wheel was looking at her, quite

carefully too, but he was talking to someone else who was sort of out of shot. 'I'm not taking her,' he said. 'I don't fancy the look of her.'

'Here, and keep the change. It's not far.'

'Yeah, great, but that won't get near it if she throws up. Nothing will – I know.'

'She won't, never been known to. Inside like a whale. If she does I'll buy you a new bleeding cab.'

'You were doing better pulling the first one.'

'Here's my card, my good man.'

'What's this mean in English?'

'Read the telephone number okay, can you?'

'All right, give me another of those.'

When Fiona woke up they were nearly there. She knew it was important for her to say clearly, 'It's the last entrance along here on the left,' and when it came to it she managed it without any trouble at all.

'No, you don't owe me nothing. Your friend paid. He's a good friend of yours, that joker, whether you know it or not.'

'Thank you very much.'

'You seem like a woman of a decent sort of class. Why do you have to get yourself in this state? At ten o'clock in the evening.'

Somebody helped her up the steps or stairs. Actually there were both, or first one and then the other, outside and then inside, in the most extraordinary way, without any time going by or anything happening in between. There were two people there, and not just giving her an arm to hold on to but pulling and pushing and having to work at it too.

'Whoever it was let this happen, whoever brought her up so called, that's who I'd like to get my hands on,' said an old man's voice she recognised. 'Right, just on the bed'll do.'

EIGHT

Harry got out of his minicab in front of the Shepherd's Hill Wine Centre. 'There you go, Harry,' said the driver, a big fat young woman with a short haircut who seemed to turn up to drive him with more than average frequency, though he doubted if she could be pursuing him in any systematic way. Her chosen form of words closely recalled those of the porter at the Irving Club not long before. The male voice on the minicab telephone, on the other hand, called him alternately 'Mr Caldecote' and 'mate'. Then there were the people at the King's. It was not that Harry minded any of it but he wished he had a wife to convey to him that he was ever so slightly marvellous for not minding, and no less so for not trying to erect pissy generalisations about social mobility, etc.

Wifely thoughts brought thoughts of Maureen, which in turn suggested taking a bottle of Gordon's up to her place off Fitzherbert Avenue right away. Like a chump he had let the minicab go – yes, gone it truly had, through a momentary bloody gap between the files of parked cars. But by the time he was inside the shop he had an alternative plan.

His errand had been to pick up some red wine for the coming evening. At home all he had at the moment was some club claret that had turned out to be too sour to offer anyone over thirty, still hanging about only because he was too lazy and uninventive to do anything with it, and the last few bottles of a 1975 first growth given him by a grateful bibliophile in Potter's Bar. He would not have said these were too good to give any guest of his whatever, just to any guest so far, including tonight's. At the off-licence shelves now he soon picked out a Chilean Cabernet that should do the trick, being quite drinkable as far as he was concerned without any nonsense about other people being made to feel they were being given any sort of treat.

'Good evening, Mr Caldecote,' said the serious, scholarly-looking youngster behind the counter – no Harrying from him. 'Just these two for now? Any spirits, liqueurs, soft drinks?'

'Not now, thanks. Oh, wait a minute – let me see. Yes, I think, er, a bottle of Gordon's gin, yes. Oh, and what was that vodka you had the other week? Stolly-something? A bit cheaper than the others.'

The proprietor, Chris something, heard the last part and called across, 'Ah, that was a bin-end, Mr Caldecote, what we call a bin-end. All gone now I'm afraid, all sold.'

The assistant gave Harry a meaning look whose meaning was far from clear. 'Ah, the Stolypin vodka, that was. Very special stuff it was. We might get some more some time if things turn out right, it all depends.'

'Oh really. I don't drink that kind of thing myself but my sister sometimes likes it.'

'Have you tried this new wine aperitif?' asked Chris, hurrying up. 'I think your sister would like it a lot.' He seemed to have abruptly lost all desire to discuss the special vodka.

Harry said something back. The younger shopman went on regarding him through his oversized glasses. On the counter between them Harry noticed an open book past its first youth with the lines arranged as verse on one page and prose on the other.

'Oh yes, Mr Caldecote, that's my Dante. With an English prose translation side by side with the Italian. I want to learn the language and I thought this might be as good a way as any.'

'How far have you got?' asked Harry respectfully, having managed to fight down any housemasterly cries of encouragement.

'Just started on the *Purgatorio*. A great sense of . . . uplifting.' Harry tried to show he knew how much that meant.

'Now you mustn't keep Mr Caldecote all night,' said Chris.

'Oh no, I'm most interested. Oh, could I possibly use your telephone?'

'I'm afraid it doesn't seem to be working.' Precisely then a telephone bell started up somewhere at the back or side of the shop. Chris widened his eyes. 'Except for incoming calls,' he said, and hastened away.

More bespectacled looks came Harry's way. 'Shall I put in a

bottle of Smirnoff with the others, since we seem to have run out of the Stolypin?'

'If you would. And I suppose you couldn't run the stuff along for me, could you?'

The shop-assistant was shocked and grieved that Harry should not have taken as much for granted. 'The moment I've finished making up this order, Mr Caldecote.'

'Marvellous. I think – I think I might as well take the Gordon's with me.'

'Are you quite sure?'

Harry was, as far as the Gordon's went. Whatever else might or might not have been at stake in that last couple of minutes he forgot about as he crossed the road with an agile step. A delicious, an almost intoxicating feeling of conspiracy possessed him, making him seem to himself years younger. In the post office he picked up more or less at random a small packet of airmail envelopes and made for the counter. Here he found he was standing next to a kind of elderly small boy dressed like a conscript in some half-starved oriental army. When an unsmiling glance of recognition had come his way he identified this person as the dreaded Popsy, girl-friend of Bunty, his niece by marriage. She seemed to be daring him to speak.

'Hallo, Popsy, how are you, haven't seen you for a long time. How's old Bunty?'

This was obviously so devoid of insight and style as not to be worth answering. She was buying some packets of coloured sticky labels of the sort that might be used (it occurred to him later) to distinguish one person's belongings from another's. Harry watched her intently while she had her purchase put in a bag, paid for it and was given change, not because he wanted to in the least but through having somehow entered a state of light hypnosis. It lasted until she had moved to near the door and he had followed her.

'Did you say something to me about Bunty?'

'Yes.' He wanted to say something else to her now, on the subject of her going and fucking herself, but stuck to his original point. 'I wondered how she was.'

'*Oh*. Well I'm afraid I'm not really up to date on how Bunty is at the moment. I haven't spoken to her for over a week it must be. She was all right then.'

'I . . . what . . . I . . .'

'That flat she's in, I'm not living there any more, I'm in South Kensington now.' To save him from looking a bit of a twit by objecting that actually as anybody could see she was in Shepherd's Hill *now*, Popsy added, 'I'm just over here to see some of my stuff being picked up.'

'You're moving out for good, then,' he said without much sense of breaking new ground.

'Life had simply become impossible.'

'Really?'

'I don't know whether you think you have any influence over her, over Bunty.'

'Oh well, perhaps I do, I mean perhaps I have.'

'After all you got her into that flat, didn't you?'

'I thought I'd made it clear I merely happened to have heard it was vacant at the right time.'

'She needs someone to tell her other people don't belong to her as if they were her private property, they have their own lives to lead.'

'I don't think I've ever met anybody in my life who needs someone to tell her that less than Bunty does.'

'In any case it isn't just Bunty. That Piers needs to pull himself together as well, in a big way.'

'I couldn't agree more, I've often tried to put the point to him myself.'

'Young lord and master. Do you know what he does for a living?'

'Do tell me, I've given up trying to find out.'

'*I* don't know, I just thought you ought to, in your position.'

'Well there are an awful lot of things I ought to know which I don't suppose – '

'There certainly are.' Popsy's bottom teeth were visible between her thin lips. Her eyes moved as if in rapid thought. 'Here's another. There was a fellow round the other day making inquiries about that Piers.'

'What sort of man?'

'I don't know, I wasn't there.' She gave a grim laugh out of a thriller. 'The sort of man who makes inquiries, I shouldn't wonder.'

'What sort of inquiries?'

'As I said, I wasn't there. But evidently they boded no good at all to Master bloody Piers.'

Harry glared back. 'Well, Miss Popsy-Poops, all I can say is that if for your own good reasons you want to make me feel fed up or concerned or frightened about Piers, who's been in more kinds of trouble than I guess you have so far, then you'll have to do a bloody sight better than that. Your trouble is you've plenty of ill-will but not the imagination or the practical knowledge or I dare say nasty enough associates to carry it through. Good afternoon to you.'

At that point the two moved apart. Her and Harry's contact by the busy doorway of the shop had not been of the closest. Now a whole repulsive little fat family, from bald bearded father to grunting bejeaned toddler, came and pushed them further apart. Popsy made a final sour grimace and was gone, leaving Harry to go back and pay for his envelopes.

She had managed to convey greater hostility, and also a more worrying message about Bunty, than anything in her words. In addition she had made him feel he was responsible for everything she had alluded to, and for much else besides, things he could never even have known about, but he was used to getting such teleaesthetic messages even from the sort of women that were supposed to like men. Something in his manner had told her, quite likely without her knowledge, that he was feeling pleased with life, and she had instinctively moved in to see about that. Well, he was not going to let himself be got down by a bloody dyke at his time of life. Not that it necessarily took a bloody dyke to . . . He suppressed this wantonly chauvinist thought.

With the envelopes acquired and a couple of ultrafine pens added for verisimilitude, he asked one or other of the brothers if he could use the telephone. The man jerked himself upright, hurried from behind the counter, steered him importantly in the direction of the pet-food and generally made a bloody disaster-movie out of it.

'Out of order at home, are you, Mr Caldecote?'

Harry was ready for that. 'Yes, and they're having trouble at the Wine Centre too.'

'A bit thick, I call it. What are those fellows at British Telecom spending their record profits on, trips to Las Vegas? There, help yourself.'

The Shepherd-Hire office was only two streets away and sometimes you got a minicab in two minutes, sometimes in two to the power of several. This evening he was in luck, or so it promised. Via the paperback stand he wandered down towards the front door again.

The same brother, or perhaps his brother, waved Harry's proffered coin aside and handed him a small leaflet of stiff pink paper. Shepherd's Hill Neighbours Help, it said.

'You've got a dog, haven't you, Mr Caldecote? This lot'll exercise it for you. Also come to visit you if you feel lonely.'

'Or babysit for me, I see.'

'Some time in the future. Mind you, I doubt whether any of those services are really intended for you. I mean you're not from a black or ethnic minority or gay or disabled like it says, are you?'

'No. No.'

'No. And you're not regardless of age, creed or religion either, are you?'

'I should say not.'

'You know what I think, I think that lady you were talking to just now, she's more the kind of person these people are anxious to involve, as they call it. Or am I completely wrong?'

'Your powers of perception are extraordinary.'

'I'm just interested in human nature, Mr Caldecote.' A hoot sounded from the street. 'Ah, that looks like your minicab there now.'

'Oh, thank you very much. Cheero.'

'Have a nice evening.'

Harry gave a suspicious glance at that, but got only an artlessly amiable one in return. Though there was no direct sunlight outside it was still quite bright. He was scarcely inside the car before it took off with a satisfying crunch and jerk, and his elation returned in full force. To be embarking on this infinitesimal adventure in this marginally impromptu way, instead of in due form from his book-lined study with old Clare round the corner, made a kind of difference he could have explained to nobody at all except perhaps Clare herself, certainly not to Maureen. The bottle of gin in its purplish wrapping-paper became less a bottle of anything than a posy of amaranth, a sealed casket from far Cathay, or one of those objects that, arbitrary or valueless in itself, must be offered up at the door of the secret garden. It was true that almost any exploit would make a nice change from sitting in the Irving hour after hour feeling sixty, seventy-five, ninety as he had this afternoon while a very sociable fellow, known and feared all over London as one who told you about small-boat sailing, went on quite unforeseeably to tell him about his financial work for the Conservative Political Centre and then, driven off that, about the by no means infrequent pianistic passages in Mozart's vocal writing, with a number of sung illustrations. He was younger than Harry.

In grateful silence driver and passenger sped (for once) up Fitzherbert Avenue, turning off near the top into a gloomy red-brick-and-ivy crescent like an old don-infested bit of north Oxford. Here was Maureen's house, north-facing and further darkened by a large sycamore in need of pruning down. Evergreen bushes, no flowering plants, filled the gravelly patch of garden. Nobody passing could have had the least suspicion of the light and warmth that waited for Harry inside. He was halfway to the front door when for a second or so he felt what it had been like to be a young man. There was no season or time of day, let alone piece of his life about it, but it showed him what he had then had so vividly and completely that he checked in his stride for a moment, but luckily for him it had gone away after that second to something he could mistake for a fleeting bit of memory, and he trotted up the couple of steps and rang the bell without any trouble at all.

When Maureen let him in and proved to be at leisure Harry realised that he had been perhaps a little lucky. Slim, scowling, smoking a cigarette, her hair hidden under a pink handkerchief, she said 'Christ' when she saw him, not her warmest greeting but by no means her coolest. He followed her along a cluttered passage into a lofty sitting-room crammed with pictures, mostly Victorian engravings of Continental buildings or statuary and all going back to Leonard's time. Unlike so many, Leonard was not dead, far from it, not so much as divorced, merely separated and not even that with any finality, turning up as he did several times a year, sometimes for days on end. Whether Maureen went to bed with him at any or all of these reappearances, as with any or all of her shifting congeries of men friends, was not made

75

clear, at least to Harry. She certainly seemed to live alone, taking up the entire commodious house in doing so, for as well as everything else Leonard was rich, had been as long as anybody could remember.

'How are you, Maureen?'

'Ghastly, darling.'

'What? You look all right to me.'

'No, it's all these bloody people, isn't it, they don't give you a chance, any of them, they say Thursday definitely, now can I take that as absolutely cast-iron, oh yes ten o'clock on the dot madam, and you stay in all day and not a whisper. Absolutely horrific.'

'You mean the people who are supposed to see to the . . .'

'There's a pool of water on the kitchen *floor*, and it's come through from the *bathroom*, because there's a leak in the *roof*, where there are some damaged *tiles*, and also a number of defective *laths*, and the people enclose an *estimate* . . .'

Not for the first time Harry remembered Maureen going into this style of recitative at her own dinner-table across the passage here in the days when Leonard was fully her husband, and Leonard's mouth had gone down at one corner in a way Harry remembered from further back, having been at school with him. He had since speculated now and again whether he might have seen and heard a sample of the trick of behaviour that had induced Leonard to leave her side, and to go on leaving it at intervals ever since. Still, while this lot was going on she had, without thanks or other delay, stripped the gin of its wrapping, unsealed it and poured two largeish drinks with tonic and ice. Harry had never to the best of his recollection entered this room without ice being available within it, half melted to be sure as now, as always, but there.

'Cheers, darling,' said Maureen.

'It's lovely to see you.'

'Listen, why didn't you telephone before you came? I might not have been here. I'm quite often not at this time, or I might have been having Bernie round.'

'Oh, Bernie, of course.'

'You know *Bernie*,' she said impatiently. She smoked with her cigarette pointed at him and her elbow against her chest, like a beauty of a bygone era.

'No, but I'm sure I can imagine him.'

'He's an actor who happens to play the guitar rather well.'

'Yes, I thought I could imagine him.'

'Anyway, why didn't you telephone, because I might easily have been having him round.'

'Well you weren't, were you, and I don't know, I suppose I didn't think, and what of it, it's only a step from Shepherd's Hill Road.'

'You weren't by any chance hoping I'd be out or otherwise engaged?'

Harry moved from the chair he had taken and went and sat next to her on the Leonard-period sofa, and she instinctively shifted up to make room for him. 'Would that be like me, do you think, as you've known me?'

'No, you sod. No, of course it wouldn't be like you. That's true enough.'

'There you are, then.'

'Made it more of a bit of excitement, though, perhaps, not knowing?'

'Well, now you mention it, I suppose there might be a bit of that in it, I really don't know.'

'*Yeah*.' She did a great scowling caricature of a wink. 'So the old bad penny's turned up again, eh?'

'Bad pennies are supposed to be things people don't like to see turning up.'

'I beg your pardon, Professor.'

'No, I just meant I hoped you weren't saying you were sorry I'd come.'

'Do me a favour.'

He leaned forward and picked up in his fingers two deliquescent lumps of ice from the bowl. They seemed to become measurably smaller as soon as they hit the surface of his gin and tonic, but it was the general idea that counted. Settling back again, he snuggled a little closer to Maureen on the sofa. 'This is jolly cosy,' he said.

When they were into their second drink she went and lowered the venetian blind over the window that looked out on the front of the house, working the twiddler at the side to turn the slats vertical or some way in that direction. The arrangement was familiar to Harry and he considered it admirably useful and sensible whichever way you looked at it. At one time, though not recently, he had wondered whether there might be a patrician class among Maureen's boy-friends with access to the upper floors. On the present occasion all was going well, in fact had already gone, when after vague vehicle noises somebody approached the house on foot, paused for a couple of seconds and went away again. Complementary noises followed.

'Bernie,' said Harry.

'Could be.'

'No doubt about it, I heard him twang his guitar in frustration.'

'Shut up,' she said, but only half scolding. 'If you really want to be an angel there's some more ice in the kitchen. No rush.'

When he brought the ice, everything was as it had been when he arrived except that she was playing an Ella Fitzgerald record on her small distortion-rich machine (*c.* 1968) and joining in with some of the words.

'Do you mind very much if we don't have that on?'

'I thought you used to like her. The Bronx and Staten Island too.'

'I did. I may have done, but I don't now. Anyway, it's not her I don't like, it's having it on. Actually I'm not mad about her either.'

'I'm not *mad* about her myself.' Maureen turned off the gramophone and tucked some blonde-coloured hair back under the pink handkerchief.

'Thanks. Sorry. How's Leonard?'

'He's fine,' she said, brightening up straight away. 'He came and took me out to dinner last week. Very full of himself, he's just taken somebody over. Or perhaps it was somebody's taken him over. Whichever it was he's made a lot more money because of it. We went to that hotel place off Old Brompton Road where it's all black glass and that Japanese beef stuff they soak in soy sauce and Christ knows what for days and days before they let you eat it. Do you know it? – the restaurant, I mean.'

'I'm afraid I don't know any places like that. Good God, doesn't that sound pompous? But there it is, I just don't, not that I feel it leaves much of a gap in my life.'

'I wouldn't either if it wasn't for Leonard. Come on, just a small one before you go. Or not?'

'Or not? Whence the sudden urgency? And what the importance? People say *or not* these days as if the sands had started running out. Yes, thanks, I'd love one.'

'This is jolly nice,' he said, parking himself on the sofa and snuggling up to Maureen again. 'Getting away from everything. Really nice.' In fact it struck him as so nice that at one stage there seemed a fair chance that she would have had to let the blind down again, but he remembered how late it was getting and the moment passed. Not long after that he said he would walk back to Fitzherbert Avenue and pick up a cab on its way down to Buckland Village. She went along to the front door with him.

'It's been lovely,' he said, and kissed her affectionately. 'See you soon.'

'Well, that's up to you, isn't it, a bit?'

'What? How do you mean?'

'Do you realise how long it's been since the last time?'

'No? Why, has it been a specially long time?'

'Not really. Well, I was going to ask you.' Her face and voice went into a sort of Dickensian-cockney travesty. 'I mean it wouldn't be, now would it, that you'd found yourself some other little fancy piece of work in Muswell Hill or likewise, what is more appealing than your poor little Maureen what you have known these many years.'

'*What*? Good God, no.' He was genuinely astonished, if only because she knew so well how lazy he was. 'What a, what a ridiculous bloody idea. At my time of life? Thank *you*,' he said, trying to follow the spirit.

'Oh well, I just thought,' she said, and hurried on back to normal and beyond, distant, distracted, set on wasting none of his time any more than hers. Not looking at him she lifted her cheek for a different kind of kiss. 'Great fun. Love to Clare. Bye darling.'

It seemed to him no time at all before Désirée was putting down her glass of Chilean Cabernet and saying to him jovially, 'It seems a benign hyperplasia of the prostate produces a fibrous growth indistinguishable from fibroid growths in the uterus. You may have known that already but the first I heard of it was when the surgeon explained it to us.'

NINE

But in fact it was quite long enough for Harry to be taxied home, have a quick shower and take a glass of sherry to Clare in the kitchen with ten minutes to go.

'Thank you dear, that's very thoughtful of you,' she said. 'Are you drunk?'

'That's a bit hard, isn't it? Have I got to be drunk to be thoughtful? Bloody hell, dear.'

'No, I'm sorry, I didn't mean that, it was an independent question. I just wondered, you were so late back from the club, you probably got through a lot of port with your judge and the rest of them, I wasn't being nasty.'

'No, actually I didn't stay at the club the whole afternoon, I went and looked some stuff up. Why, do I seem drunk?'

'Well ... you realise Freddie and Désirée are coming to dinner?'

'Yes indeed, I've remembered all along and I ordered some wine specially which I hope arrived.'

'Yes – yes – yes, compared with how you usually are when they're expected, you do seem, not exactly drunk perhaps but rather pleased with yourself.'

'I did manage to get hold of exactly what I was looking for,' said Harry, and longed to snatch it back the moment he realised how frightfully wittily and comically he had put it. From its start he had concealed from his sister as much of his amorous career as he could without putting himself out unreasonably. Well, not quite from the start, just until he had noticed how she looked whenever a fornication of his, small or large, happened to have come to light – unsurprised, quite unshocked, almost un-interested, just mildly and resignedly fed up, as if registering another one down to her sex, no more than enough to incline a fellow to keep his trap shut. The close-down policy had stopped

80

working with the advent of Arnold, who though too good-natured to harass his brother-in-law purposely on the point had seen no reason not to bring it up, just for fun and for interest's sake, when the three of them were alone together. Now Arnold was gone the black-out was back, not that there was much to black out these days. Just the odd bit.

Clare had a handkerchief over her head, not such a pretty one as Maureen's, and a very cook-like look too as she fussed at the stove. Fussing she was, with plenty of mouth-inhalation and nose-exhalation, and stray-lock-pushed-off-forehead-with-outside-of-wrist effect. She seemed short of a place to put her sherry-glass down.

'What's the trouble, dear?'

'Nothing,' in a glassy tone, was what either of Harry's ex-wives might have said to this question at almost any time, but his sister said, 'Nothing much really, it's just these damn spuds are behind, my own silly fault, anyway I left them on too low and you know how Freddie likes to sit down to eat soon after he arrives.'

'No he doesn't, not really, what you mean is Désirée doesn't like giving him a chance of standing round with a drink beforehand, but I see what you mean. How long to catch up?'

'Twenty minutes, and they're usually punctual, and I'd like to be able to take this thing off my head and so on.'

'Leave it to me.'

'Oh could you really, dear. Sort of hold them in play?'

'Holding people in play is my natural game.'

He might be a bit drunk after all, he decided on reflection, after a large glass of vintage port to help him through the sailor-accountant-singer's one-man show and another to celebrate its end, followed by a stiffy and a half at Maureen's. While he poured Perrier on to ice-cubes in the sitting-room he reflected that if it had been Gillian or Daisy who had appealed to him for support just now he would have been able to be wonderful, running through his repertoire of hugs, squeezes, little kisses, murmurings (especially them), strokings, all those, the very paragon of a philogynistic man. As it was he had merely been helpful, or got himself into position to be. Faced with the choice, of course, an awful lot of women would have plumped for wonderfulness without actual help, eating their cake and having it in the shape of a grievance still unremoved. Daisy would certainly have gone for wonderfulness, not so much Gillian. No, bugger it, actually they would both have taken the wonderfulness option. And, by Christ, *and* he was as sure as anyone in his position could be that Clare just now would have chosen wonderfulness from Arnold had it been available from him. Which made it not simply a women thing.

For a long-service-engagement husband under two wives with some other service experience on his record, Harry was unusually interested in relations between the sexes. At times he would even concede if challenged that there might be some things about them, relations as well as sexes, that he had not fully grasped as yet. But before he could think further about the interesting wonderfulness point, the doorbell had announced Freddie and Désirée, dead on time as only the dreaded can be.

Since last seen, Freddie had had his hair cut and his top front teeth somewhat narrowed by filing, though on a second glance the latter must have been an illusion. He also looked like a man roused from a deep sleep a moment before and still recovering himself. 'Well, here I am,' he said. 'Come to report, though as I understand it I'm not supposed to actually report anything.'

'Jolly good,' said Harry, at baffled random.

'And jolly good it is as a piece of obeying orders,' said Désirée with a jovial smile. '*You* know.' What was new about her was a pair of oval slate-tinted glasses instead of the old round brownish jobs. 'You instructed your brother to buy a large manuscript book and write there and nowhere else the poem he was intending to write, and he must show what he wrote to nobody. Well, I have his word that he has been writing the poem, the book exists, I know nothing of what is in it. That is all. What more could have been done?'

Harry turned his yell of horror at the reminder of Freddie's poem, which of course all his levels of consciousness had been working overtime to forget, into satisfied expectation rather adroitly, it seemed to him. Although he tried not to, he could not help picturing Freddie at his work-table supposedly adding page to page, actually doing something that could be called writing a poem. If he were, then all he would be doing would be adding more to the sort of thing there had already been too much of thirty years ago. But if he were not, if he were giving free expression to some part of the large unknown Freddie, well, what of it, except unknown woe to Désirée. Harry's mind lingered on poet-Freddie, asking itself questions like whether the old man had found a way of reconciling himself with his life, whom he hoped to be stretching out to with his words, whether he had made his mind and spirit into a plausible harmony, and horrible Maugham-narrator stuff like that. Where did one *get* these things from? As far as poet-Harry was concerned, the stuff, all stuff, all poetic stuff, was either meaningless or banal and that was that.

He became conscious that Désirée was sort of staring at him. He smiled encouragingly, instead of asking her what she bloody wanted.

'It's a little bizarre, isn't it?' she said, smiling with the ends of her mouth close together. 'He writes. He mustn't talk. I mustn't ask. He can ask me for nothing. I can tell you nothing. It's like a solemn game. Rather outré. Imagine trying to explain it to a sympathetic friend. What does Clare say?'

'You mean it's a bloody scream,' said Harry to himself. 'And so it is. But it's going on as long as it gives that poor little bugger any escape from you.' Aloud, he said jolly thrillingly, and it was a solid blessing that Désirée was ultimately to be overawed and overwhelmed with bullshit – not even all that ultimately, perhaps – 'No more words. We've said what we've said. Enough.'

'Is there some possible way I could get a drink?' asked Freddie.

'Clare need any help?' asked Désirée.

'All under control,' said Harry.

She was going to make something of that, but thought better of it, and for the next twenty minutes it was fine, with Harry only intermittently hungering for the society of the Irving's versatile virtuoso, to hear more of binnacle, unscrambling, tessitura. He reasoned too that a dog, a rat, a parrot, a crocodile could sense hostility while remaining impervious to sarcasm. The fibrous and fibroid growths stayed in the picture for a bit. No, Harry had not known about them either. Fred was a lucky man not to have run into anything like that. Oh, he had? Lucky to be none the worse for it, then. As far as they knew. Yes. Well, what clever fellows these surgeons were getting to be these days. Why, only the other week at the Irving a chap who had had a – '

'I was telling Harry,' said Désirée, and paused over a mouthful of casserole. 'How tasty this is, Clare,' she went on as if completing her sentence. 'Just on the quiet, what's the secret?'

Clare talked cookery for a couple of minutes. 'I might throw in a couple of tablespoons of bone-stock like tonight.'

'Well, I think that's absolutely marvellous. Don't you, Harry?'

'I always fancy it.'

If there was anything Désirée seemed to enjoy when she was not herself talking, it was having something explained to her. So at any rate Harry would have said. Her demeanour on being told about the casserole reminded him of the occasion when Clare, again on request and not without reluctance, had explained the flutes and other memorabilia of Arnold's she had assembled in the sitting-room alcove. Then as now, she – Désirée – had behaved like a very serious, dedicated person being shown something a high-grade mental deficient had taken a lot of trouble over. And now, at least, had she but known it, she was heading for a swift uppercut to the point of the jaw and a speedy removal in the fireman's-lift position to the builder's skip in the street outside, or possibly into the boot of the wheelless Volkswagen next to it that had for some weeks eluded the vigilance of the police – Harry would make up his mind about that detail when he got there.

There followed some more talk of food. Harry was about as much interested in that as anybody else who in the course of a normal day took some of the stuff on board three times or so. Freddie on the other hand proved to have his likes and dislikes and made no secret of them, in fact was remarkably knowledge-able and comprehensive on the subject. Clare was pleased with the response to her cooking. Désirée hardly spoke. As dinner-parties went this one seemed to be developing into a sensational success. Then Freddie mentioned oysters, and Désirée looked up, and Harry was aware of the faintest of premonitory flutters, like the string tremolo heralding the onset of the storm in Beethoven's Pastoral Symphony.

'Nothing to compare with a dozen fat natives with plenty of lemon-juice,' said Freddie. 'And don't give me any of your tabasco or chili vinegar,' he warned Clare. 'Ruin the whole thing, you know.'

'Of course there's a lot of folk-lore about oysters going back centuries, you know,' said Désirée.

'They were very cheap till quite recently,' said Harry. 'Dr Johnson's cat – '

'People used to think they put lead in your pencil,' said Désirée.

Freddie blinked and looked quite disapproving. 'What? Used to think they what?'

'Can I help anyone to any more?' asked Clare.

'Used to think?' said Freddie. 'I don't know about used to think. I was chatting to the fellow driving my minicab the other day, I told you, didn't I, darling, and I happened to mention I'd had a dozen of the large for lunch at Law's a while back, and he said, hooh, he said, bet the wife went through it that night. Eh? Bet the wife went through it. Urhh!'

'All folk-lore. Because of what they look like. I mean, I ask you, what *do* they look like for God's sake?' When nobody answered her, Désirée went on, 'Not that our young Freddie needs anything in the way of oysters or bananas or hard-boiled eggs or strychnine or Brazil nuts – oh yes, I've made quite a study of this fascinating little backwater. No, as I was saying to Harry t'other day in the pub – you were off getting drinks, darling – since his *recent operation*' – she mouthed this in the way she had – 'young Freddie's become a positive menace. Not just a matter of the wife going through it this or that night, but – '

'My darling, I really don't think Harry and, and, and, and, and Clare want to, want to hear about this. Really and truly I don't.'

'Oh, don't be so stuffy, Freddie, why should we hide these things away at our time of life, and it's not as if we're on the air, it's all, come on, we're in the family circle now, for God's sake, aren't we? Yes, well, okay.' Désirée made concessive movements with her head and hands. 'A joke's a joke. Old lover-boy here and me, we're obviously not in our first youth. Things ain't what they used to be – what's the matter, Harry? All right? Yes, but a little bit of do you know what he calls it, a little bit of num-num – well,' she said with a sort of indulgent frown, 'a little bit of num-num on a Sunday morning, then a cup of tea and a glance through the *Observer*, and then perhaps, depending on how we feel . . . That's actually our best time, Sunday morning. You can imagine.'

'Well, I expect I could if I were to put my mind to it,' said Harry.

He would have sworn that he had spoken informatively and nothing but, without audible irony, or if audible only so to somebody really good. He must have been drunk after all to have forgotten that, when they felt like it, they reacted not to anything audible or visible but to what, knowing you, you might well have been thinking or 'really meaning', or if not you then someone or other, in all probability a man. Anyway, Désirée was on him like a knife.

Smiling naively, she said, 'Oh dear, I'm afraid I didn't realise it was bad form or something for close relatives to refer very indirectly to sex in private. I am most desperately sorry.'

'It isn't that' was all Harry could think of.

'Oh isn't it? In that case I wish you'd say what it is, and then we'd all know where we stand. While you're about it you might as well let us know what else is verboten these days. Religion? Politics? We're not all pro-EC yet, you know. Perhaps we'd better be on the safe side and stick to the weather.'

'Jolly interesting subject, the weather,' said Freddie. 'Can't think how it's managed to get itself such a bad name.'

'Well, I don't think even old Harry would quarrel with being told it had turned out nice again,' said Désirée as a way of showing she had been pulling all their legs all along.

'I shouldn't be too sure of that if I were you, darling. I've known such things to stir up quite a bit of trouble one way and another.'

At this Harry went into a great roaring-with-laughter exchange with Freddie, hoping vaguely for a way out, but Désirée gave it no chance. When she went on it was in the same gruesomely bantering style as before.

'If I didn't know you better, Harry me old love, I'd say you were suffering from an acute attack of the middle-aged sour grapes.' After only a small interval to ponder this enigma, she continued, 'I expect you've heard people say that the biggest puritans are the Don Juans of yesteryear,' and left this conundrum too to take its chance. 'But that's not you, Harry me old cock-sparrer, oh dear no, I'll take my Bible oath *you've* got your little bit of frippet tucked away nice and convenient or my name's not Désirée Caldecote.' She brought off the feat of making it sound quite likely that somebody should be really so named. 'I was talking to a couple of your mates in that pub of yours the other day – but I wouldn't have had to have that to go on. Out with it, now! It'll be all round the place so you might as well tell us. Now – where were you this afternoon, for instance? Answer me that, my lad.'

There was simply no way she could have known, known about any of it, anyway that recent bit of it, but Harry had seen spot-on shots in the dark before in his time, far too many to be reduced to the babbling that tempted him. Clare, as she gathered up plates, seemed to be pausing for his answer. 'Never you mind, my dear sister-in-law, and can we please talk about something else, because contrary to what you evidently feel, it isn't marvellous and open and mellow and grown wise over the years to bring these things up like this, family circle or no family circle, it's merely silly and awful. Frivolous too. And, to use a word I'm sure you're very fond of in its proper sense for once, exhibitionistic. Nothing mature in it at all. In fact it's the other way round in a sense.'

'What do you mean by that?'

'It's too late in the day. We're too old for it to be our proper concern.'

'Oh, come, surely it's just natural, isn't it? Mentioning a fact of life?'

'That more than anything is what it's not. Unnatural to the highest degree. And to call something a fact says nothing whatever else about it.'

'I'm sorry, I'm afraid I'm too stupid to follow most of that. I can only say that, speaking for myself, that – is it all right to call it sex? – anyway, it was a great, great part of my life, I didn't realise how great until I thought it was gone for ever, the worst thing of all that can happen to a woman, and now as I was telling you I've got it back and I honestly don't see why I shouldn't say so within these four walls in 1990.'

Intentionally or not or somewhere between, Clare dropped a plate of apple pie on to the table, in front of Freddie as it happened, not really very hard, not hard enough to spill anything, just enough to make an unmistakable clatter. Her face was flushed and the skin on it looked stretched tight over the bones.

'Oh Clare dear, really, I wasn't thinking, what can I say, I simply forgot, I didn't see . . .'

And more babblings. Désirée had jumped to her feet and turned towards Clare, who turned away, in the opposite direction. For more than just a moment Harry had the horrible feeling that he had finally lost all ability to understand why other people behaved as they did, and even to know what his own emotions or wishes were beyond a longing to be by himself indefinitely, unreachable by others, not necessarily in this room, just anywhere. Then that passed and for another moment, much to his surprise, he felt physically sick, not very but unmistakably, until that too passed.

'Just leave it,' said Clare, 'don't think about it, let it go away, not a word, stand about for a minute and wait for it to just fade away, just hang around and it'll be gone.'

A scratching and bumping outside the door became noticeable. Till then Harry would never have dreamt of being glad to see Towser in any circumstances, but now he got very near running to let him into the room. The dog charged squealing over the threshold, up one side of the dinner-table, round and down the other, snorting and sniffing too, nosing at chairs, at the low table across the window, at the linen and cutlery cupboard, still prying. After a pause while he seemed to peer vaguely at those present, whom he had not otherwise approached, he trotted down to the far end of the room and peered about there. Nobody moved.

'I expect the poor old chap's wondering where – ' said Désirée.

'Harry, er Harry, er Harry,' said Freddie, 'you've got a television set somewhere in the house, surely to God, fellow like you bound to, seen it somewhere myself before now come to think of it, yes, well anyway, do you, do you think we could have a look at the News? You know, the News on the TV? It's my only way of keeping up with things, you see. Papers all such a bore these days, I find. Just can't seem to get through them. Well.'

The News, and then the Thames News, and then some of a hard-hitting current affairs programme specifically directed at the City audience and everybody connected with the financial services industry, which turned out to be not all that long. But it was quite long enough, and provided enough distraction, for

Harry to write out on a page of his diary a message that read: PUT YOUR POEM IN A BIG ENVELOPE AND ADDRESS IT TO ME AND HAND IT IN TO ONE OF THOSE CHAPS AT THE POST OFFICE AND DON'T SAY ANYTHING ABOUT ANY OF IT TO HER BUT JUST PRETEND TO BE GOING ON AS NORMAL AND THEN BURN THIS. After some thought he added the words PIECE OF PAPER in the hope of making it that much less likely that Freddie would burn his poem before handing it in at the post office. He was sitting close enough to Freddie to fold this message and manage to slip it into his jacket pocket unobserved, and some intervention of Providence or turn of good guys' luck for a change dissuaded him from bounding to his feet with a howl of surprise and incomprehension.

After they had left Harry wondered how to begin, or even whether to begin at all, but Clare soon settled that.

'Did you know, perhaps you did, get yourself another whisky, go on, did you know there's a kind of potato called a Désirée, very common, rather cheap, big lumpy sort of thing, only any use for baking and cutting up for chips. No, honestly.' After trying to think of more bad ways in which a person could be like any kind of potato, she went on, standing in the middle of the sitting-room, holding herself together as if she was cold, 'Isn't it terrible how when you find out more about someone you've known a long time and thought you knew all about, they're always worse than you thought before, never not as bad? Never kinder or more generous or ready to go to a lot of trouble. Or a bit of trouble. When you were young, there were the people you knew, who were all more or less all right, though of course you preferred some to others, and awful people you only heard and read about. Now, you're constantly tripping over them, awful people I mean, in your ordinary life, and it's not as if they were new, they've been there all the time. Have they got worse, or did you just not notice before?'

'She's not usually as bad as that.'

'No. Probably just felt like a bit of boasting. I can remember going in for a bit of that myself. Women do. She wasn't really *bad* at all in one way. I don't think there are any really *bad* people. Just awful ones. The bad ones are all in books.'

'I wish there was something I could have done.'

'What, you mean like cutting her head off?'

'I suppose I mean stopped her, but by the time I realised where she was going it was too late. Old Freddie did quite well, didn't he? If he's got any sense, any at all I mean, he'll be grabbing at the sleeping pills now with all three hands. Unless they're under lock and key there like everything else.'

Clare nodded and looked down and stayed where she was.

'I was thinking of all that stuff you must have hated so much about being a woman or whatever it was,' said Harry, putting his hand on his sister's shoulder.

'Oh, that. Because of Arnold, you mean. No, that's not what was bothering me, not as such. It was the way she was talking. What made her think you and I wanted to know about that? And the way she made it sound, what was it, a big part of her life, as if it was separate, or something she happened to have come across for herself. Don't worry, dear, she didn't hurt me, she just embarrassed and disgusted me. You know what it made me think, the poor bitch doesn't know what it means for it to be a proper no, I'm afraid I can't say it, not even to you now, but I've no doubt you know what I mean. Anyway, thank you for what you've said.'

'I'll give you a hand with the clearing-up,' said Harry, and actually picked up a coffee cup.

'No thanks, I'll do it on my own, it's just what I need to work off my temper.' She paused and smiled at him. 'And thank you for thinking all the things you thought. But you know, Harry, there's nothing about my life with Arnold that anybody could ever say or do or remind me of that could make me feel anything I haven't felt a thousand times already. So there's really no need for you to worry yourself on my account. Old Freddie, he's the one who's in trouble. Just imagine. If you can bear to. A rather unenjoyable evening. And that's an end of it, dear.'

And there was nothing either wonderful or helpful for Harry (or anyone else) to do about any of it.

TEN

Property prices were going up in and around the part of Powys Road at the top of the hill from Buckland Village. Further down towards the underground station, only a couple of hundred yards away, there stood a very serious-looking municipal block made of a material resembling petrified porridge. It trembled with various sorts of popular music for twenty hours out of the twenty-four and included within itself, as part of the ground floor of the very structure, a pub where football enthusiasts and others foregathered, chiefly though not exclusively on Saturday evenings. The houses in the rather attractive Victorian terrace opposite showed many a cardboarded-up ground-floor window and their little squares of front garden were mostly littered and overgrown. In the very far from quiet pub on that side, old-age pensioners in ones and twos sat on plump scarlet furniture among strange representations of rock stars, though nobody except those who actually went there knew who frequented, perhaps lived in, the derelict surgical-apparatus warehouse next door. But walk up to what was trying to call itself the Powys Trade Mart and you were in almost a different town, one with room for a garden shop, a health shop, a shop that sold nothing but wallpaper, a boot boutique, a pottery centre, a coffee shop where you could sit outside if you felt all right about having a mass of heavy traffic accelerate past you twice a minute from four yards off. Across the road were half a dozen more establishments with pale-painted fronts and, in one or two cases, abstruse names. Along the top of them new flats were going up.

The Café Cabana was situated rather towards the less desirable end of this development, that from which the noise of music from the hill was likely to become audible when the day's traffic had died down and the wind was in the right direction. Not that that constituted any sort of factor to the café's patrons except theoretically, in the intervals between its own tapes. Those patrons came mostly from the better parts of round about, office people, printers, shopkeepers at lunchtime including regulars like Mr Lalani from the pharmacy-cum-video-library next door, sometimes with a small circle of business colleagues. The evening trade was different. For one thing the Cabana was in the catchment area of a large bingo hall, mostly non-young women naturally but including two small obsessed men, probably widowers and ex-warrant-officers, and one large obsessed probable bachelor who had once quite frightened Desmond by claiming to have a winning system, not that he won on it. As a general clientele they were not what Desmond had hoped for and called for snowballs all round when somebody had had a good evening. But they turned up and they paid.

Desmond and a mate of his had got the premises off an unthrifty hi-fi dealer shortly before the upward trend started to take hold. The mate had not foreseen that trend and soon sold out to Desmond, who would obviously have kept his better advice to himself. It was in the middle of these dealings that Bunty, hardly the sort of person to fit into life at or around the Café Cabana, had finally moved out of their flat in nearby Lancaster Way. Not long after it had become more or less clear that this move was indeed final, Desmond had induced somebody called Philippa, who did the cooking at the café, to move in. After three or four months of the new arrangement he had found himself wishing now and then that she would move out again, but not hard enough or for long enough at a time to stir him into action. Philippa suited him in ways, or in one way at least, that Bunty did not, and then again she suited him not at all in ways that Bunty had. If, as he believed, he was cut out for the married state or something like it, why had he not done better in it so far? Working out what he really felt or intended about Bunty was too difficult, and about Philippa too boring, to absorb him for long. Most of the time he concentrated on running the café.

One of the troubles about doing that was that the place still had Philippa doing the cooking in it. When he first employed her he had thought her reasonably willing but rather slow to learn; now she seemed to him just slightly less willing, nothing to make a song and dance about, but had revealed herself beyond mistake as not in the business of learning at all. There was really not much for her to know and he had thought he had told her all of it in a couple of mornings, for instance the punters not liking moussaka (and no wonder) but liking shepherd's pie with some canned tomatoes stirred in and just enough grated cheese on top to see, not forgetting a couple of slices of aubergine, and *called* moussaka, and no, no eggs and *no*, no bleeding garlic no matter what the bag in the *Daily Express* might say. In the same way duck-liver pâté à l'orange was not really that at all.

'There's your liver sausage, right?' he would explain. 'Two or three chicken livers if you must and some of the blood out of the bottom of the container. A Bovo cube in half a cup of water, a dob of gelatin to make it stand up and a teaspoon of black-currant jelly if you're feeling energetic. Then on top of each ramekin an orange slice, a bay-leaf and not just an old bay-leaf but a *Continental* bay-leaf, in other words – wait . . . while . . . I . . . tell . . . you – a blanched bay-leaf dipped in oil and wiped so's it's shiny, and two peppercorns and a lot of parsley, all for looking at. That's on top of each ramekin.

'Just try and remember, darling, it's no kindness to give 'em the real thing, they hate the real thing. What they like is getting what they're used to and thinking they're getting the real thing out of the appearance and whatever it's called on the menu. And keep that bloody cat away from this lot unless you want to wind up clearing up after him.'

If Philippa listened half as hard as she talked she would have been all right. 'You ought to be doing the food in the army. Or a prison. An oil-rig. Where it's eat what's there or go without.'

'For your information I happen to know that the food on oil-rigs is gourmet standard, and I mean proper gourmet standard, not just half a bottle of Cyprus red poured into everything. It has to be to get the blokes there, because they can't drink while they're there. And yeah, in the army and prisons they call things by their right names.'

The salads were prepared behind the main kitchen on the old gutting-table, bolted to the floor, that went back far beyond the hi-fi era to that of a primeval fishmonger. Here a Jamaican girl of seventeen did rather better in her sphere than Philippa in hers, needing only occasional rather than continual bringings up to scratch. Simpler ones, too.

'One thing we have a reasonably good supply of here, Sandra, is water. Another is time. But there is this third factor, persistence. Using enough water long enough on as it might be a lettuce-leaf to remove coal, iron filings, animal wastes *and every other kind of shit. Then* we can start thinking about cutting it up and putting it in a bowl.'

Sandra never said much to any of that. She was only putting in time at the Cabana till her sister-in-law got her into a job at the BBC, and in any case she had heard from Philippa that Desmond's father had been a schoolmaster, as it was called in those days.

Now and then a wine rep tried his luck, not often making any impression. 'You're not going to undercut my house wines, so show me a bottle I can show,' said Desmond for openers.

'Everybody's going mad about this one, last few cases at the old price. Aren't you going to try it even?'

'What, "a white wine with a hint of sweetness from the verdant foothills of Italy's Apennine mountains"? What sort of way of going on's that supposed to be?'

'But it *is* a white wine with that from, you know, somewhere like that. What's wrong with it? You're always going on about them going for anything sweet.'

'They don't go for being *told*. You'd think the penny would have dropped by now. A full, fresh, fragrant, fruity, floral, flowery, flavoury one-of-those white wine with a touch of charm, elegance, you name it. Style. Now *this* I could take a couple of dozen of, at the introductory price, that is.'

'We're only supposed to – '

'That very nice Burmese bloke down what's he call it, the Bistro de Paris, he doesn't know a blind thing about the wine trade. Well, you wouldn't really expect it, would you? I happen to know he's going out of his mind for a round, ripe, robust, reliable red, and lots of it. Isn't it funny, I was going to give him a ring lunchtime anyway. Oh. Er, you know Philippa, don't you?'

'Telephone call for Mr Streatfield.'

'Many thanks. Excuse me for a few moments. Oh, and while I remember, Clive, I wouldn't make a big point out of that one's bouquet next call you make. These southern-area wines, their nose takes a year or two to settle down. Big, yeah, but undisciplined.'

Philippa could get more expression into her face by leaving all expression out of it than anyone Desmond had met or could imagine. Her eyes did most of it, being wide-set and almost royal blue. In fact as far as somewhere about her top lip her face was really quite terrific from some angles, though it fell away rather in the lower part. She picked up again a bit lower down still. When he compared the way she looked with the way Bunty looked he had to admit that Philippa scored out, only she had none of the funny helpless look that had first attracted him to Bunty. If Philippa were ever to need helping it was hard to think of a department where money would not do the trick.

So as not to play her game with her now he asked in an extravagantly normal voice, 'Did they say who was calling?' She was moving away and ahead of him by then so in order to express her disapproval she had to do what she could with her bottom, which was not negligible.

'Desmond? Harry here.' This was not much of a surprise, nor were the excuses for not having got in touch before. Things were always preventing Harry from doing things. 'Just an odd point I thought you ought to know about.'

It was hard to make out whether there was not much to tell or Harry was not telling much of it. One of the reasons it was hard was the eye-catching way Philippa was paying no attention to him from the part of the kitchen where the blender was, which was also the only part he could see and be seen from behind the bathroom-glass partition where what he called his office was. Nearly sure by the end of their conversation that he had fixed to see Harry later, he hung up and wandered across and watched her satisfying herself that the blender was clean or all there or something. He looked pretty ridiculous to himself not just walking straight back to the rep like a normal human being, but experience had taught him it was better to get it straight away than later. Or perhaps it was just the way he was made.

'Did you want something?'

Any fool would have been ready for that. 'Don't tell me that bleeder's sticking again.'

'Oh no.' She moved over to the stove with him following and then her looking again at him over her shoulder. 'Something you wanted to tell me, was there?'

'No. No, just no problems, are there?'

95

After asking him if there should be and what sort of problems and so on for a bit, she said, 'Ahnkle Harrair quaite all raight, is hair?'

On their one brief meeting Harry had typically started trying to explain to Philippa his relationship to Desmond, but Desmond had had too much sense to. 'Yeah, fine. I said I'd see him for a beer tonight early.'

'Sahmthing the mattah with Buntair?'

'He'll be telling me that when he sees me, I should think. I don't know.'

'Am I invited to this exotic cocktail rendezvous?'

'No.'

'No, of course I'm far too common, aren't I?'

'That's right, yeah.' Quite recently he had found that it made very little difference if in the course of getting it from Philippa he handed some of it back. Just some of it.

'I suppose it'll be quite a small select gathering, will it, no brass bands or dancing girls or any of this?'

'He didn't say.'

'Rathah a pitair reallair. Old Burlington Bertair Buntair in her topper might have enjoyed running her eyeglass over the chorus-line.'

'Yeah, that's right.' Now, when the scene was on its last legs with him coming off a proper second best, he had to go and tell her, 'And in future lay off those bloody authentic herbs if it's all the same to you. Just the bouquet garni in the teabag, wave it around in the pot and take it out and forget it, okay?'

'Always leave off while you're losing,' Desmond had several times been advised by his father, who despite having been a schoolmaster all his working life had known a thing or two. 'Never have the last word on anything. If you let them have the last word, no matter what as long as it's the last and a word, then they're happy. Even if it's "so what" or "I dare say" or "hark at him". Even your mother. Well, I say happy.'

'Funny way of showing it.'

'Ready to let the whole thing go. Out of the goodness of their heart and don't you forget it.'

Desmond put some of this to Harry when they met later in the King's. 'So I let her have her say over the tie, didn't I?'

'What, that tie? It looks perfectly reasonable to me from any point of view.'

'Well, it would do. The way she sees it, Philippa, she reckons it's an old-school tie or as good as. I'm supposed to think it looks like one or think you might think it was one, that's if you follow her reasoning.'

'I must say, even for a woman . . .'

'Harry, you've had two *wives*. The other part of it is it's a tie at all.'

'What?'

'A tie in the first place, don't you know. The way she looks at it – '

'Ah, now I'm beginning to disentangle the thread of her ratiocination. You're wearing a tie so as to be suitably upper-class for this exclusive resort of West-End clubmen with its beeswaxed mahogany panelling and historic oil-paintings.'

'Spot-on, Harry. Actually I mean precisely, old bean.'

'Has she ever been in here?'

'Oh yeah. For instance one time I brought her to meet Bunty. Went off all right too. Well, not too bad. Well, anyway. Yes, she's seen it.'

'And no doubt you've been known to wear a tie at other times?'

'Like evenings at work if there's anybody coming in.'

Harry nodded and sighed. Desmond looked at him and also sighed. Then Harry said, 'Of course, you know I think old Brahms had it worked out as nicely as most.'

'The Brahms with the symphonies, is that?'

'That's the one. He went to the same tart once a week for twenty-five years or so, then switched to her daughter on the same arrangement for as much longer as he needed.'

'M'm,' said Desmond. He seemed unconvinced. 'Where was this?'

'Christ, I don't know. Vienna, Berlin, Prague, one of those.'

'Right. And it'd be, what, a hundred years ago?'

'That sort of time. He smoked a lot of cigars too.'

'M'm. Mind you, there's always Liszt as well, isn't there?'

'Is there? According to what I remember he used to knock the birds off like ducks in a shooting-gallery, if that's the phrase I'm looking for.'

'Forget it. No, that's right, yeah. Vicar, wasn't he, Liszt?'

'What? Well, yes, I suppose you could call him that, Abbé Liszt. Yes. What about it?'

Desmond shook his head and sighed again. 'You know that Philippa, she thinks I went after Bunty and married her because she was posh.'

'So I've gathered. I wouldn't call her posh exactly.'

'All right, a bit posh, you know what I mean, compared with Philippa. But I didn't, did I?'

'Well – I don't think you did, not now. Not that I'd call it the biggest bloody atrocity in the world if there had been a touch of that to it once upon a time. Anyway, what of it? If you say you didn't you didn't. Simple as that.'

'Well, no, Harry, er, that's just it, it's not as simple as that, that's the whole problem. Sometimes I get to thinking, perhaps it was that without me knowing. Perhaps it's still that and I can't see it. Perhaps, perhaps there's something in what Philippa says.'

'Listen, sonny,' said Harry, glaring and grating a little. 'We do quite enough we know the reasons for without having to start worrying about what we do that we don't know the reasons for, in other words when we do something for a reason we don't know about it's the same morally as not doing it for that reason. Shit, but you see what I mean.'

'Yeah. Thanks.'

'To put it more simply, you start thinking there's something in what Philippa says and *you're fucked*.'

'Now you're talking. Same again?'

'All right. Bit early in the evening, isn't it, to have got down to this kind of thing? Not that I'm objecting, my dear fellow. Perennial fount of interest.'

'You and I don't seem to get a lot in the way of later in the evening, do we? I'll just get these in now before she comes.'

There was a gap at the counter in a loose knot of middle-aged men all wearing different types and colours of hat, which somehow emphasised the solitary look of each. You often got a completely different lot in after work from the midday crowd, people were always telling Desmond in pubs he happened to go into, but to him they all tended to fall into the same categories, like no-hopers, louts and often sheer kids, meaning young kids, also females who brought the kids into the place with them as one way of demolishing another bit of blokes' territory, a more wholesale way than just coming in themselves. There was a kid, a fat little bugger in a sort of beret, lolling on a stool at the bar now, trying to kick his leg by accident. Of course when you got to Harry's age you were out of the way of most of it. Not all of it, though.

The group of fellows in hats might have been more cronies of Kenneth the landlord, or more likely he just pointed his head their way when the mood took him to unburden himself. 'Not that I've ever been one to mince my words,' he said, thereby giving Desmond a faint sense of unreality. 'In my experience it does nothing but harm. So – when I see a lime bitch, I tell her so. I say you're a lime bitch. In my opinion half the trouble in this world comes from people not calling things by their right names. Two of a kind, they are. Which makes you what, I asked him,' and here the landlord turned his matt-surface eyes on Desmond, 'a lime bastard pure and simple; yes, sir.'

Desmond decided to give life best and take off while he could still speak. At least Philippa had not been there to miss the point but get the score. They took everything from how it looked and sounded, like dogs.

'More deglin a mall,' said one of the hatted men a moment later.

'Ass not same much,' added another, and a third said something about seem boh sides, so perhaps they really were cronies of some sort after all.

'Harry keeping well, is he?' the landlord asked Desmond in the course of serving him, and proceeded, 'I don't know how he does it with all that on his back, I really don't.'

'All what on his back?'

Perhaps encouraged now by his first clear sight of the controversial tie and its shirt and jacket, Kenneth leaned gradually and confidentially forward, then, seeming to glimpse or recall something of importance overlooked, straightened up again and moved off, his right hand raised as if in farewell or benediction but actually, as Desmond saw when he turned away with the drinks, to reach out to replace a newly empty bottle of Southern Comfort that hung inverted as one of a row in front of his crowded shelves.

Nothing more onerous had happened to Harry in the

meantime than that Bunty had joined him, as planned but a few minutes ahead of time. Desmond tried not to notice her starting to struggle up from the little round table, remembering not to and resettling herself. At the same time she reached out and over and gave him a kiss that muffed everything except a dab on the ear and a flash of a smile.

'I'm sorry I'm early,' she started at once, 'I was telling – '

'No you're not,' said Harry. 'You're spot-on to the second.'

'It's because I – '

'It doesn't matter. Nobody minds. Now you're having a glass of white wine. No you're not, you're having a Campari soda, I remember. Typist's drink. However. Don't move from here.'

When Harry had squeezed and pushed out they told each other enthusiastically how marvellous he was, marvellous both considering and anyway. She was wearing a not very successful kind of informal nurse's rig and clearly found the collar about a quarter of an inch too high for her, and Desmond tried to remember if he ever noticed things like that about other girls. It crossed his mind that it might do her good to take up smoking – no, give her something to do, but then she would always be finding more things to apologise for about it.

'Of course, he's very fond of you, you know,' he said, trying not to make this sound like a good or any other sort of Harry's marvellousnesses.

'Well, he took me on, didn't he, when he – '

'No, I mean he's concerned about you, he worries about you.'

'There's no need to worry about me.'

'Well, no, all right, maybe not, not at this moment, but it didn't look like that the other day, did it for instance?'

'You mean those silly label things Popsy was supposed to have been going to go round sticking on all the furniture that belonged to her? But that was all just a stupid misunderstanding, she was in a bad mood and didn't really realise what she was saying, I explained all that. I'm sorry you were upset but there was absolutely no need.'

Desmond started gearing himself up to protest that he had not been upset, that it would not have mattered if he had been, that the question was neither here nor there, and if he had ever got that far might have tried to tell her that Popsy's buying of the identity stickers, described to him by Harry, witnessed to

100

something more than any kind of mood, and how would it be if everyone carried on like that, and look at the mischief that might have been done all round, and catch him opening his bleeding trap in future. 'Oh that's good, I'm glad to hear it,' he said. He remembered as a boy reading in an encyclopedia where it had said that for every word in the Bible a million other words had been written on the subject – on that of the Bible as a whole or in some part, presumably, rather than on each successive word of its text. A tough one to shoot down, had been an early thought of his on the point, followed not so many years later by a supplementary to the effect that in the human or material sphere the nearest comparable disparity was between the number of words that women said and the number that would have to have been said about what they had said in order to produce a full or clear or straight account of any matter. But he had not expected to find that statistic in any book at all. 'Just a fuss about nothing,' he said.

She caught a bit there, but only said, 'Is this, us getting together, was it both your ideas, I mean yours and Harry's?'

'Well, Harry rang me – '

'Of course it doesn't make any difference really, I only just wondered whether perhaps one of you had some special reason for getting me along, some particular thing you wanted to ask me or tell me.' And if anybody had, it was not going to be about anything like her winning the ten days for two in the three-star hotel in Tenerife or even the 98-piece set of handcrafted Georgian hallmarked silverware in display cases. Not old Bunty. She knew that much.

'No, just Harry was thinking it was a long time since he'd seen you and if I was free and you were free we could the three of us have a couple here and perhaps slip over the road later for a bite at Odile's or . . .'

'No, I'm sorry Dezzie darling, such a lovely idea but I'm terribly sorry but I simply can't, in fact I can only stay a few minutes, just, just for the one drink and then off.'

'But you said you were going to be – '

'That's why I had to pop in early like this, just to say hallo.'

'Harry's going to be very disappointed,' said Desmond, wondering as he said it why it sounded so untrue. 'It means a lot to him, keeping up with how you are, knowing you're getting on okay, all that.'

'Oh, all that. But all that's always the same, there's never anything to report about all that. What have you got there, can I have a sip? I don't mind – anything. Listen darling, before Harry comes back, he's a dear man, and I'm fond of him, and I think he's fond of me, but I don't think he really wants to hear, not *really*, what I'm doing or how I lead my life or anything really about me, how I actually spend my time. You know, get through the day.'

'Oh for Christ's sake, he's always on at me asking – '

'Please shut up darling just for two seconds – he'd hate to be told about my life because it's all to do with *her*. That's right. It's no good, Dezzie.'

He noticed on the wall behind her the tinted cinema still, showing a helmeted gladiator with a short sword ready to plunge into the throat of his fallen opponent, while in the background an emperor in purple toga and laurel crown dramatically lowered his thumb. Desmond said rather mechanically, 'Nobody's going to ask you anything or talk about anything you don't want to talk about.'

'And what's Harry going to talk about, what are you going to tell me, look what an interesting time the rest of the world's having, you know, where the real people are, doing what people are supposed to do, getting married and having families and the young mums getting together, and taking the kids to school and all going on holiday, and all the couples in the pub and everywhere, and shouldn't I be trying to take things seriously for a change and behaving like a grown-up woman instead of, well, instead of not. Being reasonable.'

'There's your conscience talking now, I suppose you realise.'

'Oh, God knows I've got plenty on my conscience but nothing to do with that, not ways of living your life or anything. All people.'

'Harry would never hint at the least suspicion of what you were saying. The whole thing's your imagination, that part. Nothing but you reading into it.'

'Every word he says brings up the whole issue whether he means it to or not, he can't help it. Yes, it probably is me as well, and I can't help it either. Well, every word that's more than like reading out of the newspaper. Like my mother.'

'Like me too, I dare say.'

As they spoke the last couple of phrases two people got up and left and another two or three squirmed themselves some distance round the luxurious powder-blue banquette, so that Desmond was able to move over beside Bunty and be something more like alone with her, even in the noisy pub. He half rested his arm against hers and at once felt as if they had just exchanged many more in number and far more intimate and affectionate words than they had in fact. If she felt the same she failed to respond, not moving herself away but speaking in an immediately harder tone.

'Of course one wouldn't expect Harry to give more than a selection of whatever he'd call it, ordinary life, normal life. Nothing about the wives left to bring up the kids on their own, or the girl-friends dropped like a hot potato after ten years with a couple of thousand quid because the chap's decided it's his duty to keep his marriage together after all. Or all the careers given up or forgotten about or just . . . laughed away. He's not going to go into any of that, not a man like Harry.'

Desmond had never heard Bunty talk like this before, in style or sense. 'Have I said something?' he asked, as the first one he happened to think of out of the four that also included his not having said something, his having done something and his not having done something.

'Saying something won't make any difference.'

Routine stuff now, though still not her brand. To his instantaneous regret he said, 'Now you sound like Popsy talking, at least – '

'Oh for Christ's *sake* can't it ever be *me* talking! You're all the same, nobody can ever think of anything for themselves, it's always got to have come from someone else. We do just occasionally have an idea of our own, you know. Can't you see . . .'

Her voice stopped with as complete a break as if a hand had been clapped over her mouth, or more realistically as if she had caught sight of Harry returning belatedly to their corner as he now was. He had just had time to say something not intended to be momentous about slow service when Popsy appeared in her

103

turn, soon enough to effect briefly the larger illusion that the two might have been hob-nobbing at the bar for the last couple of minutes.

She was wearing an ungathered greyish dress suitable for a stage production designed to suggest some unlocated limbo about the time of the Dark Ages. Taking from his unresisting hand the glass Harry had been carrying, she said, 'Ah, a Campari soda if I mistake not – a sadly underrated concoction,' and drank the top half of its contents in a single swallow. 'Now I'm well enough aware that a lot of you *men* rather look down on it, in fact I once heard a well-known male science-fiction writer describe it as an innocuous fucking drink, but let me say this to you – try one when you're putting your feet up after a hot Saturday morning's shopping and twenty minutes' standing on the 23, preferably in a tall glass with not too much ice and an orange-slice – and you'll find it really coming into its own.' She raised the forefinger of her free hand. 'Not that it's not got a lot to be said for it at other times. Like now.' Having drained the glass she put it down on the small table near her, 'Well, it's been fun, but now we really must be going. Harry. Desmond.' Popsy nodded to them one after the other in German-American fashion and stood courteously aside to let Bunty depart first.

Almost at the last moment, and for almost the only time since Popsy's arrival, Bunty's glance met Desmond's. She looked troubled, upset, any of those that any thickhead could have seen and named – not taken by surprise, though. And accusing. He could not make that out at all. The people round about noticed something had happened rather than the event itself, not so much the stroke as the leave. But not for long either way.

'Would you like to start?' he said.

'What about Christ on a bicycle? I think this is where we move to the bar, don't you?'

'Sorry about that,' said Desmond when they had done so.

'You'd do as well to save your breath for apologising for the weather, but thanks most awfully just the same. What do you want to do, after the next couple, that is? Not go home? Go home?'

'Yeah, but not for a bit. I've got the feeling me and Philippa are due for a trial separation. Ninety-nine years would come out about right. You know, like a lease. How much of that bloody fandango do you reckon was prearranged?'

'Well, there again you might as well ask me to simultaneously pinpoint the position and measure the speed of a subatomic particle, but yes, most of it.'

'I was hoping you'd say the sheer speed and ruthlessness of it took poor old Bunty properly by surprise. Or even that . . .'

'Come on, you can tell me.'

'All right, that she wasn't actually absolutely dead certain, not like a *certainty*, er, that Popsy would come popping in out of the blue, just it was on the cards, and then when . . . No.'

'How old are you, Desmond?'

'Thirty.'

'Well, there we are, then. She's a woman, you see. Which is a proud and yet a wretched thing.'

'Some bleeding quotation, beyond a doubt.'

'Of course wretched was a much stronger word in those days. Base, contemptible.'

'And what days would those have been, Professor?'

'Whenever they were is the answer to that. And if you mean do I think Bunty went along hook, line and bloody sinker with all that stuff, no I don't. But not all willy-bloody-nilly either.'

'I took a bit of anti-man crap off her just before.'

'That was her radar picking up a blip from the homing Popsy. Now I take it we are having another here.'

'Being like that must mean they've got a bit of man in them, right?' asked Desmond later.

'I don't know about *right*. But yes, in the sense of you might as well go on.'

'Well then, why doesn't that make them that bit more reasonable? Or less unreasonable?'

'Well, just off the cuff, it gives them more to go on about and so to be unreasonable about. And, still off the cuff, it's more queer they've got in them than man in the normal sense.'

'But hang on a minute, that ought to make them fancy blokes.'

Harry made no reply to this, perhaps finding any beyond him, but a couple of minutes afterwards he was saying, 'I suppose you wouldn't happen to know what they get up to, would you?'

'Actually I've never asked.'

'No, I meant in general, you know, when a pair of them get together, what they actually . . .'

'I'm afraid I've no idea, no more than anybody else.'

'I just thought you might have happened to hear something from someone in the way one does.'

'No.'

'But I mean after all you must admit it's an interesting point on intrinsic grounds.'

'Maybe to some.'

'Sorry. No I really am very sorry, Desmond, that was thoroughly tactless and vulgar of me.'

After another minute or so of talk, Desmond said, 'I'll get her back.'

Harry made no reply to that either.

ELEVEN

The light was showing behind Rob's front door, but that meant nothing – it had been showing the morning last year when two of them broke the door open at the end of his five days out of the game. This time it had only been three, and the key was in its place under the half-brick in the corner of the area. Water flowed from the drainpipe giving off vapour or steam into the dark pool round the ferns, a fact which meant nothing either, but today's lot was pretty certainly not going to be a bad one.

Fiona went inside and sniffed, with nothing much worse than the expected result, then listened, to hear a young woman's voice scolding and wheedling in alternate phrases at top speed, though not very loudly. Moving into the sort of kitchen Fiona made a place for her shopping-bag on the table, switched off the television, put the telephone back on its hook, and listened again. Quite soon her ear was caught by an irregular series of groans that were half low cries of grief and dread, signifying no mere physical agony but recognition that the world was a cheap, mean, messy, petty little place as well as one of horror and an unending sense of loss. Fiona nodded, switched the TV back on and turned the volume up higher than before, changing the channel after a moment to a cartoon full of explosions and crashing machinery. Next she took out and lit a Marlboro and, giving off smoke as if for some warlike purpose, entered the bathroom. Here things were frankly not at all good without having actually crossed the borderline into being frightening. It became clear why the hot water had been left running, even if the difference made was not that great. He had done his best in a way.

The next half-hour went smoothly, as though to a timetable. When Fiona had finished with the bathroom she got most of the stuff from the kitchen into a couple of the My Mum's black sacks she had brought with her and carried them out and up to the corner of the square, where they would presumably either be collected or, on a longer view, become part of the scenery. She was unpacking her shopping when she heard Rob in the bathroom, clearly enough and more even though a full-dress air-and-sea battle was raging on the television screen. She turned the sound up another notch.

Soon afterwards he was saying rather irritably from the doorway, 'Look here, would you mind terribly if we had that a little quieter?'

'No, not a bit. Sorry.'

She let him do it and went on making instant coffee. Very pale, sweating on the upper lip with the effort of continuing to breathe or something on about that level, his gaze drifting nowhere in particular, he stood about with his hands in the pockets of his once peacock-blue dressing-gown. Grievously stained and ripped as it was, it still looked expensive, a birthday present, he quite often said, from the richer of his two ex-wives, the one now married to the egg millionaire. Not long before, somebody had given Rob a black eye. He was always collecting such things, being pugnacious by disposition though undersized and of poor physique. He was twenty-eight, while naturally looking rather older. But what he looked like most was a very unfit man of about forty with an incongruously boyish or girlish hint about the eyes and mouth.

'I hope none of that revolting stuff is intended for me,' he said when he had taken in what Fiona was doing.

'You needn't drink it.'

'Oh I say, thanks awfully.'

Strolling up to the table, he looked through her purchases with a tolerant amusement that turned brittle now and again. The tins of soup, the tubes of fruit pastilles, the pot of honey, the sliced brown loaf, the lime-flavoured Perrier, even the Silk Cut and kitchen matches he passed over. The three pairs of underpants in their plastic, the three pink toilet-rolls and the packets of J-Cloths puzzled him a good deal, and he glanced to and fro between them and Fiona in doubt whether she might have misdelivered them. (What on earth could he have made of the bottle of Domestos and fourth toilet-roll she had left on the bathroom tank?) Then, whereas he favoured *Private Eye*, *Time*

Out and *Screen* magazine with the kind of half-smile that suggested he might well skim through them later, there was naked hostility mingled with incomprehension in the way he stared at the four-pack of 440-ml Special Brews.

'What's this muck doing here?'

'Sorry, I'll stick it in the fridge.'

'Don't . . . bother.'

With a grand yet careless gesture he swept the tins of lager aside, though not as far aside as the edge of the table, and presumably dismissed them from his notice likewise. The quarter-bottle of Yellow Label, however, was not to be seen off so lightly.

'What do you mean by bringing this filth into my place?'

What do I *mean*, you stuck-up little drunken twit? *of course* she wanted to shout, and bugger your stinking *place*, and *come off it*, and an infinity in the same strain. But she had never yet tried that on with him because word said he slung his fists rather more effectively with the ladies than with the gentlemen. So she silently made her way over to the little table near the door, the one he sometimes used as a desk when the time came round for him to remember to pretend he was a film man, and dropped the vodka there, ready to leave behind when she went. It would in fact have been more tactful to put it on the toilet tank with the other stuff. But never mind.

'Well, that's, that's better,' he said vaguely, half mollified, and seemed to hang about.

'Oh . . .' Fiona took a five-pound note and three pound coins out of her purse and laid them on the main table.

He saw, nodded twice and gave a brief smile. 'Thank you,' he said affably – 'thank you,' like the squire acknowledging a hand-up to his carriage from a forehead-knuckling cottager. 'Very nice of you.'

She hesitated and said, 'How are you feeling, Rob?'

'Feeling? Ha. Well, I've felt better in my time, no question, but I dare say I'll survive.'

'I'll be off, then. Give me a ring if you want me.'

'Yes. Yes. Very nice of you to call in.' He spoke absently, his eyes on the Contents page of *Screen*.

It was not any actual thanks you looked for, just seeming to be recognised or registered. That was really why she had asked him how he was feeling. At that prompting at the latest another woman would have softened, come clean after a fashion, perhaps humiliated herself a little on purpose to make a kind of return signal. Fiona hoped she would have done, hoped without much confidence that that was how she behaved at such times. But perhaps pretending ridiculously to be above the whole thing was a man's way or Rob's way of being brave and that sort of made it all right all round. She was quite prepared to admit that being brave was not something she knew very much about.

Whatever she made of any of that, there was no doubt that planning this do, writing and rewriting the list, buying the things, getting over here and cleaning up had taken all her attention and energy since about News-time the previous evening, and now there was nothing left. It no longer seemed neat or important that Rob's three days out of the game corresponded to her three days off the stuff. She had let herself forget what he was like, forget so much that she had been counting on a bit of a chat or something, say half an hour, a chance to relax and work out where to go and what to do. At the moment both were covered by walking back to the bus-stop. She concentrated on that and on what there was to see and hear around her, only just then nobody seemed to be about, not a thing moved in the empty street and not even one noise was separate from the rest. The sun had gone in or perhaps had not come out that day. For a second or two Fiona was quite near having to start to run, until it dawned on her, and so easily too – home, home, because telephone and telephone-book. The trouble with leading this sort of life, it made you stupid.

After twelve minutes of wonderful busy bus-ride and a couple of so-so ones walking, she got to her telephone and picked it up to hear the sort of silence that went with there being nothing at all connected to it. She punched Marilyn's number just the same and went on doing so. At this stage Fiona realised more of what she had forgotten or ignored while carried away by her Rob stunt. The easy one to face was that he was never going to pay it back even by mentioning it to a soul, let alone go into the odd detail as Marilyn or Linda would have done. Fiona suddenly saw and heard herself being told by that Father Czerny at Sean's friend's presbytery place that God knew the whole tale from first to last, and letting him go on to ask if she would make an honest effort to believe that, and saying she would.

That was better fun at any rate than thinking for instance about having hardly any money left, not much of anything in the flat, nowhere to go and no way of finding anybody and nothing to do. Unless something came up pretty soon it was going to be possible for her to start wondering what it would be like to try a small glass of light white wine from as it might be the western tip of Sicily, in other words to have to start the old blacking-out process going, to have to *be* that sort of drunk, without the means of getting there. Whatever had protected her against that case before was missing now. What would it be like to fade away, vanish, go out for good? – the actual moment, not the one before, no intention to go, no feeling it might be close, just wondering. Then she could not remember why she had wondered or very much about what, and ran the comb through her hair and even put some colour on her mouth, and went out in no great hurry.

Roger Greenhough was in. He always was. Although quite active enough at short range he had something wrong with a knee or perhaps an ankle that indirectly got all his shopping done for him. He opened the door of his flat to Fiona's ring with what at almost any time would have been a rather horrifying promptitude. There were white patches on his forehead where, as he had explained to her, he twice daily put baby-powder on his eczema. After a question about how his girl was that fine morning he backed off from her in a half-crouch, his weight distributed on the balls of his feet, reminding her of other explanations of his about unarmed combat in the army, in which he said he had been a physical-training instructor. She felt she could hardly blame anyone she had met in the past couple of years who got into a defensive posture at the sight of her.

'H'm. Yes. I see,' he approximately said in a high-pitched appraising drawl. 'So. We're off it, eh? I say we seem to be off it,' he repeated a good deal louder, though without having given her a chance to mishear or ignore the first take. 'Child's play, you know. To anyone who can read the signs.'

Fiona kept her head meekly lowered while he crossed and recrossed his kitchen, squinting down at her with his chin in the air. Unlike all its surroundings, the kettle he filled and set going was dirty and battered. There would have had to be a reason, perhaps unexpected but undoubtedly cogent, why it nevertheless kept its place among his utensils. Old people had a reason like that for everything they had and did. She did not ask this one or any other. This was chiefly because the entire scene in here seemed new to her, no matter that she had probably seen some of it more than once before, and she needed a couple of minutes to finish arriving.

'I had a mate in married quarters once had a wife like you. I've told you about her before but you won't remember. This time it might stick I dare say. Just as well if it does. Yes, it was the gin with her, of course to us in those days it cost next to nothing. I can't help having reason to know it's the wine with you, dear. Well, it comes to the same thing in the end. Now when d'you have your last drink?' She told him. 'All at once or tapering-off job? Just like that. I see. Tell me, Fiona, you notice anything unusual happening night before last, yesterday, perhaps last night?'

'Well, I don't think I've ever felt like that before. I don't think so.'

'But nothing like *happened*, nothing you might want to tell me about.'

'I don't want to talk about it even.'

'Okay, okay, fair enough. Just, my mate's wife said things went a bit peculiar once or twice and she wished she'd taken it more stage by stage. Tapering off, they call it.'

He paused and looked at her with an expression his face seemed unused to, possibly doubt about whether he should say more. Then the kettle started to whistle, as any kettle of his would have had to, and he started making tea. Unable after some thought to envisage any reason he might have against it, Fiona sat down on a hard chair at the kitchen table. A child's footsteps ran irregularly across the floor above their heads.

'Did she go back on it, the wife?'

'Oh yes. There's a certain percentage does. Inevitably. To and fro.'

'What happened to her?'

Again Roger hesitated. 'I never did hear the full story. My mate got a posting. Don't be a blithering idiot, I said, what do you want to go and do that for, we're all used to her ways here, I said, you'll only have to break in a fresh lot. Says she wants a fresh start, he said. Well, there was nothing I was going to say to that, you may be sure. Oh by the way dear, before we go any further I should tell you, if your phone's down and you were wanting to use mine, mine's on the blink as well. All the ones in this part of the block are. Someone put a pneumatic drill through a cable if I'm any judge.'

If he had told her that on her arrival she was sure she would have had to just get out straight away or burst into tears, probably both. As it was she managed to say at what felt like random while she was saying it, 'Actually I was going to ask you but it's not important . . . and it's not the only reason I'm here. I was wondering if you had any bits of shopping or washing or cleaning or anything you wanted doing. You've done a lot for me and it's time I did something for you. I've got some friends who are like me and we try and help each other out. That's what I've just come from doing. I know this isn't the same.'

'Go on,' he said when she had been very much hoping not to have to.

'Well . . . there's nothing I've got to do now, so I thought what could be better all round than me giving you a hand while I still can.'

He drew in his breath with a long wincing noise and let it out slowly. 'Four very sad words. Oh dear. While I still can. Oh dear. That does sound a little bit like a signal of surrender I must say. You do realise, do you?'

'I'm only being practical. Going by what's happened in the past. I suppose I'm just one of the percentage.'

This too he took badly, pacing the floor while the tea went on brewing as if forgotten. Presumably he had things to remember and was doing some of that now. Fiona made herself look at the special egg-cup, the special egg-timer, the special fat-strainer, the special oven-cloth, the special mat at the outside doorway, the special light-shade, the special blind with the thistlehead bobble at the end of the cord, and forced her eyes away again. It was impossible to believe that this horrible little snuggery was in size and all other basics the duplicate of her riff-raff-hutch next door. There were photographs on the walls here – people in hats, overcoats, a military cap. Roger had moved behind her. Perhaps he was lining himself up to push her over to his immaculate sofa.

113

Well, stranger things had happened to her, not by a hell of a lot, perhaps, but a couple or so. It was of course impossible that this very one had and she had forgotten, but impossible was not one of her favourite words.

If he had had any such intentions he held their execution over for the moment. When, placed rather like interviewer and interviewee, they were sitting at the table with their cups of tea, he said scornfully, and contentedly, and inevitably, 'Why d'you do it, Fiona? Why d'you drink like that?'

'Well, one answer is I start feeling too frightened not to. The other is I just don't know.'

'What are you frightened of?'

'The only answer to that is I really don't know.'

That little exchange had run more or less true to formula. Although she said so herself it was pretty neat and terse, hard to shorten as a way of making people feel they had asked this hopeless lush their jolly decent concerned questions and got about as much answer as they might after all have expected. Next there usually came a few seconds' respectful silence and then a wandering-off into stuff about strain and stress or altogether out of sight, but Roger slipped instead into low-grade social worker nods.

'No husband in the background, I take it?'

'No.'

'Parents together, are they?'

'Divorced. My mother's married to a businessman in Coventry who won't have me in the house. My father's in America. He lives there with his new wife. Well, she's quite an old wife now, I suppose.'

'Any other kin?'

'I've got a sister but I'm not to go near her with her two young children in the house.'

'Tell me, who's that middle-aged fellow looks like some kind of scientist, Harry is it, Harry? comes round here sometimes? What is he exactly?'

'He's a relative. A sort of uncle.'

'Going by appearances I'd say he was a well-off-enough kind of man. Can't he pay somebody to look after you the way you need to be?'

114

'Full-time? For the rest of my life? And he's got other obligations.'

'That's what people have always got, isn't it funny, other obligations. They'd like to buy a blind man's matches, they really would, only unfortunately they've got all these other obligations. There's stacks of help around but it's got this way of always having to go to someone else.' He banged his cup down in the saucer. 'Can't you get treatment or something on the National Health?'

'I don't think you realise how bad you have to get before they take you. Really quite bad. And as soon as you're not quite as bad they throw you out again, so what's the point?'

'That's defeatist talk. Mood talk. You're not drinking your tea.'

'Sorry.' She started trying to put it all down in one, but stopped after the first swallow for fear of throwing up, not that it was bad tea as tea went. 'It's nothing to do with mood,' she said as she wiped her watering eyes with her fingers. 'I never feel any different about that ever.'

With straight-backed movements he got up, went to a shelf where a box of tissues sat and, with a smart scraping sound, pulled out a handful which he unsmilingly put before her. But his voice was still sorrowful when he said, 'There must be an answer somewhere. Surely to God.'

'Why must there be? Why should there be? What makes you think that?'

'All right, what made you come off it the other day?'

'I was disgusted with myself, but then I always am. I don't know why I felt enough like that to come off it.'

'Any more, I suppose, than you'll know why you feel so frightened you've got to go back on it. Right, well I think I've heard enough for now.' He had not gone back to his chair and was again standing behind her. When he went on it was in a stiffer tone than before. 'My granddaughter'll be here in a few minutes to eat a bit of lunch with me so I'll say this to you now. I'm very sorry for you, Fiona, but I can't do anything for you more than I do already. You need a kind of care I can't provide. I'll be on the spot when you need it and see you safe indoors but no more than that. And yes, many thanks, you can pick up an evening paper for me should you be going in that direction and that's all I'll be asking of you for the moment. You said you believed in being practical, well, so do I.'

Fiona had taken in the necessary parts of this and clenched her thumbs in her fists in a private sign of triumph. In her right mind, whatever that was, she would never have dared to seem to let her hair down to this jaunty old ruin and risk the result of being endlessly watched over, comprehensively taken care of, doggedly thought the world of, believed in through thick and thin, above all talked to. Against the odds she had renewed her lease, so to speak, got out of him another couple of months' worth of being scooped up off the floor and washed down, got it with no strings. She kept her head down in further pretended humility while she waited to be let out.

He had strutted to and fro as he talked but now halted facing her. 'There is one thing I should be failing in my duty not to draw to your attention. I didn't tell you the full story about my mate's wife that time. I did say she came off the booze in a tearing hurry once and wished she hadn't. Well, you see, I don't understand the ins and outs of it, that can have rather unsettling results for a short time. It did in her case. She didn't actually *see* anything, that was effectively ruled out,' he conceded, 'but she did hear one or two funny little bits and pieces. People talking when there weren't any people about. Voices in the same room, in fact from quite close to. It wasn't they said anything much out of the way, it was more them being there at all she didn't like, if you see what I mean.'

Fiona dug the nails of her index fingers into the flesh at the base of each thumbnail. 'Yes, I see what you mean.'

'They called them the DTs in those days, I don't know what name they've got for them now. It's a widespread misconception that they're brought on by an excess of alcohol. Well, so they are in the long run, of course, but the *immediate* cause is a sudden and complete *withdrawal*, right, er, of alcohol. Evidently they start to appear about forty-eight hours after that if they're going to, in pursuit of which was why I got on to you pretty sharpish about when you took your last drink. In fact to tell you the truth,' he said, and paused to reconsider at some length the wisdom of telling her it, 'when I first saw you I wondered whether you'd come to tell me you'd heard something, but of course if you had, well, you'd have been in a very . . . Anyway I considered it my not very pleasant duty to let you know those facts while you were in a state to take them in, so you'll be that much better informed next time round.'

His last few words were half obliterated by the front-door buzzer. 'This'll be young Debbie now,' he said, smiling with lively pleasure as he moved to the door. 'So just you remember, Fiona,' he went on over his shoulder, 'take it step by step next time – tapering off's the way, just to be on the safe side. Hallo my love, how's my gorgeous girl, rotten old day it was till you came along with your sunshiny smile, ooh what's this, come on, you never made it all yourself, not with this beautiful oak-leaf is it, ooh my word, I should say so. Er, this is Fiona just popped in from next door, my granddaughter Debbie. Say hallo to Fiona, my love.'

Debbie was about fifteen, with incredibly straight and shiny dark-brown hair that hung down from the centre of her small head in two identical cascades over the sides of her face and over her shoulders and upper arms. Not smiling now, if ever, she peered wordlessly out from inside her hair like a timid little monkey, the sort to have your finger off given half a chance. Fiona started circling round her towards the exit.

Her grandfather was still talking. 'Fiona's just off, aren't you, dear? Tell me again, Fiona, when did you have your last *portion of strawberry ice-cream*? Oh, that long ago was it, oh well, you won't be coming down with that *nasty stomach trouble* now.' He quelled an inner doubt in a moment and said very positively, 'No, you'll be all right now. Remember I'm here if you need me. Really need me.'

The television came on like a light in the sky and Fiona left to a wild outburst of applause from it, with affectionate whistles and yells. She went back into her flat and held her hands under the cold tap until they had almost stopped shaking, and dropped on to her bed and started thinking about stabbing herself, not too dangerously, just enough to have to go to hospital. Enough to have to be taken to hospital would have been longer-lasting as well as grander, and it would have been fun to see Roger fucking Greenhough knocked off his perch for the first time for sixty years at the sight of a cut artery waved in his face, but silly too, because you could die of one of those, which on the whole she had no great desire to do as yet. Then she decided that just giving

117

herself a bit of a nick with the breadknife instead would be silly in a different way, though no sillier than expecting being sober ever to be as nice as being drunk, or rather getting drunk, or rather setting about getting drunk. Then she tried not to think anything, because she had already thought everything there was in her to think, some of it twice over or more, between lying down here the previous night with the TV on without the sound and the moment the Rob thing had come into her head and set her hunting high and low for pencil and paper at twenty past five in the morning, but that was done now.

Then a great peace came upon her, or alternatively she fell into a half-stupor or freak-out, so that when someone seemed to come on to the balcony outside she just thought it might be one of the little girls from one of the other flats – well, it was only there for a second and it looked more like a little girl than it looked like anything else, so she just forgot about it. Then she fell asleep.

TWELVE

Kenneth of the King's of course knew near enough who Fiona was. Also it would have taken someone far less learned than him not to know about her. As against that she had never become disorderly or fallen down in his house, whatever she might get up to elsewhere. So when she asked him in an ordinary voice for an apple-juice he paused weightily and served her, saying as he handed over her change, 'If you're looking for Harry, er, he'll probably be in in a few minutes,' as a sort of recognition-cum-warning signal.

Anyway that was how she took it. One of the things about being sober was what a lot seemed to be going on at any given moment – another point in favour of being drunk. 'Right,' she said, and tried creasing her face into a smile, 'thanks.'

At the name of Harry someone who had been on the point of leaving paused and turned back. Fiona had a quick impression of tunic collar, metal buttons and a female but unfeminine face with a mouth that suggested some small gnawing mammal like a beaver, none of it stirring any memory or any pleasant expectation either. 'Hallo there,' said a hoarse voice, 'sorry, I'm absolutely hopeless at names, but we have met, haven't we?'

Fiona supplied her name. She was used to such questions from apparent strangers, if not as used as she was to seeing equally unidentifiable persons taking the shortest path to the door or hurrying across the road at her approach. 'I'm trying to think where,' she said, which was just about true.

'Yes, that's right – Fiona, you're dear old Harry's niece, aren't you?'

'Well, in a way.'

There followed a close-to-the-body handshake with knuckle-crushing grip nevertheless and more patter about fancy seeing her in this neck of the woods, but if there was a name anywhere

119

then Fiona missed it. What was to be detected was the presence of something personal, something over and above the non-friendly curiosity she was used to.

'Well, Fiona old girl, you probably don't remember the last time we ran across each other.'

When no more followed Fiona muttered thickly to herself and reached for her apple-juice under the momentary delusion that it was a proper drink.

'Wait a minute . . . it was Monica's down in Chelsea just a couple of weeks ago. Out in that pretty garden there.'

'I expect so.' Fiona flinched as a heavy-duty unpainted lighter was thrust up at her cigarette, held in position and extinguished with a small crash.

'No no, that was the time the ballet company were there. Got it – Steve's in Kew.'

'What? Oh yes.'

'You made a great play for the ginger-haired Iraqi poet.'

'Did I?'

'Well, if it wasn't making a great play I don't know what is. But he told you he already had four wives at home.'

'Yeah.' If Fiona had been drunk she could have coped with this, nipped it in the bud, had a wonderful time in fact, bashed the slag if it came to it, but as it was all she could think of was wait for it to go away. Her way to the door was blocked.

The woman in the tunic put her hands on her hips and her head a long way over to one side. In that pose she reminded Fiona of something in one of those plays with very stark lighting and no scenery and probably from East Berlin that she had been taken to years ago, before all this started – there too the characters had had no names. In a wheedling, almost caressing tone the hoarse voice said, 'You haven't the remotest idea in the wide world where we met or who was there or what happened, have you, my darling?'

'No. And could you stop.'

'Or even if we've ever met at all. Which we haven't, hadn't. And what of it, eh? Eh? Who cares, my love? None of it's worth remembering anyhow. You've got the right idea, my sweetheart. Get smashed out of your mind and *stay that way*. Now just to show there's no ill-feeling let me buy you a nice glass of wine before I go.'

120

'It's apple-juice,' said Fiona. 'And I'm sober.'

'Oh *super* – good for *you*. How *marvellous*. It'll be all the more fun going back on it, won't it? Well, my sugar, in the present circumstances I won't press you. So . . . Have a nice evening. And be sure to give my love to Harry.'

'That's Popsy all over,' said Harry to what Fiona told him on his arrival.

'What? Who?'

'Bunty's girl-friend. She presumably has a surname but I've never heard it. I must have mentioned her to you. More than mentioned. Nobody could just mention Popsy and leave it at that.'

'You identified her just from what I said?'

'That and seeing her coming round the corner from here a moment ago. Nasty. What you need now is a couple of stiff . . . No, it isn't, is it? Er, look, you mustn't take old Popsykins too seriously. She's got a lot of grievances. Against heterosexual women for a start, and no doubt a lot of non-heterosexual women too if her chums on whatever the opposite of the distaff side is are anything to go by. And men, of course. Quite a set. She was just having a go at a couple of those in her own way.'

'Stop being so bloody *understanding*, Harry. It doesn't do any good, it just complicates things, making allowances. Anyway I obviously haven't got across to you how bizarre it was. Just from hearing your name. Her mind must work like a chess-player's.'

'Yes, I've had some of that myself. Short-notice discomfiture.'

'What if I'd set on her? I'm bigger than her.'

'Kenneth's regulars would have pulled you off her and thrown you out and you wouldn't have been able to come in here again. Score two to her side. But you wouldn't have, would you?'

'It's funny how people want to score off other people. I never do.'

Fiona stopped, conscious of having sounded as if she thought she was better than someone. She could feel Harry running his eyes over her, presumably taking in how sober she was. According to her mirror before she came out, she had lost her habitual look of somebody who had gone without food or sleep or human contact for a couple of days and might now be thought to be fairly well on the road to recovery from a serious illness, or else starting to sicken for one. She was wearing the black woollen dress she was almost sure Harry had bought her on a birthday or kindred occasion. Its state of cleanliness, which would have much surprised Marilyn or Linda if noticed, came from its having been kept hung up for untold months in plastic, held firmly in reserve for important contingencies like a visit to the head man at the office that paid her her Giro money or Harry's funeral. With it she wore no jewellery or other ornamentation, not out of good taste or any of those but because everything she had ever had in that line had been sold or stolen or, most often, lost. Or as good as lost – there was a quite decent Georgian cameo ring, once the property of an aunt as it might have been, that Fiona was nearly sure was still where it had fallen down the back of something somewhere in the flat. If she had been quite sure she might conceivably have done something, but she was never quite sure of anything now.

'Well, Fiona,' said Harry, smiling at her. He had a good smile, partly because you could see he had kept his teeth and they were in pretty fair nick and the effect would have been even better if he could somehow have forgotten about it. 'Can I get you, I won't say a drink, but something to put in that glass? Or another glass?'

'I'd love a tomato juice. With a lot of Worcester so you have to force it down a bit like a proper drink.' But not much like one, she thought to herself as Harry moved off. She had once read of something called absolute alcohol, and wondered now what it would be like to force that down.

But she would have had to try, or at least she would have had to say she would, in front of the crowd, among whom it passed for a point of honour never to refuse any proper drink while you could still get it as far as your mouth. All that, and the crowd themselves, seemed a thousand miles away from here. She and Harry had settled down not in the usual semicircular alcove among the gladiators and legionaries but on a little wall-seat for two, set back and sheltered from the door, where they could not be got at. Left on her own for the moment she looked round the half-crowded bar without much curiosity and without any uncertainty at all. Harry was over at the counter between the old boy with the Asian son and the old girl with the Yorkshire terrier, pocketing his change, pausing for a word with a fellow in a very swagger light-grey suit who looked like a Pakistani or one of those. Fiona spent most of her days and a lot of her nights looking forward to getting to the end of whichever bit of either she happened to be in, but this was one she would have let go on as long as it liked.

Usually when she was in public, out anywhere, among strangers, in other words people who were not going to say 'Hallo, Fiona' or 'That's old Fiona over there' – that was when she felt something might suddenly happen that she could neither get out of nor deal with nor even understand. In the days when they were still sending her to shrinks and people, one of them had asked her if she had ever as a child been dumped down in some big place, say a railway terminus, to wait for a parent or some other adult who had turned up very late or not at all, so that she had given them up and not known what to do, and she had not been able to remember anything like that actually happening to her, but it was the best description of how she felt or was liable to feel at certain times in public. She had started to tell the shrink bloke that, but he had gone straight on to questions that boiled down to whether she had ever been beaten, starved, raped, physically or psychically abused or tortured, chained up, shut in a cupboard, played with, made to watch while her mother/sister/other kin were subjected to indignities, and other possible adventures she had not had and he had ticked off in a long column that ran down one side of a green card he had had in front of him.

'This is very nice for me,' she said when Harry had rejoined her on their seat. 'Being in here, I mean. It's so nice that I feel all right. Can I tell you about some things? I want to while I can.'

'Well, yes, of course you can,' he said, doing a fair job in the circumstances.

'I may have said every word of them before. I don't think I have, but I may.'

'That's nothing. People repeat themselves all the time.'

'What you think of me when I've told you about them isn't the point, I shan't be minding. Except I wouldn't like you to think I feel sorry for myself because it's meant to be very unattractive, everybody knows that. But the real point is I don't feel sorry for myself. I suppose I must have worked it out. To feel sorry for yourself you have to feel you don't deserve what you're getting, it shouldn't happen to you or it shouldn't happen to anyone.'

She paused. He had taken her hand and was putting everything he had into looking and sounding serious and sympathetic and not bored, and very shitty it was of her to be thinking so.

'Right,' she went on. 'I deserve what happens to me because I choose to do everything I do, however hard it might be for me to do differently. Alcoholism is not a disease. But I'm getting away from what I was going to tell you. How did I start?'

'Something about wanting to tell me something while you –'

'That's right. While I could. Meaning not only – you can't think how extraordinary it feels to be able to remember two minutes back – meaning yes, while I'm sober and you're here, but also while I'm *all right*, and that's extraordinary too. It means I can tell you what it's like to be me without making things up because they sound good or interesting. The point is there isn't really anything to say. Like madness. Which along with alcoholism is the great bore of the twentieth century.

'Do you remember, did you ever see that film about the drunk chap who thought he saw the mouse coming out of the wall and the bat flying at it and you didn't really see what happened, but there was blood all down the wall? Anyway, the chap was supposed to be a writer or trying to be one and at one stage when he wasn't seeing mice and bats there he was, sitting at his typewriter and he typed "*The Bottle*, a novel by Don Birnam" and then he got anxious and couldn't go on, couldn't start in fact and had a drink and that was that. Well, at the time I thought they just meant he couldn't face the strain, and the chap I was seeing it with, he was a writer and he told me you didn't have to be a drunk to feel like Don Birnam when you were starting on something. Perhaps that side of it got too much for him, because he's in public relations now, or was when I last heard of him, which is quite funny, isn't it?

'Anyway, when I thought about Don Birnam more recently I thought it made much better sense if what was holding him up wasn't nervousness or anything like that but *realising there was nothing for him or anybody else to say*. The rest of the film hadn't got anything to say either about being drunk, how could it, it was all about wanting to be drunk or being ashamed of it or various put-upon non-drunks. I tried myself, you know. Before I really got going I tried to write a story. "Getting Nowhere" it was called. Good title. Then I think there was another one but I

124

must have lost it. Yes. It's having everything going on and being able to take all the meaning out of it and thinking you're free, but then you find what you really are is lost. And the funny thing about it, it's not even particularly horrible, except in a paltry, second-rate sort of way, like things in a dream that would only horrify you if they were really happening, and that's all. Not nearly enough for a book, unless you filled it up with all falling downstairs and stealing and getting arrested. Padding.

'It's not my fault and no one can help. Sending me anywhere is no good and so nor is worrying about me, Harry. If I ever get better it'll be the luck of the draw. You know, fate. God – though you'd have to be a bit of a bloody fool to believe in him and be me. I don't know, though, people who thought they were damned didn't stop believing in God, did they? Can I tell you one more bit?'

'You can tell me as many more bits as you like.' He was really being very good, and what if he did know it?

'My sister who died, Elspeth, I don't think you ever met her, did you, she ran her car into a wall. Ten minutes to ten one Monday morning. Well anyway, we were going through an old photograph album together once, family thing, and she suddenly said, Fee, there's somebody who looks just like you, even the hair, absolutely exactly like you. Annie, it said, our grandmother took a lot of trouble with those albums, writing in everyone's name with a sort of white pencil on the black surround, and we worked out eventually Annie was her elder sister, our great-aunt, and I went into it out of curiosity, and I found out that Great-Aunt Annie died of a liver complaint at the age of forty-one. Liver, cirrhosis of, no? Great-*aunt*, notice, so no ancestor of mine, but what about Great-great-great-grandfather Archibald or Percy, not that I'm saying it started with him or that I'd blame him if it did – *blame* him, good God. Only it does make you feel a little bit sort of hemmed in, a thing like that, even if you weren't already, and start thinking about brain transplants.'

'But you've given it up, Fiona, the drink, I mean. What is it now, the sixth day?'

'Yes, and before that it was nearly six weeks altogether, and I forget how long it was before that. Nobody knows how long Great-Aunt Annie gave it up for, if she ever did. But I'll tell you one quite interesting thing about her, or rather about that photograph of her. You see, I agreed with Elspeth that it looked exactly like me, down to the hair, as she said, but our mum didn't. At least she said it wasn't a good photograph, not a good likeness of her Auntie Annie, who she remembered quite well from when she was a little girl, in fact a medium-sized girl, say ten or eleven. Different-shaped face altogether for one thing I remember she said, so the effects of drink can't have come into it. So perhaps . . . perhaps the original drunk, Great-great-great-grandfather Percy or whoever he was, was an ancestor of hers but not of mine, and handed on his face to only one of us, and his hopeless drunkenness with it. You can see I've thought about this quite a bit.'

Harry looked at her and nodded and drained his glass.

'I didn't mean I don't try to keep off the stuff, of course I've got to try, I just mean trying on its own's no good. I can't help it if that sounds mystical. Everything they say about going on the booze sounds mystical in one way or another. Telling you that lot has cleaned me out, so we'll switch to just chatting like old pals, which you'll find quite easy after a minute or two, you'll see. I had a great evening once with someone who'd just had their husband run off with some floozie because we went into it and then she made me forget it. I know it's not the same but you don't mind that.'

And she told him about Rob when he was being a film producer, and old Mr Greenhough with his funny old ways but not things like his funny old information about his wife's mate in married quarters, and Sean turning into a sort of foul-weather friend, only putting in an appearance when Father Czerny or that Father Kinsella had been telling him it was his duty to, but she did indeed seem rather cleaned out by her monologue to Harry and presently said she thought she would make for home and bed. Yes, there was some food in the flat.

'Will you be all right?' asked Harry, and Fiona knew he knew it was one of the most fart-arsing questions anybody could ask anybody in the circumstances but forgave him for asking it, especially since a certain amount of money came with it.

It was still quite early, not yet dark at any rate, when she went and stood by the balcony window of her flat at the point from which she could see down into the street. Cars went along it all the time with their lights already on, a taxi or two, now and again a bike, not stopping, indeed accelerating hard, speeding up as they moved past away from the corner, set on being somewhere else as soon as they could. She was on the point of giving up when a car did stop almost across the road from her window outside one of the houses that had been turned into flats. These were not flats like hers or the others in her building but old ones where some people with proper jobs still lived, for the time being at any rate. The stopped car, which was black or dark blue and looked newish, had rock music coming from it, not very loud but audibly enough to get to Fiona. She hated rock or whatever it was now called – it seemed to be everywhere and she could only put up with it when she was well away and could no longer separate it from whatever else was going on.

A couple of toots had come from the car as it pulled up and now, as she watched, a fellow, a youngster climbed out of it and went up the steps and rang the bell, and after only a few seconds a female appeared, with shiny pants on and earrings that caught the light, and one after the other the two of them got into the car. They and perhaps others were talking and calling out to one another. The internal light showed faces, shoulders, arms and was gone.

'I want you all to be in a war,' said Fiona very distinctly, though there was nobody to hear her.

With its offside winker winking fussily the car waited for a couple of others to pass it before pulling out and away and accelerating. When it was about to disappear Fiona said in the same voice, 'I want you to have to beg in the street and to have to let horrible things be done to you for money to stay alive.'

On the table stood a bottle of White Nun with a glassful or so out of it and there was more, much more than enough more, where that had come from. The glassful or so was inside Fiona. Later, a little later, she would speed up but so far she had taken it slow, prolonging the best time, when you had started and you knew nothing was going to stop you going on the whole way, which was why it was always best, *really* best, on your own. Perhaps this evening it had been best of all in the pub, feeling all right, feeling safe, feeling doubly safe with this to come, certain to come out of the cash Harry would give her. She seemed to remember that there in the pub she had had some idea of telling him the truth, her own piece of truth, because she thought it ought to be told and he was the one to tell, but that was getting pushed out by the idea that she had been making herself seem worth more of his attention, interest, concern, all at 100p in the pound. Anyway it had mostly been true as far as it went. One thing it had not gone as far as was the other photograph of Great-Aunt Annie her mother had found and shown her and Elspeth – near the back of a group under a tree, not in good focus, rather dark, but still surely, unmistakably, not much like Fiona at all, different-shaped face and everything. It must have been lost years ago, that photograph, but she could still see it in her mind's eye, and as long as she could do that and still went on not mentioning it to anybody – well, it might mean something.

She emptied her glass and refilled it. To be back on it so soon was honestly not very good, but this last one had been a funny one to put it mildly. She might even so have been able to get through it all right if it had not been for those noises. The first one had jolted her awake when she had been asleep for half an hour or so after getting back from next door. Then she had gone through the stages of thinking it was the plumbing, then someone imitating the plumbing, then putting her fingers into her ears even after she had reasoned that if what she had heard had not really come from inside the wall then fistfuls of cottonwool would not keep it out. She had got her door open and her breathing back enough to make it to the street, where blessedly not a hundred yards away a gang of men had been working on the road surface with pneumatic drills and another, bigger machine that thudded loudly and steadily. After standing on the pavement right by them for some time and ignoring their stares, the sort of thing she was in a class by herself at these days, she had felt up to going in search of an unvandalised public telephone, running Harry down in his club with almost the last of her change and setting out to walk over to the King's.

Whatever noises might come out of the walls now, she knew she could handle them, and she still felt it was best on your own in a way, but at the end of an hour or so she began to feel something else, the familiar loss of attention to whatever was on TV and the corresponding impulse to wander. And her telephone was back on.

While she waited for the minicab she sang a little – a hundred years ago she and her parents too had thought she might make a singer, which was a laugh if ever there was one.

> '*Und ein Schiff mit acht Segeln*
> *Und mit fünfzig Kanonen*
> *Wird liegen am Kai . . .*'

She had known some German too at the same sort of stage, which was another laugh, even bigger when you thought about it, but she had long forgotten what it was exactly that the ship with eight sails and fifty guns got up to after reaching the quay, though she did remember that at the end the crew asked the girl Jenny who was supposed to be singing the song how many of the people in the town she wanted killed and, speaking not singing the word, she answered, 'Alle!'

All? Everybody? On the principle that charity began at home if anywhere, what about the old head of the clan? Thanks for asking – fuck the Hon. Iain Menzies Carr-Stewart *for a start*, and *go on* fucking him. One of the episodes from the alcoholic part of her history that Fiona remembered without any trouble at all – it was an early one, true – was the speed, thoroughness and irreversibility with which the Hon. Iain had ditched her when he found out about her and the bottle, not even the whole bottle, just the beginning of it. Her mother, on the other hand, had just not been able to bear any of it from the start, darlings. Her stepfather managed with a choice of three things to tell her, namely to get out if she was there, to stay away if she was not there, and not to forget that whatever anybody said and never mind the rights and wrongs she was over eighteen wherever she was. Elspeth had gone before any of it had got properly started, and was only any good really to mention to people like Harry and to use as a bit of an excuse or extenuation for ending up a drunken wreck. As for Harry himself, he was good, he was kind, he cared, and more than any of that he actually spent money, and there were more reasons than there was tea in China why he could not have actually so to speak really as it were in point of fact gone as far as literally *helping* her. Who could? – but who could or no who could, all. 'Alle!'

The doorbell rang without making her jump, thanks to the start she had made on her third glass of White Nun. To tell the truth it would have been rather fun to have silly old Elspie around to fribble with occasionally and suchlike. Fiona opened the door to reveal the minicab driver. He was really quite something, in the sense that other women might have been looking at him even when sober. Further, he gave no sign of recognising her either directly or from the sort of verbal artist's-impression of her that had presumably been going the rounds among the local companies since very soon after her settling in the district.

'I'm afraid I'm not quite ready,' she said to him. 'Would you mind awfully coming inside for a couple of minutes?'

THIRTEEN

Harry sat reading a well-documented, cogently argued attack on the training methods that had produced the new generation of British hairdressers, whom the writer pronounced to be a disgrace to a civilised country and a substantial cause of our diminished cultural standing among the nations of the world. Mrs Thatcher, he went on, had defeated the miners' and the printers' leaders, but unaccountably left on their perch the little Hitlers of the hairdressing union, an omission which if not repaired in time would cost her his vote at the next General Election.

Part of Harry's interest in the matter was its possible use as a bore-counter at the Irving, partly it was in line with his self-delibrarianisation policy, designed to give him the comforting illusion of knowing something about how other people lived, but mostly it was to regale him while he waited his turn at Andy's Hair Bar and enable him to keep his *Daily Mail* to read with his supper. And he used Andy's because it was cheap and near and it itself had bore-stopping and self-delibrarianising potential. Anyway, if he had not been there that morning he would have missed something, and not only he.

Andy cut Harry's hair in person, not because he was Harry but because he was next. He got round the last lot in what felt like about three and a half minutes, impressively in that the lot included not only quite a lot of hair from the scalp but also lesser quantities from eyebrows, nostrils and (a recent innovation) ears. Then Andy brought his oblong mirror and showed Harry the back of his, Harry's, head, no doubt to solicit his approval. It was while he was trying, for perhaps the thousandth time in his life, to think of something, anything to say in this situation, that Harry glimpsed for a split second a reflection of part of the face of his brother Freddie, like something seen in a clever film and so

131

of course not meant to be recognised, understood or even particularly noticed. When, a moment later, he tried to pick up Freddie by direct vision he had some trouble finding him at the far end of the bench for waiting customers and on the far side of someone who also recalled the art of the screen, a 100-kilogram American Red Indian, say, fresh off location in some piece of cinéma-vérité crap. He would never have spotted his brother but for that chance flash in Andy's mirror. Chuckling slightly to himself, he trousered his change and moved without undue ostentation over to the corner where Freddie lurked.

'Morning, old boy.'

Probably no human being has ever shied much like a startled horse, especially not from a seated, even slumped posture, but anyone who saw Freddie just then might have been forgiven for thinking along such lines. When he had finished doing something like that and looking to and fro for some seconds, he said, 'Harry. What brings you here?'

'The same as you, I imagine, getting my hair cut. Or are you just sitting there for a bet?'

'What? What sort of bet? A bet?'

'Oh, for . . . Or I suppose you might have dropped in for a shampoo and blow-dry.' Harry at once slightly regretted saying that, for the best part of Freddie's hair lay homogenised in a grey-brown fillet across the top of his otherwise naked skull, the result of too much vanity, or not enough? Harry shelved the problem and said, while all in earshot seemed to hang on his lips, 'Actually I'm just off, I've finished here. It is Tuesday week we're seeing you, isn't it?'

'If you're not in the most absolute tearing hurry for the next few minutes I should be terribly grateful for a quick word.'

This, which would normally have taken about three-quarters of an hour to wring from Freddie, came hurtling out at the same time as two or three assorted summonses to a now-vacant barber's chair, notifications that he was next, please, and after Harry had told him twice that of course he would see him and asked him twice where would be convenient, and been told over again that Freddie would so appreciate a brief chat with him, the name of a café or snack bar just down the road was successfully transmitted.

Andy, who had about him something of the look of a Venetian

magnifico, and in view of his birthplace might well have carried some such blood in his veins, courteously held open the shop door when Harry at last left.

'You know my cousin Chris keeps the off-licence near you?'

'Sure, I often buy from him.'

Drawing air in through his nose and shutting his eyes, Andy shook his head and his index-finger slowly to and fro in a complicated cross-rhythm. 'He's got a bad sense of humour, has Chris. It doesn't tell him when to stop.'

'What can I do about it?'

'You, you do nothing. You see this bottle of stuff,' – some high-gravity brownish fluid in a transparent flask was waved fleetingly under Harry's nose – 'supposed to make your hair grow. Now: it doesn't matter whether it makes your hair grow or not. What matters is it costs 98p. I tell you it costs 98p. If you want it you give me 98p and you get it, if you give me 78p you don't get it, you've got a bad sense of humour. You understand?'

'Completely,' said Harry, trying to make it do equally well for thanks for a timely warning and for caving in not without dignity to a gentlish threat.

One way or another it seemed to serve. 'Great,' said Andy, smiling affably, 'take care now,' and, his invariable valediction, 'Please give my best respects to Sir Alex Guinness,' whom Harry must be presumed to consort with in his high-society club.

All that would probably have made perfect, obvious sense in Greek, mused Harry as he looked about for his rendezvous with Freddie. After a short while he came to the conclusion that in his directions Freddie had been doing a Freddie, or one of his Freddies, one of the sort whereby an expression like 'just down the road' could turn out to mean 'somewhere in Greater London I expect the fellow meant'. Harry had about decided to give it up before buggering off across the bridge to a glass of sherry at home when his eye at once fell on an establishment too frankly and repulsively lower-class to have reached his conscious mind the first time round. Its name appeared on a brightly coloured tin sheet that gave more prominence to a type of cola drink and also what might have been the proprietor's name, though it seemed to have more syllables in it than anybody's name ever. He was still dithering round the door of the place when Freddie, his three and a half minutes of treatment done, came hurrying down the hill towards him, moving with unaccustomed decision and speed.

'What a horrible place,' said Harry when they had settled themselves at the back of it, near the counter. This took Harry a little longer than Freddie because he was not used to bolted-down furniture. Each received, brought to his place, a cup of ginger-coloured tea, but Freddie could be heard muttering some further requirement to the statuesque Levantine matron who presided.

'Well yes, I suppose it is really,' said Freddie, at once conceding a point obviously new to him. 'The thing is, you see,' he said, gesturing at the twenty- or thirty-strong mixture of races, colours, creeds and no doubt other variables that sprawled or lurched in the far from extensive area close by the bar, 'that nobody ever comes in here.' As he spoke he ducked his head for a second under a cardboard-box-lid full of cups of tea and assorted eats being carried to customers outside the walls. New arrivals pressed forward up the aisle, sometimes calling out to one another.

Harry took his brother's meaning and quickly guessed more. 'Where are you supposed to be?'

It was in Freddie's favour that while distinctly more likely than not to fail to understand what you said to him, he never pretended to. 'Prideaux's,' he said, referring to an establishment in Duke Street St James's that had been cutting the hair of gentlemen and of other persons of sufficient standing for a hundred years or two. 'Down there in the minicab,' explained Freddie, 'hang about waiting for your turn, fellow with the scissors treats you as if he was painting your bloody picture for the Royal Academy, lucky if you're out of the place much under the hour. Then finding a cab back and so on, call it ninety minutes door to door minimum. Whereas this way I'm in and out of Andy's in fifteen minutes, about the same in here, leaves me just about a full hour to myself.'

'What do you do in that time? Just go on eating?'

'Ah, now that's the most extraordinary part of the lot. If it hadn't been for Hartmann, Leafe there'd have been no actual objective to the whole enterprise. I mean supposing he confined himself to British Empire and Protectorates or even Europeans and Possessions. Plenty of 'em do, you know, even today. Or what if he simply hadn't been there at all? I'd have had nowhere to go. Nowhere in the wide world.'

While Harry expressed what sympathy he could at such a predicament, a voice called loudly, 'One bacon butty with fried tomatoes on the side.' It had called similarly once or twice before without any response visible to Harry, but this time Freddie's hand shot up like a know-all schoolboy's. An ugly but far from graceless dark girl in a fairly clean overall, on obvious nodding terms with Freddie, came and laid in front of him a considerable plateful of fried slices of white bread and thick salty bacon with all the rind left on and ancillary tomatoes, as specified. Fats swam and bubbled there.

'My God,' said Harry with a remote envy. 'Butter too.'

Freddie shook his head as he picked up two of the three varicoloured plastic dispensers before him. 'Butter, who said anything about butter? This is *marge*. Very hard to get these days I can assure you. Oh yes. *Marge*.' He made converging jets of mustard and brown sauce play on what he was evidently about to eat. 'Are you quite sure you won't have anything?'

'Quite sure, thanks. What would you call this? Not your breakfast?'

'Oh I never eat breakfast,' said Freddie severely and with several pauses. 'No no, this is my middle-mornings. Don't have a great deal in the way of lunch after this lot. Sardine or beetroot or so. I've got it fixed so there are these times when I somehow don't seem to feel like more than a bite of anything at all when lunchtime comes round. Just as well too. We all eat a damned sight more than can possibly be good for us these days, I expect you agree.'

Though Harry readily gave his agreement, Freddie must have realised he had still left a good deal out of his self-explanations, though what he said next, after dragging from his mouth a strip of bacon-rind the thickness of sash-cord, still sounded less than basic.

'This, this hairdo of mine,' he said, identifying it with his fork. 'I expect you think it looks a bit damned silly, all scraped over the top like that.'

'To be perfectly candid I haven't given the matter a great deal of thought.'

'She now has the whole thing finally organised. On the first

Thursday of every month she gives me six fivers and sends me down to Prideaux's to get me hair done. Then the other week the fellow driving me down there in the minicab said, "My pal Andy'll fix that for you in five minutes, scissors and a hot comb, you could near enough do it yourself," he said, "whole thing cost you a fiver including tip." Well. I don't mind telling you that set me thinking. The first time I tried it I just walked about after Andy had finished with me, looked into a few shops, bookseller's and a couple of others, till it was time to set about getting back. But it was the being where she didn't know I was and the not doing what she thought I was doing that was the thing that put the, put the, the *sting* into it, you know.' He laughed gently, resavouring his triumph, then turned businesslike again. 'Twenty quid to the good, too.

'Then the *next* time, I can't imagine how I missed it before, I walked slap into Hartmann, Leafe. Moved up from their old place in Cecil Court only the previous year. Old Hartmann's gone now, but the son remembered me, remembered my field, too. "We've got the new Belize issue complete but you've never cared for first-day covers, have you, Mr Caldecote?" Of course stamps, *postage* stamps, were always a great interest of mine at school, you know.'

Some quirk in Freddie of humility or derangement had often caused him to inform his hearers of facts they had known at least as long and as well as he in the manner of one imparting a close secret or perilously neglected truth, like his father's full Christian names or how to tell the time. Harry had thumped him for it when they were children and wanted to now a bit, reminding him pari passu that actually he, Harry, had spent more than half the money and done more than half the work on what had been their joint collection until pressure on his time from model aeroplanes and girls had caused him to sell his shares for a nominal sum – so fucking nominal a sum that the memory could still rankle. But he only said, 'You kept it up after school, surely. Till your marriage at least, wasn't it?'

Freddie nodded sombrely. 'Yes, I rather dropped it after that.' He stared down at his plate, which prolonged wipings with pieces of bread had brought to good-as-new condition. 'Do you know what I enjoyed most about that snack?'

'The marge?'

'The fact that it wasn't beef Stroganoff or sole bonne femme or steak en croûte or tripe à la mode de Caen.'

'I see. Aren't you going to have some afters?'

They looked over at a blackboard advertising spotted dick — roly-poly — syrup pudding — plum duff. Freddie shook his head sadly. 'I daren't. I'll have to eat some sort of lunch, and anyway it was time I was getting down to Hartmann, Leafe.'

'Mind if I stroll along with you?'

Freddie made no objection. As they left the snack-bar he went openly through his money. There would be a little more of it today than usual, since by his old magic he had beguiled his brother into paying their joint bill. Harry went on alert not to find himself forking out for a Penny Black or one of those triangular Cape of Good Hope jobs when the time came. He asked, 'What made you drop it and then take it up again after all these years?'

The way Freddie glanced at him before answering had the effect of reminding him how long it seemed, must in fact have been, since they had last talked to any purpose à deux. 'What made me drop it was Désirée. Like a damned fool I showed her my stuff, told her about it, got her interested. And she did get interested, she's an intelligent woman in her way. The only thing was, when it came to the stamp collection, I wanted to do it with her, to share it, and she wanted to run it, so before you could say Jack Robinson there she was running it. She didn't really see eye to eye with me on Latin America, either, thought the Pacific had much more of a swing to it. One day it wasn't my stamp collection any more, so I dropped it. Does that sound most frightfully bloody childish and silly?'

'Not to me,' said Harry. He had been reminded more than once of the conversation he had had with Clare about Freddie and Désirée and how Désirée would insinuate herself into the writing of Freddie's new poem or poems the first time the subject had come up. Unwillingly reminded, needless to say. Purely as a delaying measure, he asked, 'Did Désirée keep it up at all, the collection?'

'Dropped it even more stone cold than I had. No fun without me, she said. I had quite a bit of explaining to do.'

'How did you explain it?'

'Can't remember now to tell you the honest truth. Something

else must have come along. Something always does in a marriage, doesn't it? Early on, anyway. The shop's just at the end of the row here. As for me taking it up again, that was easy. I simply stepped in through the door, and there it all was. I just felt . . .'

'Like stout Cortez, when with eagle eyes he stared at the Pacific.' Harry remembered arguing with Freddie in their schooldays about how much a difference it was supposed to make that Cortez had eagle eyes while all his men presumably only had ordinary human ones, and so their wild surmise might be meant to be not worth much.

'Well not quite Harry, I mean Cortez had only the vaguest idea of where he was and none at all of the extent of what he was staring at. However.' Freddie looked suddenly at his brother in some sort of new way or closer way – not than ever before, it could not have been than ever before, just than most people would have thought possible at that moment. 'Harry, I've got an hour and twenty pounds a month, that's regular, something I can count on, though there are other little bits at odd other times that's all I can count on. I've got to get away from her more than that. Sitting in a room supposedly writing a poem with her waiting in the next room and not asking me about it afterwards isn't enough. I've got to get away from her more than that, I don't mean for ever, I've got to have some, some, some place to go or an evening off or a motor-boat or something, and that means money, doesn't it, money, and she won't give me any. That's what I wanted to speak to you about. Is there any chance that rubbishy so-called poetry might earn me a few bob? – *a few bob of my own.* Is there any chance at all of that?'

They were waiting to cross a side-street and Harry looked at his brother closely too, or perhaps he merely remembered a lot of past impressions – anyway, he saw the face of the gentlest and most vulnerable person he had ever met, also the biggest fucking fool and the most self-serving by disposition. More to the point, the plea just made would mean that he, Harry, instead of getting Freddie's muck printed in some hoary cathedral-close quarterly that existed to supply the genteel unread at 50p a pamphlet, which was as far as his thoughts had taken him, would have to show it to a real publisher or two and get hold of a couple of real rejections. Or something. Automatically, he said, 'It'll take a long time.'

'I've waited a long time already.'

The two reached the portals of Hartmann, Leafe. Millions of stamps of innumerable kingdoms, republics, principalities, federal territories, associated states and island groups, of all shapes and sizes and hues, or wildly varying face and sale values and of one total and totally uniform boringness to Harry were spread out before them. Well, he had lost interest in model aeroplanes too.

'You just have a good look-round, do you?' asked Harry.

'Oh no, I buy. In a very small way as things are at the moment, of course.'

'Where do you keep your, your albums or whatever they are? Not at home, surely?'

'Good God, no, I couldn't think of it. Here. They let me have part of a little sort of cupboard.'

'So you just see them once a month.'

'If you care to put it like that, yes. For the moment. I'm, er, I'm working on that. Coming in for a quick once-over?'

'No, got a couple of things to get off before lunch.'

Freddie blinked and seemed to turn his head away at the last word. 'I shouldn't have eaten all that bread in that butty I had, you know. The thing is, one gets so fed up with all that vile wholemeal high-extraction stone-ground stuff or whatever they call it that's supposed to be good for you. All that filthy wheat-germ and calcium and iron. When I see a proper bit of old-fashioned sliced bread made out of decent white flour, and soaked in all that cholesterol . . .'

'Wouldn't it help if you skipped breakfast on haircut days?'

'Not a chance of that, she thinks I need building up for the long haul down to St James's and back. Bran flakes. Even a kipper. That reminds me, this morning I managed to wrap half a kipper up in a page of *The Independent* while she was on the damned telephone.' He reached inside his coat. 'Don't watch me.'

But Harry could not stop himself watching his brother pull out the folded grease-stained packet, look left and right, hesitate in a way calculated to attract any spare attention for yards around, and with mingled defiance and furtiveness drop the thing in the gutter and turn wordlessly aside. If Harry could somehow have known how much of that defiance and furtiveness was real and how much an act, he would have known silly old Freddie in a way he probably never would now.

FOURTEEN

'I really do wish I could get you to change your mind, dear. I can easily get them to – '

'Yes, I'm sure you do,' said Clare, 'but this is one you have to get through on your own.'

'No, I just mean it would make a bit of a change for you in the most harmless ordinary way.'

'Nothing's ever in any sort of harmless ordinary way with Piers, as you perfectly well know. If he'd wanted you to bring me along he'd have asked you to bring me along. He wants something from you, either something that at the end of the day turns out to be what boils down to be a really not very sizeable sum of money – either that, or else some money.'

'Whereas you've never been known to slip him a tenner in your life,' said Harry.

'All right, what if I have, this is something on a bigger scale altogether and in every sort of way I don't want anything to do with it. Sorry.'

'I merely thought you might like a bit of lunch at the Irving, that's all.'

'No that's not all, there is that but it's not all, you wanted me to share the responsibility of whatever it is and also because Piers embarrasses you slightly and you wanted me to be there too as a mate or a sidekick or a batter for your side, and I don't blame you in the least. It's nothing to be ashamed of. To ride shot-gun with you. He embarrasses the hell out of me too, always has, right from a small child.'

'What nonsense,' said Harry with as little conviction as he had ever brought to anything, if that was not too huge a statement.

'But I'm not saying you're not also thinking in a nice way it would be fun for me to have lunch out somewhere some time. So it would, but there's nothing urgent about it. I'm not somebody

141

that needs having something done about them. Honestly.' Clare smiled at her brother and touched his hand quickly. 'I have chums and children and things, you know. Mostly rather a long way off but *there*. I don't *need* taking out. In fact I only really . . .'

'Perhaps the week after next, there's not a lot on then,' said Harry, before she could go on to call to mind that the only person she had really liked being taken out by was Arnold. 'Oh, I must remember to ask the chef about that mustard.'

It was funny, thought Harry, how different it seemed to be to have a living but absent wife, in fact two of the same, compared to having a dead husband. He himself was constantly running into one or other of his exes, from mentions to quite long bits of conversations with them, in memories of a couple of moments in a bus and of whole blocks of years as long as school, all of it much of a muchness with the rest of his life as he looked back on it. And if he were to hear in the next minute that Gillian or Daisy had died, would it all change? Of course not. But why not? Would it make a difference if Daisy, say, had left four months or four weeks before instead of four years? Yes, of course, but a *great* difference? A big enough difference to make him feel like Clare about Arnold? – whatever that was. Had Clare loved Arnold more than he had loved Daisy (or Gillian)? Yes, or rather very likely, or rather quite likely, but a *lot* more?

Harry was constantly getting about this far with his reflections on this subject and no further. He might have said he was trying vaguely to work out something comforting to say to Clare, or perhaps more to think to himself. And after all these times he was getting clearer and clearer in his mind that he was never going to be able to do any better than, dear God, that it had been a mercy when the suffering had ended. And there had been dreadful times, not so many nowadays, luckily, when Harry had wondered whether even that was true.

Of course life would not have been livable, let alone worth living, if Arnold's shadow had been as low and as dark as that for more than a second or two together. Now, this bright morning, with frothy crisps of white cloud flowing upwards into the intensified blue sky like paper streamers, he and it seemed as far away as he was ever going to be. At such times the Irving Club and everything it stood for seemed expressly designed to negate all such possibilities. For a little while it still seemed on the face of it worth trying to pull oneself up a measurable way from the primeval muck and murk.

'Drinking club this Irving place, isn't it?' asked his driver, a young man encountered before who regularly made Harry feel very humble about his acquaintance with the growing majority of modern youth. He had gathered, and found it most believable, that all these fellows did at least one other job besides their minicabbing (of course paying tax on nothing whatever like everybody else). This particular instance, who must have been about thirty, could from the look and sound of him have spent half his working-life as anything from a ball-bearing operative to a valve-trombonist.

Harry guffed smartly back with the standard candlclight-on-polished mahogany vignette of fellows in lace cuffs savouring this and that out of crystal decanters proffered by obsequious servants, but it went over less well than it would have done even quite recently.

'Yeah, but you knock 'em off pretty cruel in there when you get going, don't you?' Not a particle of irreverence or anything but a studious matter-of-factness entered the driver's tone. 'I mean I've given one or two of your porters a hand before now with an old gentleman who's been doing very-nicely-thank-you-indeed so he could use a couple of extra legs. And I'm not talking about the odd two or three, I'm talking about waiting in that little bit of Lyceum Court eleven o'clock at night *midweek* and hearing the din coming out in waves, in positive *waves*, like, well, I wouldn't really know what to compare it with.'

'Boat Race Night?'

'Yeah, I dare say, whatever that was. Well, not unlike a little bit of Trafalgar Square on New Year's. You know, like a little posh bit of that.'

Harry took a pride in being tremendously egalitarian with his minicab drivers, but the next bit he could hear coming out a bit cold while it was still coming. 'If you don't mind my saying so, I think you must be confusing us with the Garrick Club, which is just round the corner from the Irving. I have heard that some of the members there – '

The driver pulled in and pulled up so decisively that for a distinct moment Harry thought he must surely be about to offer to fight him. Then, 'Harry,' he said, quietly and slowly, leaning over the back of his seat, where there hung a red-ringed disc-shaped notice thanking the world in general for not smoking – 'Harry, believe me, the last thing in my intentions was causing you the slightest offence. My object was merely to make a social observation devoid of any moral comment whatsoever.' After a couple of paraphrases of these disclaimers he asked, 'So can we take it from there?'

'By all means. I mean right on.'

When they moved off again the driver's manner had reverted entirely to the businesslike detachment it had held earlier, indeed had hardly lost. Even perhaps a hint of dreaminess could now be heard. 'I find it interesting to observe it on its way out, what you might call the whole drinking culture, because it is, isn't it, obviously. Smoking's on its last legs, drinking's going the same way. Oh, it'll last your time, Harry, but it's kind of funny, isn't it, to think that one not-so-distant day drinking'll be, not illegal, but something you'll have to go somewhere special to do, like, well, I can't really think of a good comparison, like going off to get whipped, or, well, I suppose getting whipped would do as well as any.' (He was courteously refraining from what was usually coupled in such contexts with getting whipped, thought Harry, i.e. getting peed on.) 'That will cost you four-fifty, Mr Caldecote,' continued the driver, pronouncing the name in its owner's style as from the very first time – 'it's gone up again, I'm afraid, which is one of the penalties we pay for having a strong government.'

Harry just had time to catch a brief, confused picture of himself as one of a small, persecuted band of taxpaying heterosexuals eating bacon butties, drinking claret and reading hardbound books in a songless, televisionless cranny in the bowels of some underground Irving of the future before the marble, brass and plush of the reality enfolded him. The great actor as seen by Watts in the part of Lear loomed down as ever from the half-landing, the authority of his glare a little blunted to this day by the slash inflicted on the canvas by a member of the women's suffrage movement who had taken it for a likeness of David Lloyd George, then Chancellor of the Exchequer.

'Your guest's waiting for you in the morning-room, sir.'

Even assuming this visitant was not some surprise-packet bore kept out of Harry's diary by Freudian intercession, there was something definitely not-all-right afoot here. No quest for money, however naked or however well wrapped up, had been in all history enough to get Piers along to a rendezvous at a stated time, let alone ahead of it. Harry felt something of the uneasiness of a young man in Waugh's Africa who fears that a remark about the lateness of the rainy season, say, may be taken as a request for the person of a favourite wife of the chief. This feeling sharpened at the sight of Piers – for it was he, not instantly recognisable in a suit of morello-coloured flannel, cut perhaps by the best man in Rio de Janeiro – striding forward with splayed hand, obviously ahead in everything – salary, service, destination – except age. 'Good to *see* you,' he kept saying, and 'Come and sit *down*,' as if this conferred a rare intimacy. 'I'm afraid I've been a wee bit naughty with the tipple, but a most frightfully nice man asked me what I'd like to drink, and I said I wasn't a member, but he said any son of Mr Caldecote's will always have his wants met in this club, and before I knew where I was . . .'

Harry noticed straight away that the tipple in its silver bucket (a gift from Beerbohm Tree) was not only champagne but the Cordon Puce, the club's priciest (think yourself lucky it's not a bloody Rehoboam, he reflected grimly), and took hardly longer to admire the skill with which he was being manoeuvred into the position of the one being stood the treat, done the good turn. Would that champagne be all right, for instance? Because if not . . .

By some similar process of shuffling, the flat shared with Bunny and Popsy, once a rather peachy little spot however questionable the company, now seemed devoid of all charm, while the erstwhile poky little basement chez Caldecote had miraculously expanded into just the spot for the rather exciting desk-top venture he was about to give a trot (with a few quid spent on it of course). Harry began to get anxious. There were not enough noughts in this for Piers to have asked himself out at the Irving for. In particular, his imitation of Popsy going on about the nobs who visited the Camden Town gallery, while adequately horrifying, would butter no parsnips. Then he said, 'Actually there was something rather particular I wanted to say to you about those two while we're on the subject. Just to lay things on the line.'

This intensified Harry's mild feelings of alarm. Piers was famous through most of the English-speaking world for his habit of threatening to come to some unpleasant or at least revelatory point without ever actually doing so, but this time he looked and sounded as if he meant to. Especially looked. Harry was no great one for suddenly realising things or even for realising them at all, but given the leisure and the inclination he might have been able to set down how his son was looking at him just then, without the sort of peering of the muscles round the eyes, half-squint, half-glaze, that unless hostility was present always had the hint of a smile with it, perhaps a not very affectionate smile – seriously, in fact. Harry tried to seem expectant. What else was he to seem?

'Popsy,' said Piers, refilling his father's glass with his own champagne in a lordly way, 'is by way of being a bad lot. It'll come as no news to you that I know a bit about bad lots. There are,' he went on, smiling now, but without any hint of superiority or sophistication, 'different sorts of bad lots. Popsy's sort likes fisticuffs, so to call them. With other ladies. That sort of thing is likely to impede my own activities. But more to the point, a consideration that may sound strange to you coming from me, Daddy, and I apologise for bringing this up with you at all, but the situation has reached the stage where Bunty must be detached from Popsy for her own well-being. How, I haven't the smallest idea. You may. That unpolished but by no means unamiable person representing himself as her husband whom you produced on a couple of occasions conceivably may. And now I see that His Honour Dafydd Onslow has risen to move to the luncheon-table I suppose we'd better follow his lead. I remember the same system applying the very first time you brought me here, though of course it was a different old josser in the green chair then. That must be nearly twenty years ago. How time flies, to be sure, though I must say *how little happens* would be a more appropriate way of putting it. This is a lovely ceiling, isn't it? I remember it from that first time.'

Piers had somehow got them a window table, a move usually thought of as desirable, though Harry had never much cared for the view it gave of a tattered thicket of dark shrubs. According to him the country should be left in the country.

'You took me to Lord's that summer,' continued Piers, 'and

146

Westminster Abbey and everywhere under the sun – you were offering me what you had, and I appreciated it, I mean I appreciated your doing it, and then there came the horrible moment when I realised *I didn't want it*, not any of it. No, this is fine, I always take the cold table whenever I happen to lunch here. It's a thing that people never seem to allow for, that two chaps can lead quite full and interesting and up to a point satisfying lives and not so to speak overlap at all, or anywhere it matters. Like yours and mine, both of them equally – what's the word they all use? – equally *valid*, though it's true that the law might think that parts of mine were rather less valid than parts of yours in certain respects – not that I propose to embarrass you about that or anything else. It's a pity we haven't turned out to have had more in common, but there it is. Ah, now, Cyril, you're never going to tell me that you still manage to get in those wonderful Maconochie's potted shrimps as you always did in days gone by.'

'Ah, well, no, Mr Piers, I haven't seen you in here for a little while, have I now, I'm afraid those fellows of Maconochie's have gone and faded away in the meantime like a lot of other nice old things in the world. Pemberton's which we take now are perfectly eatable but the money goes on to the wrapper instead of into the wrapper if you follow my meaning.'

Cyril was gone before Piers could slip him a lucky silver threepenny-bit for his youngest's youngest. His attempt to evoke from the wine waiter, even in memory, a Chandon de Briailles not on the list was a failure, and his half-called exchange with a passing third party – 'sorry, just assumed everyone in here knew Charlie' he apologised to Harry – too short to cut much ice either. After that, and a considerable pause, something very rare in conversations with Piers except as accompaniment to a threat, he returned to the serious face he had inaugurated with his Popsy tip-off. More silence. Then, in a tone not so very different from usual, he said,

'This is where you'd be expecting to get more talk of my own concerns in Piers-type detail, abundant and uninformative at the same time, but on a sort of crescendo, as if real information might be somewhere on the way.' He carefully poured out some more of the actually rather good but not at all competitively priced Château Tahlbik Goulbourn Valley Cabernet Sauvignon

Private Bin that was that month's special recommendation of the Wine Committee, and said,

'And now, dearest Daddy, I am now about to tell you what egregiously *monstrous* con I have lined up for you this fair morning.'

Harry burst out laughing. Afterwards he told himself it was a reaction of pure embarrassment, such as those reportedly betrayed by Orientals on hearing of examinations failed, parents incinerated in defective tower-blocks, etc. 'Well, yes, I am admittedly *on pins* to know,' he said when he had thoroughly finished laughing.

'The idea is simplicity itself. Does one still have to wait until after two o'clock before one may smoke in here?'

'I'm afraid so, and should you be happening to fancy your churchwarden you'll have to stay in the card-room, the billiard-room or the garden no matter what the time.'

'The possibilities are too rich,' said Piers, laughing himself, indeed drumming briefly at the green-and-gold-carpet with his heels. 'I was reading just the other day, heaven knows where or why, that the world record for uninterruptedly smoking a tenth of an ounce of tobacco – lit by a single match, note – is something over 126 minutes. The scene was needless to say somewhere in the United States. You know, in a curious fashion I find my ability to recall that fact at this moment as telling a piece of evidence for the existence of God as any I've ever come across. One can't help wondering why one should have that feeling. Now, Daddy, the scheme is that you scrape together every spare penny of your cash and give it all to me, and I take it all away with me somewhere I shan't be telling you or anybody else about, and then I come back and give you half a dozen times the money you gave me in the first place and then we all go off and have the most marvellous party somewhere together. Now then, what do you find yourself saying to that?

'And while you're rehearsing some of the things you find yourself saying to that, I'll just see if I can't catch Cyril's eye and persuade him to part up with a couple of those angels-on-horseback Mary used to do so beautifully. Nowadays they always seem to give you a prune instead of an oyster inside the bacon which to my way of thinking makes a devil of the thing instead of an angel. Ah, I'm afraid Cyril's in the right of it and there's a lot of nice things that are passing away.'

'That do be passing away, and that's the truth of the matter, begob, you mean. Look, sonny-boy, or rather Sonny-Boy, there may be all sorts of things about you I don't know but one of the ones I do know is that you're no sort of fucking Irishman.'

'And haven't the pair of us had to learn there's more than one sort of fucking them. But no, you're right, you and I are far too devious in our different ways for anything but a couple of bloody Saxons, Daddy. No, it's just my tendency to slip into whoever may be in the air at the time, which trait you'll admit might have come in quite serviceably for me at certain stages of my career. But haven't we been digressing?'

'Nevertheless I remember perfectly well the point we'd reached. You'd just offered to take all my spare cash off me in return for your promise to pay it all back to me a few days later at a rate of several pounds in the pound.'

'Something of that sort, yes. All that part is quite straight-forward. The difficulty arises when it comes to the question of security. This consists in the first place of my personal effects, which would just about fix you up with a couple of drinks and a newspaper, in the words of another piece of reading I seem to have been doing recently.'

'And am I supposed to say back to you, "And in the second place?", or are we thinking about a rather better class of reading-matter?' Although he still spoke lightly, Harry felt the beginnings of a leaden hope that this was going to turn out to be no more than a fairly funny way of taking a swagger lunch off the Old Dad and showing what flights of fun these old Terrible Two (*fl.c.* 1955) could still get up to on their day. He knew him better than that. Surely.

'For Christ's sake, Piers.'

'What's the matter, Dad?'

'Bit of a round unvarnished tale, isn't it?'

'Oh, I'm not joking if that's what you think. Calm down. Don't let the size of it daunt you. Consider now. You and I have after all been through a certain amount of this before. Admit it. How many times have you co-operated with me to facilitate, or rather render perfectly certain, some method of picking up some unattended cash?'

'Four.'

'Four! Oh. I see, you mean you're counting Bunche-Babington.'

'Only numerically, so to speak. Not morally. It was worth going down for the little I went for to imagine the look on his face when he heard what had happened.'

'Spoken like a true Caldecote. He had got an unusually horrible face, hadn't he, poor old Bunchers. Do you remember those red bristles on his cheeks? I've often thought about them. You know, I think some perfect fiend of a girl must have told him they were rather attractive. Sort of masculine. I can't imagine any other explanation. Anyway, that's one Bunche-Babington, one that really should have gone like a bloody Technicolor dream if there were a particle of justice anywhere in heaven or earth . . .'

'Which one was that?' asked Harry curiously.

'What? The plastic marble.'

'Oh, that one. All right, go on.'

'Well, then there was that so-so one, where if it hadn't been for – '

'If you ask me there was a bloody sight more so than so about that by the time everything was squared away. And finally there was one debacle so complete and spectacular that you swore you'd never ask me for another bloody bean.'

'Not me. That was you. You swearing I'd never get another bean out of you.'

'It comes to the same thing in the end.'

'M'm, I suppose it does a bit.'

'Right, so totting 'em up that comes to one Bunche, one not too bad, one not too good and one fall of the house of Usher. Doesn't sound very encouraging, does it?'

'Not put like that, no.'

'Well, how would you put it?'

'Less colourfully. But now listen, Dad. You like a bit of a gamble, a little flutter. I may not have inherited much in the way of your temperament or tastes but I've certainly got that in full.' Piers had gone back to his serious face. 'I'm putting all I can raise on this but it's different for me. You lay out what you can afford. I promise you, if you'll pardon the expression coming from me, that you won't regret it. You see, Dad, just for the time being I've run out of clever things to say to you.'

Harry was slightly disconcerted, but he said only, 'Well, we can at any rate proceed a little further on a theoretical basis. This, er, this proposal, it is I take it entirely legal?'

'*Legal?*' Piers's voice shook when he pronounced this word. 'Did you notice anything when you mentioned the fall of the house of Usher just now?'

'I don't think so. Why? Oh, I did think you farted slightly but that was probably just my imagination.'

'*No,*' said Piers, crossly now. 'It took me back – when I was once briefly detained in an interview room I remember thinking I could hear the doors of the bloody gaol grinding shut behind my back.'

'I can well believe it would be rather a frightening experience, but, er, what's it got to do with the fall of the house of Usher?'

'Don't be so literal-minded. There was this awful sense of impending doom, you see, everything going all . . . And by the way it's no joke, Daddy dear, if that's your feeling on the matter. I don't suppose you've ever been to prison, have you? Spent a night in the cells?'

'Not so much as a cup of morning coffee.'

'Well I have. Just the one. Quite enough. There were no end of apologies the next day.'

'On their part?'

'No, on mine. They were in the wrong as it happened but I didn't let that stand in my way. If asked the most amazing thing I have ever heard I think I might mention the fact that some people go to prison more than once, and yes I rather *would* like a glass of port.'

They moved to the card-room where, in the manner of rooms in men's clubs, cards had not been played in living memory, though a great deal of port had been drunk in this one. Piers chose the 1967 Warre rather than the 1960, which Harry privately considered to be showing off rather, and outlined his scheme.

He had heard from one of his many nameless sources that he could buy for £50,000 fifteen per cent of a company engaged in importing something called Gospodin vodka. From a quite separate but equally nameless though rather more drunken source he had heard that there was soon going to be an enthralling Press campaign extolling this same Gospodin vodka – the source had gone all lyrical over poems being plastered up in the Tube. The shares were to be introduced into the pig-pen – the abstruse technical expression signifying the unlisted securities market, the one accessible to the general public – quite soon, certainly before the end of the year.

'I see,' said Harry. He did too, or partly did, or might for the next five minutes or so. 'Well, where do I come in?'

'Ah, now that's the easiest part of the whole lot. You come in with the £50,000 – yes, I know, but that would be the ideal picture.'

'But as much as I can.'

'*Please*, Dad. Another word from the distant past.'

'Well . . . First of all, why come to me for any of it? I'd have to get nearly everything on a mortgage, as you may perhaps not have considered, I don't keep drawersful of five-pound notes. And as for reasons we've been through old times' sake.'

'A good question. So that I can do you down a bit, Daddy. I can get away with giving you less in return than I could a more orthodox supplier.'

'That section I find wholly convincing. Any other reason?'

'Well, I want to keep third parties out of this. There's not a lot written down about it. And you don't know anybody to go behind my back to. Convincing?'

'Sufficiently, if not very attractive. Now: what's this Gospodin vodka?'

'What? I don't know. A horrible type of muck distilled out of sawdust, rotting cabbage-stalks and peasants' boots in some slave-state, rendered free of actual poison and popular with people who don't like the taste of drink but like getting or being drunk. You know. Vodka as prepared at the court of the royal house of Ruthenia.'

'Is it legal?'

'Dad, what the fuck, *legal*? You mean the said horrible type of muck? On a British excise licence? It wouldn't be if it were left to me but of *course* it's *legal*.'

'Sorry. Isn't there some stuff called, what is it, Stolypin vodka?'

'Very likely. In fact I'm sure I've seen it advertised. What of it?'

'Well, I just wondered if it had any connection with this other stuff, what is it, Gospodin, because apparently there's quite a bit of shady dealing in the, the *Stolypin* stuff going on round where I live, and . . .'

A minute and a half later Piers was saying, 'So the fact that some Turk or Greek may or may not be flogging half a dozen bottles of one brand of filth a few bob under the odds means you don't want to hear any more about a legal transaction a million miles away related to another brand of filth. *Dad.*'

'What's that supposed to convey? Professional disgust?'

'Oh, nothing so severe. Professional disappointment at the amateur.' Then his expression lightened. 'Why don't you just say you're windy? You can to me, you know. And I can't say I blame you. But you really should have wanted to know more. Like how much you stood to pull in. Well. Thanks for a sterling lunch. And reflect that I wouldn't have asked you if I weren't sure. And also that half of £50,000 is £25,000.'

They came out on to a landing where theatrical memorabilia stood in glass cases and where, at the sesquicentennial celebration a couple of years before, Clare had spent nearly a whole half-hour with a fairly famous actor without his once letting her know that he was any sort of actor at all. The man hanging about there now was quite a different one, though not perhaps as different as could be, a friend of Harry's, in fact the one once described by Clare as a funny old publisher, a stocky fellow called Will Morrissey with an appearance that suited his calling, or perhaps rather better that of a venal city official in some corruption-disclosing American classic.

As soon as Harry laid eyes on Morrissey, before he had the least inkling of the reason, he knew he had to keep him away from Piers, and set about edging him past towards the stairhead. But, by an instinct no less finely tuned, and particularly useful to him in his line of occupation, Piers was as quickly aware of the pressure and set about resisting it. At the same moment Morrissey recognised him.

'Ah, the scapegrace son,' he said.

'That's me.' Piers was obviously not going to bother with this part of Morrissey. But the three of them were halted together now.

'What do you think of this?' immediately demanded Morrissey in the hectoring style he habitually conversed in and mistakenly thought caused club servants and others to regard him as a bit of a character. The 'this' that he had been hanging about staring unfavourably at was a sort of portrait bust in yellowish stone on a greyish sort of pillar. 'Bloody revolting,

153

isn't it?' he went on as immediately, to save either of the other two the embarrassment of voicing a mistaken opinion of what was before them. 'I agree it doesn't look in the least like Charlie, which is a relief, even so I can understand Prunella not wanting it in the house, but I'm buggered if I see why we have to let her present it to the club and not only that but have it where people can't help seeing the bloody thing all the time. You're on the Works of Art Committee, aren't you?' he asked Harry.

'No. I'm afraid I really must be – '

'Never mind, you can write a letter to the Chairman explaining why you think it would be much more in keeping in the servants' shithouse. You're good at that sort of thing.' Then, after an instant when he might have left them after all, he went on, 'Oh, just while I've got you, Harry, that poem of your brother's you pushed my way. We've had someone else look at it and the upshot is – '

'Already? But it was only about last Tuesday – '

'That's the extraordinary thing. You dropped it on my lap in here, I took it to glance at on the train and the bloody thing broke down for an hour just outside Sevenoaks. I had nothing else to read.'

'Give me a ring about it, Will, I've got to – '

'This'll only take a minute. Might amuse young Percival here too. Your Uncle Freddie has written a conspectus of the twentieth-century consciousness, from the Somme to Sharpeville, a long poem or bit of poem-shaped crap that'll fit beautifully into our *European Poetical Testaments* series. We've got a dozen in print already by various Poles and Latvians but there's always room for another. Freddie turns out his version, brother Harry out of the goodness of his heart or having been through Mrs Freddie in the past – all right, all right – gives it to me, and there we are.'

'What?' said Harry. 'Where are we?'

'Here. Subject to this and that, we'll be making an offer for it. I thought you'd like to be the one to pass on the glad tidings. But not till after next Monday if you don't mind when we hold our rubber-stamp financial meeting.'

'So you like it,' said Harry at last. 'You think it's good.'

'I know exactly what you mean, Harry, and you surely know

that the answer to both your questions is that we think we can do reasonably well with it.'

'How well?' asked Piers, all nephew anxious to learn the full extent of his uncle's good fortune.

'Publishers hate mentioning money unless it's the reduction of an author's advance or a cut in his share of the paperback proceeds, so the answer to *that* is reasonably well.'

This produced a pause which produced the departure of Piers. The other two settled down to a final glass of port.

'*European Poetical Testaments*?' asked Harry.

'That's right, yes,' said Will Morrissey. 'In English, of course. If you want me to put your mind at rest and tell you that your brother's poem is crap, I hereby do so. Crap it is, in Renascence cursive upper and lower case. But my opinion of literature is worth nothing, as everyone agrees. However I can tell you that with a title in Hungarian or Czech (but easily pronounceable in English) your brother's little volume will draw a highly respectable sale from middle-aged to elderly intellectuals who want to feel part of an international community of philosophers and seekers after truth. Also that *European Poetical Testaments* strikes a lot of people as a better class of series title than *Things from Underground* (another very good line of ours) or *Tales of the Whip*. But perhaps you had already noticed that yourself.'

FIFTEEN

'Try and think of it as a treat for Freddie,' said Clare. 'A day off school and up to see Mum.'

'I am,' said Harry. 'That's how I've been trying to think of it ever since I woke up this morning. Without carrying much conviction. It certainly won't be anything else for anyone else. I can't see what she gets out of it herself even.'

'Then try harder. First, the obvious pleasure to be got out of the buggering-about, as you might put it in your quaint patois, of three grown-up human beings. Oh, did I tell you the little thing in that new Portuguese bistro offered us game patois the other day. Quite good it was too. We might try a – '

'It still doesn't seem much return for Mum having her house occupied for several hours.'

'That's all you'd get out of it yourself, agreed, the sheer power thing. But try and look at it from her point of view.'

'Oh Christ, must I? You know how I hate doing that. Even trying. From anybody's, not just hers, though hers more than most, admitted.'

'Very short-sighted. The usual result of looking at something from someone else's point of view is to see how much worse off they are than you. Can be quite cheering actually.'

'And bloody quit philosophising. I can't take it at this hour of the morning and it makes you sound like a wife. I've told you before.'

'In the sense you mean there never was a man who needed a wife more than you. But don't let's squabble, dear.'

'We're not squabbling, are we? Sorry, I didn't mean to be.'

'No no – but just while we've got a minute, there she is, she'll be eighty-nine at the end of the summer. She likes thinking of herself as a sort of materfamilias or whatever it is. I wouldn't but she does. For various reasons the grandchildren are blessedly unsatisfactory or not about, but her sons and daughter are in range and reasonably tractable and she can be a sort of matriarch to them every so often and keep her book up to date. We bore her stiff and she doesn't much care for any of us, but she does like the thought and it's about the only thought of that kind she's still got so there we are. No no, I've told you you're not coming,' she added to the dog Towser who stood with them at the sitting-room window. 'Mrs Osborne will give you your lunch,' she added as if this would lay his mind decisively at rest.

Tufts of his hair clung to her heavy black skirt but she had nothing else to wear that she felt was funereal enough. He looked from one of them to the other with the slightly huffy incomprehension, as if nobody could have accused him at least of having failed to play his full part in the communication process, that more than any other expression of his made her wish him at the bottom of the Marianas Trench without as ever any disposition to consign him there personally.

'This driver's late,' said Harry. 'I'm going to have a quick one.'

'Bit early, isn't it? And there's always plenty there, isn't there?'

'To answer your questions in reverse order, yes, there is or appears to be, but you're never quite sure where it's been. You know that house.'

'Where it's been? What are you talking about?'

'Well, Freddie told me he was given a gin cocktail there once that had a compass-fluid base or he was a Dutchman, and he did his National Service on the briny as you know, and there was some story about a bottle of walnut brandy I'd rather not go into. It's all these awful people who go to see her.'

'Oh. What about my first question?'

'What first question?'

'About it being a bit early. Or *its* being a bit early as you'd probably put it if left to yourself.'

'Oh fuck off. I mean it's at least a minute less early than when you asked it. And well over a minute nearer encountering Désirée.'

'What? She never comes to these do's, Mum won't have her. Or has something awful happened?'

'She'll find a way.'

So it proved. Désirée could never simply not be around – when the others called to collect Freddie she offered unwanted coffee in an advanced state of preparation, hunted for, sometimes successfully put her hand on, samples of recommended new products, telephone numbers, paperbacks, called out messages from windows, excelled herself this time by rushing from the furthest part of the back garden to remind Freddie to bring home some commodity she proved on nearer approach to have forgotten the name of, only to remember it half a minute later and come bawling it distastefully after them down the street. The driver, a dark-skinned Asian in suit and tie, behaved with the exemplary tact and patience of an aristocrat reduced to menial work by some relative's improvidence or fraud. He knew the address they were going to, too.

'So you see I was right about needing that sly G-and-T,' said Harry to Clare in the back seat, rightly confident that Freddie would not bother to wonder what was meant even if he happened to be listening. He was unprepared however when Freddie said, after a pause, 'Frightfully nice young fellow that young Piers is, isn't he? I'd quite forgotten. What a nice young fellow he is, I mean.'

'Yes, he is quite a nice young fellow,' said Harry, feeling it was probably safe to go that far.

'I hadn't come across him for what seemed like years, and then the other day I just seemed to sort of run into him.'

'How did you do that?' asked Clare.

'Eh? Do what?'

'Seem to sort of run into him. I mean, your paths don't cross in the ordinary way I shouldn't have thought.'

'No, and you'd have been *perfectly damn right*,' said Freddie with a sudden access of what sounded like venom. But then he went on mildly, 'We just happened to bump across each other in a little pub I sometimes pop into when Désirée's in the market.'

'Which he also happened to have popped into.'

'Yes, on this occasion. Anyway, he was very charming to me, as I was saying. He seemed, how shall I put it, *concerned* about me in a very touching fashion. Seemed particularly anxious that I should be all right for money.'

Sitting close together in the back seat of the minicab, Harry and Clare each felt the other stir and draw in breath. Much conference, moving between bacon butty and Gospodin vodka and back again, had determined that however much or little might fall into Freddie's pocket from the poetical testament, it must remain there to be disposed of as he should decree, neither swallowed into Désirée's purse nor scooped up by Piers to be dropped heaven knew where.

'I told young Piers it was a funny thing he should have happened to ask me that just then, because you'd just been telling me about this windfall you'd got me from writing this poetry rubbish, do you see. By the way, did I remember to say how staggered I was when you slipped me the news? Haven't recovered from it yet. Well, Harry, to be fair you've always said publishers were the biggest bloody fools anywhere off the stage and the High Court and I suppose this must be some of it coming true. To think of any grown man not merely being able to get through what I wrote but apparently seeing his way to making some money out of publishing it . . . well . . . do you know what I thought I was doing when I was, what would you call it, smearing, plastering down the rubbish, like kids dancing in that Irish style or doing pictures of Mam-ma and Dad-da' – the childish pronunciations he gave these vocables indicated some-body entirely wilder than the person who had been doing the rest of the talking – 'erm, erm, turning out the sort of thing Désirée would think was jolly clever and important and worth having up for people to see. It's all Désirée's . . . grotesque, I can't tell you. Sometimes I . . .'

He paused so completely and so long, his eyes drifting over the mechanism and upholstery of the taxi rather than anything outside it, even though this was changing fast enough, that Harry was quite alarmed when he started up again and said, or more nearly shouted, 'But what's it matter if it brings in a few spondulicks, a few dibs, a few shekels, a bit of boodle, a bit of swag, a bit of loot, only this time it's not going into Désirée's bloody exchequer, it's going on a great flutter, a great *bonanza*, a great . . .' He seemed to have no word extravagant enough. At the same time Harry thought he saw him start to fiddle with the catch of the door.

'Stop the car,' said Clare, but the driver had already done so. Freddie had his door open now. Exactly at that moment and point on the pavement a white-painted barred school gate began to swing open beside the car-passengers, faster and faster as more and more children crowded through alongside, mostly very young, between five and seven, mostly little girls, mostly from the Caribbean or Asia, all brightly dressed, under no visible supervision, kicking or kneeing or shoving along with them a couple of largeish brown-and-white balls and of course making a great deal of noise of a shrillness and ferocity barely to be imagined. Freddie was among them now, running among them, neither greeted nor ignored, probably yelling too but not separately heard to be so, part for no more than a dozen seconds of an intense riot of clamour and excitement that reached a corner and vanished into a few individuals running, hardly hurrying across a bare yard with a few small empty carts in it. From here he strolled back unabashed to the others, already seeming to begin to smile deprecatingly.

'Jolly little load of beggars, what?'

'What was all that about?' asked Clare, looking from face to face.

'Yes, funny, wasn't it? You know a lot of people don't seem to have much time for all these black and brown people who've come over here to live. Oh, I know they can be a pest, like that Indian woman who plays her television next door to us, but I think most of them are terrific fun. Like that jolly little load back there. I couldn't make out quite what they were doing, though, could you?'

'We'd better be getting on,' said Clare. 'You know how Mum hates to be kept waiting.'

'Well, I suppose as a woman you might, must do, but I've never really found that,' said Harry, still standing reposefully by the car. 'More they like being kept waiting so they can go for you about it and all the times you went for them for keeping you waiting. Still, yes, anyway.'

With a final wave to a small coal-black boy who might or might not have been one of the original party Freddie took his time about getting back into his seat. Little was said for the remainder of the journey. Clare and Harry were thinking how puzzling Freddie's behaviour had been without coming to any explanation of what he had 'really' been doing, trying to say to them or to the world at large, etc. The only person present who seemed to have seen nothing strange, however reprehensible, in that minute or two was the driver, and he was not consulted.

The car turned in at a battered red-brick gateway similar in style and date, and only a few hundred yards in distance, from Maureen's gloomy mansion. Where however hers was a bit battered this one was battered good and hard, not overgrown enough by the look of it to date from 1939–45 but too thoroughly to be the result of a single excavation or subsidence, the leavings perhaps of some forgotten terrorist atrocity of the 1950s. Harry had quite a clear mental picture of its better days but such a different one that it reminded him only in parts and at fleeting times of what had been. Anyway, old Mrs Caldecote was not going to have her grounds mucked about with for no return except a lot of disturbance and there, while she continued to rule the estate, the matter stayed.

Not that it was much of an estate except in an estate-agent's sense. As they drew up at the lichen-spotted porch the old girl herself came out to greet them. Nobody ignorant of who she was would have taken her to be the mistress of anything, in mere just-for-the-moment charge of anything from a house and its garden, however run-down, to a plastic-protected tin-and-cardboard shelter. It was not so much her smallness and narrowness of shoulder as her lack of colouring, unabundance of hair, absence of expression, cheerful or glum. And the incredibly dull and, for all anyone knew, unique, three-quarters-length olive-brown overall-dress featuring black press-studs that was never clean and newly ironed nor in imminent need of a change. She had a syrupy voice that even after all these years Harry was liable to find suddenly surprisingly too much, as now.

'Hallo, Mum.'

'Would it make more sense to fix a time now for the driver to come back?'

It might have, it might not – Harry had soon forgotten. While they were still arriving, while they moved into the house the four of them started to exchange information about those present and absent that they had no interest at all in acquiring and in many cases would have paid some small sum to be excused hearing altogether, as with families the world over, Harry thought, or perhaps not in Ulan Bator as an uncommon exception. Among the first of those missing in the body but there in word was Piers.

'Charming fellow, that,' said Freddie, shaking his head in whole-hearted appreciation. 'Perfectly charming.'

'He's a very *cheeky* fellow,' said Piers's grandmother in her over-sweetened tones. 'Popping to and fro like that as the fancy takes him. Such a pity he seems to have to spend so much of his life abroad. And the nerve of him. Just yesterday I had a letter from him from some place in Prague or was it Budapest. And do you know he had the cheek to ask to be cabled some money.'

'How much?' asked Freddie. 'As a matter of interest.'

'Five thousand pounds.'

'Did you send it?' asked Clare.

'*Some* of it,' said her mother with a roguish look. 'It's not good for young men to be given just what they ask for.'

'He's not much of a young man any more,' said Harry.

'Well he certainly is compared with you, compared with anyone else in this house for that matter or anybody who's been inside it for a decade or so. Anyway Piers sounded very excited. On to something big, he said. Look, here's his letter.'

'Something like ten years in a labour camp,' muttered Harry as this communication – on very down-market paper, he noticed – was passed barely glanced at from hand to hand and finally tucked away again in a compartment of a sort of portfolio, one of several that lay on perpetual display, or in mild chaos, on a big mahogany table by the drawing-room window. This, or a part of it, was the 'book' of family doings spoken of by Clare as being notionally kept up to date by her mother or at any rate used as an excuse for curiosity. Now, at family speed, i.e. at about one-quarter that required by a party of high-grade mental defectives previously unacquainted with one another, the talk shifted from Piers's money, money, the constant disappearance of money, to Freddie's money, the money from Freddie's poem, originally brought up in conversation with Mum no doubt for shortage of anything else to talk about or keep Mum quiet with. How much money? Yet to be determined. Mum quietened down when she had taken that in. Harry sensed that she was getting one of her ideas, or even about to fall asleep.

Drinks were brought in during this stage, overseen by a tall handsome woman in what might almost have to be called a gown, with a full neck and cuffs. No civilised person seeing her beside Mum could have doubted that the one was the mistress and the other the servant. Harry proceeded with caution. The binnacle cocktail was probably an exaggeration or a fantasy on

Freddie's part, but he himself had once been served here one of the most interesting mouthfuls of his life that had turned out to be a mixture of marc and Puerto Rican rum. (In those days there had been a sort of butler.) The party, if that was what it was, went on. Harry could see Clare trying to be a daughter with shops and shopkeepers but it was a struggle, not appreciated, only something to be resented if not adequately given a try. Then after dismissing in its entirety some range of sauces or sanitary fluids Clare had been painstakingly discriminating among, Mum indicated to the housekeeper that the lunch, or what was to pass for that, could now be introduced.

The lunches were always the same too, a vegetable soup of at least identifiable ingredients followed by platefuls of salad-type stuff that might have been the failed products of some dietary research establishment, spotted broccoli, multi-coloured celery, barbed watercress. They tasted all right, though, to those bold enough to try, and the cold meats were always fresh out of the tin, often with part of the label still adhering. Where this course really did the trick, drew the eye, though, was in the crockery the chatelaine-figure served it on. Every plate was different, distinctly different too, and yet with an unmistakable family resemblance of thickness, curvature, glaze, something. An incident on a Boulogne steamer when a schoolgirl had driven Clare to the theory that the Caldecote dinner-service (second-class and children) was the accumulation of years of steady piecemeal thefts from Continental boats, trains, especially boat-trains, and an occasional resort hotel. No lettering in any language was to be seen on any piece, so there was no help there. Like so much else, it was one of those things in one's childhood that one accepted until it was really too late to ask about it. As for the wine at lunch, Harry avoided it altogether. It said that it was a Romanian Tokay. He had managed a quick slurp on arrival out of a sealed bottle of White Horse and that was going to have to see him through. In the past he had tried one or two smuggling schemes with Freddie only to find that he had the wrong brother in yet another field.

After lunch Mum continued her digest of family information, more freely interspersed now with lamentations about what the world was coming to. Into one of these chronicles there fell a mention of Fiona, a rare event at these gatherings and only picked up and passed over now because some acquaintance claimed to have run across her in a doctor's waiting-room, presumably that of one who had still not known about her up to that point. The reference was gone in a moment but hearing it in Mrs Caldecote's gooily sorrowful tones was enough to depress Harry's spirits, not in any case near their zenith at the moment. It was not actually raining and he wandered out into the ruinous garden and tried to take in the broken bird-bath, the fallen-in bit of grille over that bridge thing, the hollow oak tree in whose uncomfortably shaped cavity nothing of the slightest interest or importance had ever been done or said. Or so he would have been prepared to bet. Was everywhere really like this when you came down to it, a place where childhoods and adolescences were got through like so many terms of military service, or were they just the scene of a string of vague but luminous wonders, bits of emotion, some of it glad, some of it miserable, remembered when the occasion was long forgotten? Or was there no difference? What did he remember from here? Stuff like spending hours looking for a lost ball or wandering for just as long and with no sense of purpose through some horrible garden fête or show his parents had organised in aid of some boring grown-up thing where there was nothing to eat and nowhere to play.

One object new to him in that he had never seen it in its present transformed version was a dried-up ornamental pond. In days gone by he could remember it filled with dirty water and its surface largely covered with brown-edged plants resembling lilies and decaying leaves with a clump of rushes or sedge at one end. Now all that was gone and a tiled floor was revealed, many of the tiles gone altogether, others patchily covered with a hairy dark-green weed. Only one area was more or less clear, showing two naked female figures hand in hand as if swimming or floating in mid-air. The girl on the left turned her face in pale blurred profile back towards her companion, whose figure was overgrown with the weed above the waist but for a hand that seemed to reach long fingers out and grasp for something. Something approaching? Something drifting away? There was no way of guessing that or anything else and not enough to stir any image or memory. Two girls hand in hand, one half-obliterated. Just that. Desolate, though. Some day, Harry had

164

been told often enough, the whole of this property would be not his, far from his, but at the disposal of some concern designed to improve the lot of horses in Guam or Haiti or thereabouts.

He caught sight of Freddie making his unpurposeful way towards him and, being unable to conceive for the moment of ever wanting to exchange a word with him about anything under the sun, made his own way by a collapsed culvert back to the side of the house. Here there was a structure rather like an ironing-room where tea was also made, and the fact that tea was even then being made or rather brewed in it by the housekeeper meant that in half an hour or so the visit could be suffered to draw to a close. The housekeeper was called Mrs Eastleigh or Eastley – after this long time, however long it might actually be, Harry was still not sure of the spelling, and of everything else about her he knew almost nothing at all. She kept herself to herself. It was a very long time since he had stopped trying to imagine what she did in that state. As she turned her head, not to look in his direction, he caught sight of a prominent mole on the side of her chin with a flourishing tuft of hairs attached to it. He had not noticed it before though he must have seen her on how many previous visits here? Fifty? Three hundred and fifty? Two? He stopped in the passage and stared out of the smeared window into part of a shrubbery, wondered what it was about them all, or was it just about Mum? Or him? He felt he must go, not wait for the car to be brought round and laboriously filled but down and away by any available path to the street. But after a couple of strides he ran into his mother, sitting with Clare at the big window-table where the albums lay. Purely to give an appearance of activity he picked up and opened one of these, an old one but in good condition, a heavy affair, pale green leather darker at the edges.

His mother caught the movement at once. 'That one goes back donkeys' years,' she said. 'To your grandmother's time I shouldn't wonder.'

'They used to take the most marvellous photographs in those days, some of them,' said Clare, proclaiming her loyalty to the idea that an ordinary conversation was being conducted.

'There are some very strange people in those books, I can tell you. I can't tell you how some of them got there.'

Harry turned a page or two. The photographs were carefully

mounted in an antique style and names clearly printed in white on the black. This stirred a memory somewhere but he had no idea of what. He turned another couple of pages at random and at once set eyes on someone he knew. What? Somebody he recognised without ever having seen, ANNIE as the white lettering proclaimed, Fiona's great-aunt, the very picture that Elspeth, Fiona's sister who had died, Elspeth who had driven her car into a wall at ten to ten one Monday morning, Elspeth had said was the image of Fiona, absolutely exactly like her. But – he remembered it all now – their mother, Elspeth's and Fiona's mother, had said that was not true, that aunt and niece had not been much alike at all, that the shapes of the faces had been different. And here, now, in Mum's drawing-room, Harry could see that mother had been right and Elspeth wrong and poor old dead drunken Annie and living Fiona were not really alike, not in any way that counted, and that Fiona's fears of having inherited Annie's fate along with her looks were mistaken. And he felt if he could somehow get this picture to Fiona and make her see the difference there was a faint chance he might bring her a message of hope, help her to feel she was not locked into her dreadful downward spiral of sickness and hopelessness and death. But how tell his mother, how explain something so flimsy to anybody as resistant to anything so finespun and fanciful? For a moment he felt utterly helpless, a state of mind he very rarely experienced.

From somewhere out of sight there now sounded an incident or accident involving a stepladder, a large dustbin and a pile of sacks of oatmeal. Whatever it was drew a cry of alarm or warning from the housekeeper and a kind of cackle or prattle of abuse in Freddie's voice. It also got Mrs Caldecote hurrying out of the room. Without seeming to think at all Harry ripped from the album the page with Annie on it, folded it across, tucked it into his jacket pocket and in three seconds was looking into the album at a row of middle-aged people, all evidently on a mental-home outing and standing in attitudes of pugnacity or bewilderment on the front at some South Coast resort like Worthing or Eastbourne.

'What are you – ' Clare started to say, but then immediately stopped, thus behaving quite differently from the way either Gillian or Daisy would at such a juncture. Gillian would at once have piped up to ask Harry loudly what he thought he was doing, tearing pages out of old and rare and valuable books like that, whereas Daisy would have waited until more people were present before taking him to task for behaving like some kind of lout or vandal, with perhaps a query thrown in about who he imagined he was. Clare looked at him, in a familiar way that meant curiosity no less insistent for being deferred, quite the contrary. 'Well, anyway,' she said, gesturing outside the room, 'it would be a pity to miss this, whatever it is.'

Actually it turned out to be disappointingly little, a burst sack or so and one of the steps of the ladder broken away at one side. The echoes of the dustbin had died. By the time Harry got to the scene the taxi-driver had already taken efficient charge, organising the sweeping-up, looking round for a hammer to repair the ladder. Freddie was keeping up a patter of apology for whatever it was he had done, veering in and out of mild accusation for lack of forewarning, defective materials, etc. Within five minutes they were on the move, calling to one another for the giving of love and remembrances to aunts, cousins, nephews never mentioned except at such times from one year's end to the next. By now the driver was making little pretence of not having a difficult and potentially dangerous trio on his hands that he had better get out of the way before worse befell. At last the taxi lurched out into the roadway, sending a discarded health-tea tin skidding into a ditch.

'Funny sort of woman, that Mrs Eastleigh, is it,' said Freddie. 'Anybody could have seen that pile of stuff was going to come tumbling down at any moment, and she must have known that ladder was in a dickey state, but it wasn't until it finally dawned on her that I was in mid-air that she let out any sort of yell or even took in what was happening. I was lucky not to crack my skull in there,' he ended, with an irresistible suggestion that if he had they could no longer get away with treating his various difficulties and disadvantages so lightly.

'Have you got that list of stuff for Désirée?' asked Clare.

'What stuff?'

'The stuff you were supposed to pick up for her at the market.'

Freddie cottoned on and produced it and handed it over with the disconcerting speed he sometimes showed when his own interests could or might be advanced by prompt wordless action.

'Pull in here, will you?' said Clare to the driver. 'Right down to the end.'

They had halted outside some huge fearsome building in front of which spindle-shanked carts heaped high with groceries were being pushed to and fro, often by people who seemed much too small for them, on the point of passing under their control. Loud metallic crashes filled the air.

'You two get out,' said Clare to her brothers, 'and go and have a drink in that pub while I fetch the groceries. You heard me. It'll only take longer if you come with me.'

'But it looks a disgusting place,' said Harry truthfully.

'It'll be a disgusting place,' said Clare, 'but you'll see no one you know there and for another ten minutes or so it'll still be part of Freddie's treat. Or at least day out. Which was what we decided this was going to be, if you remember. Go on, now.'

'I can't get over what a peculiar woman that Mrs Eastleigh seems to be,' said Freddie as the two men crossed the strip of concrete desert to the door of the pub. 'But then I suppose living with Mum week in week out like that would tend to bring out any peculiarities you might have dormant in you, so to speak. Do you know the only time I've seen Désirée lose control, fly into a rage?' He waited while Harry opened the pub door for him; he always let the other fellow let him go first. 'Oh yes, it was when I suggested we might take in a lodger.'

'You've got fifteen minutes,' Clare had called after them, 'and then as soon as possible after that I want to hear exactly what that photograph is and why you tore it out of that album and hid it away like that.' She had only actually spoken the first five words aloud, but the remainder got to Harry as clearly as any that had ever reached him by sound-wave.

The brothers entered the pub, Freddie in front now by several yards. Harry's unrehearsed reaction to what he saw and heard and just about as powerfully smelt was to look for the nearest means of escape, but of course Freddie was striding eagerly forward into the land of the bacon butty in butter and with fried tomatoes on the side, where nobody he knew ever came.

SIXTEEN

'So they decided they'd better have me in and see if I could suggest some brilliant solution. I told them frankly, I said if Tony's stumped and Selwyn can't come up with anything and Winston seems to have thrown up the sponge and Alec's caved in and Rab's come a cropper and Peter's beaten into the ground and Harold's for showing the white flag and even *Harold* hasn't a word to say for himself, well, it's not very likely that poor old yours truly can wave the magic wand. Then I suddenly had a brainwave. Yes?'

The Senior Parlour at the Irving was restricted to those who had been members of the club for twenty-five years or more, though like much other fact and fancy about that institution it was a small mystery how that supposed rule had come into being in the first place and how transmitted subsequently, since nobody ever mentioned it in any form and should it have occurred to anyone to look for it in any rule-book he would certainly not have found it. Indeed it was not easy to find any hard information in most departments of the Irving, where for instance the legible part of the menu seldom aroused anything more concrete than hopes or fears and the wine list was thought to be revised perhaps four or five times in every reign. It had been said that, royalty apart, only a duke, a marquis, an earl or an American could visit the Irving in the complete certainty of unself-consciousness.

Harry Caldecote had only the previous year become eligible to sit in the Senior Parlour and had gone there quite a few times since, in the first place to sneer at those not yet 'senior' enough to do so (nobody at the Irving was ever 'old' in that sense) and partly out of a kind of sense of wonder, tinged now and again with horror. Only a small minority of course of those who had governed and otherwise helped to run the country over the past generation and a bit were ever to be seen and heard holding forth in the Senior Parlour of the Irving Club, but if they were at all representative ... Harry would not have called himself a particularly cynical and certainly not an unpatriotic man, but every few minutes there he found himself marvelling slightly that the country was still a going concern at all, that it had not fallen years before into penury, anarchy, communism, fascism or some set of beliefs and practices too bizarre to be conceived by one as librarianised as himself. With disproportionate curiosity he sometimes found special wonder in the fact that the profession of actor continued to be held in tolerance, let alone esteem, but a fellow-member who understood these matters had assured him that there were much quieter, more harmless ones round the corner at the Garrick.

The old fart of a Cabinet Secretary or Chancellor of the Duchy of Lancaster who had been boring his small, distinguished audience halfway to coma for several minutes had stopped speaking. He had been irreversibly shut up by one of the club servants, the most elderly of all that elderly band. Harry had seen this man in action before and come to the conclusion that the silencing agent was a kind of hypnosis. The servant fixed his gaze on his victim and advanced on him in steps measured in millimetres and separated by a second or two, all the while by imperceptible degrees dilating his mouth, eyes and nostrils and raising his significantly substantial eyebrows. This had the effect among other things of drawing all attention away from the speaker and his words. Now, after an immobile pause like that of a matador before a kill, the servant said,

'Please pardon my interruption, my lord.'

'Very well, Humphrey, what is it?' This was said quite pacifically – the old fart could bide his time, and he was only an old fart, not an old shit as well.

'Is Mr Caldecote in the club?'

This piece of standard procedure showed the Irving at its best, really, and in no time the old fart had resumed unscathed his unforgivable story and Harry had slipped away to the kind of Edwardian sentry-box where the telephone was.

A woman's voice, unrecognisable to him, spoke. Harry answered up like a man to one of the many isotopes of his surname he had had to learn to put up with over the years.

170

'I'm afraid there's been some trouble. I live downstairs where that niece of yours is she called Bunty lives with that other woman. They said at your house you'd be at that club.'

'Yes, well they were right. What's the trouble?' This would be the old girl who lived in the bottom flat and whom he now dimly remembered. As crouched. As awful.

'It's that husband or the one who says he's her husband. Desmond something. He's drunk and he won't go away. Bunty got me to ring you.'

Harry had not come across Desmond drunk before, or not to a degree that this little old girl would notice, and the thought was unpalatable. 'Is he violent?'

'Pardon?'

'Has he hit anyone?'

'Not yet but he's smashed some things, china and that.'

'Why won't he go?'

'Pardon?'

'You say he won't go away. Why not?'

'He hasn't said. He just says he won't go away. And Bunty says please don't call the police. She asked me to impress that on you particular.'

'Anyone else about up there? You know, Piers? Or that other woman?'

'No, just me and Bunty and that Desmond.'

There was a minicab waiting in Lyceum Court round the corner and although Harry had never been any good at effrontery and things like that as a rule he turned so horrible and important and upper-class on the driver that for once in his life he pulled off a hijack. 'I am member of Queen's Bench Division,' Harry kept bawling. 'I am High Court Judge,' he snarled.

Suitably impressed, or perhaps just taking these demonstrations as signs of insanity, the driver drove. For a cloud of reasons Harry would have found it hard to explain even to members of his immediate family, which for this purpose would not have included Désirée, he kept up the High Court Judge persona, not making quite enough of a fool of himself by pretending to study official documents but peering responsibly to and fro, constantly looking at his watch, finally paying the fare and computing and paying out the tip with stone-faced precision. If this alleyway had ever been the haunt of a High Court Judge it would have had

171

to be where he kept one of his lower-grade wives or dependants. The street lighting was rudimentary but plenty of illumination came from uncurtained windows. Music of more than one sort and in more than one sense, some of it doubtfully classifiable as music at all in any strict meaning of the term, came from sources both outdoors and in. Harry remembered the house at once and was able to go straight to it, a course far preferable to having to ask directions from any of the people standing silently about in twos and threes and, so he fancied, fully ready to receive just such a one as him.

Then, as he rang the bell and waited on the step, he had time to jeer at himself a certain amount as a dried-up old frump from the Irving Club who considered he was too elevated for conditions lived in by millions of people, a bit garish for his taste no doubt, a bit noisy for quite a few more than him, even a bit rough by any standards, certainly by those of twenty years ago, but Bunty lived here, *Piers* lived here, the fellow who owned the flat lived or had lived here, Mrs – yes, he had the old bag's name now – Mrs Brookes lived here without apparently coming to any lasting damage. And then again, at the moment the door opened, he heard from near by the voice of a girl in her twenties or so utter a quite long and elaborate phrase that exactly (by coincidence, no doubt) reproduced what he had once on his National Service heard a regular quartermaster-sergeant use to reduce to utter silence a bunch of drunken Jock orderlies on a wet and windy railway station – remembered it as if it had been yesterday. So perhaps the Irving Club were not wrong every time about things going to the dogs.

'Mr Caldecote? I don't know what good you think you can do but Bunty give me your number and ask me to ring you and Chris round the off-licence let me use his phone.'

'Where's Bunty now?'

'Locked in the bathroom isn't she?'

They had moved into Mrs Brookes's terrible and pitiful sitting-room and Harry asked, 'Where's Desmond?'

'That bloke? When I last looked he was sitting with his back against the bathroom door. And he won't be shifted whatever I do.'

'Has he gone for you?'

'Him? No. Not laid a finger on me. Smashed a jug or two but that was just temper. You know how they are.'

'Where's that what's-her-name, Popsy?'

'Oh, that one, she's away for the night. That's how all this started.'

'What about my son?'

'What, that Piers? No sign of *him*.' Mrs Brookes made it sound, very justifiably in Harry's opinion, that if there was one thing to be relied upon about Piers it was that he would always be on the far side of the hill from any trouble, however produced.

'I'd better have a word with Desmond then.'

'I don't know what good you think you can do. You're not Bunty's father, not her father, are you?'

'We're related.'

Mrs Brookes shook her head, in incomprehension, in all-encompassing disapproval. Then with a great parade of fairness she said, 'I got nothing against her. Keeps herself to herself but always polite. How'd she get mixed up with a bloke like that Desmond?'

'Nobody knows. Now you lock yourself in here and don't come out till I tell you.'

When Harry got to the top floor Desmond was standing with his arms folded and his head a little on one side, like an amateur actor being a desperado. He seemed to be overdoing the defiance a little but that might have been because he was drunk, and it was impossible to say at this stage how far he had come along that road. Further than Harry had seen before, or so he thought.

'You can turn right round where you are, Harry, and go back wherever you came from. I'm not leaving and you can't make me and we got nothing to say to each other.'

'Oh, I don't know about that. I'm not going anywhere either and we might as well fill in some of the time by you telling me the story so far.'

'Absolutely no point. Wouldn't change anything.'

'We won't try to change anything. But we might as well be comfortable and you know very well you've got a lot of things to say even if it's only a case of letting the world hear about them and I don't know about you but I could do with a glass of beer if there's one in the house.'

This gave Desmond pause, as well it might. He wanted to talk, he was dying to talk, but he could see that to do so would forfeit whatever moral advantage he might think he had won by taking up arms, so to speak, going in for direct action, being one who broke things and broke into things. At the same moment it became clear that however much he might have drunk earlier in the evening a certain amount of its effect had receded.

'All right,' he said with a fierce voice and look. 'I'll tell you what I'm doing and you can listen if you want but nothing you say's going to change me. My mind's made up.'

In the kitchen Desmond remained on his feet, indeed exaggerated the militarism of his posture, while Harry found a tin of Foster's in the fridge and lounged by the window. 'I'd realised the time for reasoning and persuasion was over and it was time to take action,' said Desmond in the same clipped tones, setting Harry thinking unfairly about him holding forth from the platform of his school debating society. 'Then I got my chance. I heard, you know, locally that the Popsy female was going to be out of the way all right, so I came along and forced my way in here . . .'

'How did you do that?' asked Harry interestedly.

'Well, I rung the bell and Bunty let me in . . .'

'Oh, I see.'

'And I said, I've come to take my rights.'

'How did you actually put it? I mean, did you actually say to her in so many words, "Bunty, I've come to take my rights"?'

'Of course not.' For the first time a shade of real anger touched Desmond's face as the wing of the ridiculous brushed at the edge of his mind. 'There are other ways of putting these things to people.'

'Like trying to rape them, you mean? I'm sure you've tried much gentler ways of taking your rights off Bunty without getting anywhere either. And she's no flyweight, our Bunty. You wouldn't even get her bloody legs apart unless you laid her out half cold, which you'd find quite enough of a proposition on its own, as you know well enough without being told. I'll bet you didn't have that little red mark under your jaw when you came in, correct? All this is ridiculous and you know it and the sooner you admit it the sooner we can get Bunty out of the bathroom and all have a nice chat and go home.'

In a tone though not words that conceded defeat, Desmond

said, 'Somewhere in that woman there must be a woman's normal instincts and I owe it to myself and her to try every possible means of uncovering them.'

'Including the least promising anybody could think of in case anyone should ask you if you could swear you'd tried the complete set. Now sit down and have a beer.'

If Desmond had drawn in his breath to say that he preferred to stand he let it out again without forming the words and settled at the table with Harry and another Foster's in surroundings that an expert might have subdivided into the creation of one conscientious but not very capable manager, one sloven who would not bother to drop a cigarette-packet into a bin and one Martian. Desmond sat and waited for the ballocking he clearly knew was his by right as well as just on the way.

'I suppose it started with Petronella acting up.'

'Philippa. Poured a whole large drum of olive oil over the kitchen floor five minutes after I'd hot-dried it for the week.'

'Why? All right, never mind why.'

'Then the lamb wholesaler got a fault on his outer unit.'

'Then some beer.'

'Yeah, then some beer. Then some vodka. Then some more beer.'

'Then you thought at least I'll show that Bunty who's master.'

'Only after I just happened to hear in the King's Popsy was away and there she was, Bunty was, just round the corner, wasn't she. The trouble is, I fancy her, you see. And I just can't get away from thinking she . . .'

'She fancies you.'

'No, I *don't* think she fancies me. I think she thought, these blokes I've met so far, I don't fancy any of them, but compared with some this one doesn't seem so bad, and he certainly fancies me. Perhaps I can learn to put up with him, she thought. And I still think she could, if I could find the way to show her or let her see it.'

'Raping her, for instance.'

'Harry, I must have forgotten to say I can see now that wasn't a very good idea if it was an idea at all, but I can. But there still must be a way.' Desmond picked up a half-eaten ham sandwich somebody, probably Piers, had left on the table, and put it down again.

'Now Desmond, pay attention. I'm being the schoolmaster now. You answer only the questions I ask you and don't put in anything of your own. Right?'

'All right.'

'Have you ever really admired and liked and hero-worshipped a chap of about your own age, a best friend and more, someone you really looked up to?'

'Yes,' said Desmond without hesitation. 'Jim Butcher. I haven't seen him for years now but he was at my school. A really lovely bloke.'

'Clever, good at school work, all that?'

'Yeah, popular, nice-looking, all that, but that's not really the point. It might sound funny, but I really loved the guy. Him and me, we were really . . . Oh Christ.'

'Yes, you can see where we've got to now, can't you? That's right, suppose Jim Butcher had said to you, Dez, there's something a little special I'd like you to let me get up to with you, something I'd enjoy a lot but you probably wouldn't, but then you think I'm such a super chap you wouldn't let that stand in your way, surely now, would you, and after a bit you might get quite used to it, and *I'd* be having a real treat, and all because of you.' Desmond had been nodding his head and crying so thoroughly by the time they got that far that Harry stopped it there.

After a time, Desmond said, 'What she must think of me.'

'What are you talking about? She's devoted to you. Why else would she go on seeing you, a strongly heterosexual man whom she knows to have very serious designs on her whatever-you-call-it. You're her ideal person except that you happen to be the wrong sex. It's not a particularly nice thing to have happened to either of you but it has, and there's nothing to be done about it. Of course you could go on seeing her on the basis of your abandoning all designs on her whatever-you-call-it for ever. Perhaps she's hoping that might happen.'

'Thanks for coming up, Harry.'

'Now I'll just go round the house telling the various females that it's safe for them to come out now, and then I'll be off, but I'll leave you with one godfather's prediction. After this lot you're going to find uppity little Philippa miraculously easy to deal with, and just to allow an old man his fancy,' he quavered, 'let me add the detail that that change in your relationship will be apparent before either of you have spoken a word. Do look out for that if you can be bothered to remember. Ah, the ways of men and women are infinitely strange, and will never be fully understood as long as this world shall last. Good-night and thank you for watching.'

Harry had expected his own house to be in darkness when he returned to it, but there proved to be lights all over the place. He was confronted by Clare with an overall about her and a turban or scarf on her head. Rugs had been pulled back and the alcove in the sitting-room stripped. 'Not a gas-leak for God's sake?'

'Something I've lost and if I don't get it back before the room's cleaned it'll be gone for ever. Did that old girl get you all right?'

'Yes, thanks. That sort of thing always gets through. Tell you tomorrow.'

'Then somebody called Leonard rang. I've written it down up there.'

'Leonard who?'

'He did a lot of shouting, though in a perfectly friendly way.'

'Leonard – ah, of course, Leonard Preveza, Maureen's bloke – fancy him turning up. You remember Maureen?'

'Perhaps I do and perhaps I don't, but surely that's another one that'll keep till the morning, for heaven's sake. Sorry, dear.'

'What's upset you? Yes you are, don't be silly, of course you are, all got up for spring-cleaning at this hour. Have a drink and tell me.'

'Could I have a thimbleful of that nice Armagnac? What's upset me is something very small that you for one man in the world won't think is in the least small. Bless you.'

'By God, you certainly are upset. Snuggle up and tell me.'

'You know – well, there's no reason why you should, but I've got a very pretty baroque flute of Arnold's with a nice little piece of green chalcedony, I think it is, sort of sunk into it as an ornament which is supposed to be carved to look like somebody called Fraschini who it belonged to, the flute I mean. At least it was there until some time last week, the inlay that is. Now it isn't. I've asked Mrs Osborne, I've looked high and low. I can't think where it could have gone. I could get a sort of replica made, I've already established that, but it wouldn't be the same, or do you think that's silly?'

177

'No, but it's what you might find yourself stuck with in the end. How big is the thing?'

Clare held her thumb and finger a couple of centimetres apart.

'Oh, then it shouldn't be hopeless then, should it? Bright green?'

'Fairly.'

'Right, well, assuming it hasn't walked out of the room already it's still here, so we finish our drinks now and leave everything as it is and in the morning we start ringing round for ideas. Piers might be the sort of chap. We're not going to have it said we didn't do everything possible.'

SEVENTEEN

They spent many hours and much ingenuity looking for the Fraschini inlay, but it was nowhere to be found. Clare put all she had, instead of being absolutely marvellous about the way she was putting all she had, into concealing the fact that she had given up hope that it ever would be found. The very next morning she had intended to set about the making of a replica, but before she had risen from the breakfast-table Harry came in. Apart from Clare herself, or somebody come to read a meter, say, Harry's early-morning contacts were close to minimal, but his hair was always neat and the silk dressing-gown he wore (choice of three) was evidence of a more spacious and stylish past.

That morning the morning mail had arrived in the morning for once and there was a fair pile of it by Harry's place – letters, packets, brochures of every shape and hue he would dearly have loved to destroy at once and en masse by some peculiarly demeaning method were it not for the smoulderingly resented thought that one of their number *might*, just physically *could* have been the invitation to the sultanate of Brunei, haunt of dusky limbs, night-black hair fragrant with sandalwood, etc., from which Harry's mind could never with total probity be certified as free. Today's collection was thinner than usual, so that there stood out from it a large airmail envelope edged in red, white and blue and festooned with stamps and labels. He examined it cautiously, almost with foreboding.

'Adams,' he said, still not opening it.

'Who's he?'

'He and it are and were many things, including the second president of the United States and what I read the other day is the largest industrial concern in the world. It's probably less well-known as a state of the American Union somewhere in the Far

179

West and much less still as a university in or of that state.'

'Well? None of that sounds like a good reason for not opening the letter it's sent you.'

'M'm,' he growled. 'It gives me a nasty feeling.' But he got the envelope open eventually, damaging a fingernail or two and imperilling a tooth in the process. Several things fell or could eventually be wrested out. Clare picked up a photograph of a small town on an island in a lake which had snow-capped mountains in the background, a partly deciduous forest in the middle distance and here and there some of the bluest water anyone was likely to come across anywhere. The whiteness of the sails of the few small boats hurt the eyes. There might have been more beautiful places pictured or in reality but Clare could not call any to mind at the moment.

'Presumably that's it,' she said, and read out, 'The Adams Institute of Cultural and Commercial History.'

'M'm.'

'What's the matter with you? Aren't you going to read their letter?'

With a theatrical gesture he picked up the two nearly-full pages typed on paper of a quality more readily associated with European royal houses in exile than seats of learning, however opulent.

' "Dear Dr Caldecote," ' he began. 'You don't want the whole thing, surely.'

'Later. The gist will do for now.'

The gist was that the Adams Institute wanted him to do whatever he wanted to do, 'only of course it's called pursuing "a bold and innovative extension of bibliographical progression along paths you yourself shall determine", I haven't added up the various salaries and honoraria and allowances and grants but they must come to something like the annual budget of Venezuela, and as regards the hours I seem to get a month off every week and an expenses-paid trip anywhere in the world every month. I can terminate the agreement . . .' Harry's voice trailed off.

'Sounds too good to be true.'

'Yes, doesn't it? It is, too. Adams – the Institute, the industrial corporation, the state, the President too for all I know – is in the far West up by the Canadian border. I can't go there.'

'Have you actually been there?'

'No, but I still can't contemplate going there. It's impossible.
Everybody knows. It's just not on. And anyway what about you?
How would you make out on your own here, in this country?'

'That's got nothing to do with it. Of course I can make out on
my own. Look, before we go any further, Harry, dear, seriously,
now, you mustn't let the thought of me and my future and how
I'm to live influence you in any way. Have you got that? I'll
always manage.'

'If you think you can put pressure on me to go to this place by
letting it get about that you put pressure on me to go by making
me feel I'd been showing you were putting pressure on me to stay
if I didn't go, then . . .' For a moment Harry contemplated the
elastic cocoon he had spun about himself and finally made do by
bawling, *'you're wrong!'*

'It's just the novelty of the idea that's putting you off. You'll
love it when you get there. You know what marvellously
hospitable people Americans are.'

'Ah, I haven't finished with that. That's just it. Some
Americans are all right, though they do tend to go on a bit. The
sort that you're thinking of. Your idea of America is New York
and San Francisco and LA and places like that. All very fine and
bloody good fun but the rest, places like this Adams Institute, is
full of hicks.'

'Hicks?'

'Hicks. Peasants. Rubes. Affluent, superficially educated
farmers' children, often energetic and vivacious but devoid of
wit. And more often just unstoppably talkative lumps, especially
the – no, I'm not allowed to say that. You meet enough of them
over here, thinned out by the locals. With nothing but them
around me I'd go mad in a month.'

'I think before you decide anything – '

'In case you think I'm trying to be funny, I once, well to cut a
long story short in New York one time I picked up one of the
most attractive girls I've ever seen in my life, with the most
marvellous, anyway, and we were having dinner and chatting
away like idiots and everything was going swimmingly except
that she was so, sorry dear, fucking boring, and then she said
something about not being able to wait to get back to Toronto
and the next thing I knew I was in a taxi halfway to the airport,

well no I wasn't actually but it was where I should have been if I'd had any sense. And to look at, to meet, even to talk to at first . . .'

'Isn't Toronto in Canada and rather over on the other side?'

'With a thing as fundamental as that,' said Harry impressively, 'what do a couple of thousand miles matter?'

'Harry, this is all jolly good fun, and no doubt a lot of them up there are a bit keen on the debating society, as they are in Yorkshire as I have good cause to know, but they can't all be, and if you can't sort them out from the others then there's nobody who can. The rest of it sounds like what you've always wanted. You've been waiting for it for a long time and now it's here it's thrown you a bit. You'll feel differently when it's had time to sink in.'

'M'm.' He had been reading further in the various papers before him and now said, 'Evidently they keep a glorified mechanic called a Principal of Bibliotechnology with rank of full professor in charge of department (golly) to look after all the computers and other ironmongery. And . . . a fellow I used to know called Martin van Oudheusden is there and I'll be able to get the low-down off him. It's probably all right, a place like that, when you know your way around a bit.'

'That's more like it.'

'And what a place to escape to if you had to get out in a hurry. I wonder if Piers knows anything about library books.'

'Now I must get on.'

Clare was making her second attempt to leave the breakfast-table when the telephone rang from its station on the hall table. Harry groaned slightly. In the past, in fact till quite recently, the instrument had been associated in his mind with nice things, ordering food and drink, arranging trips of parties, even, if one went back far enough, making arrangements to see girls: now, it had become the means whereby horrible people gave reminders of mislaid bench-marks, untraced pamphlets, books of which he knew nothing for certain save that he had no idea where they had last been heard of. Simultaneously it had become a means almost entirely of incoming communication, though he was occasionally aware of the logical weakness of this view of the matter.

He picked up the handset and made into it a noise designed to leave in doubt not only his sex and age but his organic nature.

A woman's voice, speaking like someone trying to sell him a washing machine or a particularly unappealing flight in an aeroplane, said, 'I'm extremely sorry to bother you, but would it be possible to speak briefly with Mr Harry Caldecote?'

Boing! Menace hung over that one like a drunken promise come home to roost, but what could he say? He said it.

'*Ah*, now this is State Enrolled Nurse Atkinson reporting to you on the condition of Miss Fiona Carr-Stewart.'

Harry very nearly had a very serious fall involving the tablecloth, the telephone-cord and that of his dressing-gown in an attempt to get Clare back into the room before she should, so to speak, have fully left it, but to no result, good or bad. There was really no hope of conveying the sparkling oiliness with which State Enrolled Nurse Joyce Atkinson had reported to him, nor the glossiness of the tasselled brochure which would very shortly advise him of her institution's charges for the treatment and other commodities now being administered willy-nilly to Miss Fiona Carr-Stewart (not including VAT and extras). But hold: he had had a good deal of experience of this type of transaction and could sense that some undertone or sonority was missing from this one. Not difficult, really, once one was over the shock. 'What is the name of this establishment,' he said in a voice like that of the head of Interpol, 'and who is the principal doctor?'

An address lacking in great precision was given and the names and qualifications of two doctors both of whom were said to be beyond immediate reach. (Nevertheless when Harry checked later he found them both to be real enough practitioners though no more than previously available in the flesh.) More questions produced a more hopeful view of the condition of Miss Carr-Stewart and what soon became somehow equally or more important, a belief that she was actually somewhere tucked up in a bed in a real room with people close by, and not about to choke or to die of a heart attack or a fit. (She had once suffered one of the latter, fortunately while he had been in Morayshire examining the proceedings of a society of local annalists.) As Harry talked he became more and more certain that what he was talking to was not a true hospital but some sort of hostel or more likely just private house in which very recent ex-drunks like Fiona were been nice to by relatively antiquated ex-drunks like

SEN Atkinson, there being so many alcoholics of various degrees and persuasions in the kingdom that no one system or series of systems could have looked after them all even part-time. Eventually Harry said, after a speech of thanks and congratulations whose tone would not have been overdone in the case of, say, the rescuer of an orphanageful of children from the Khmer Rouge, 'When would it be possible to see Miss Carr-Stewart personally?'

'I'm afraid not for several days. I can get any message to her more or less immediately.'

'I have to get this to her literally in person. There are certain legal requirements.'

Still no good. With regrets and best wishes they broke up on that note. Harry was left with quite enough telephone numbers and extensions and alternative lines and not-before and not-after times to ensure he would never find anybody who had ever heard of anybody who had anything to do with the case. This lowered his spirits in some way. Somehow the thought of being utterly and irrevocably out of touch with Fiona had lost some of its usual appeal. Who would have thought that day would ever come?

When he got back from his lunchtime call at the King's he found a message in Clare's ridiculous but very clear handwriting saying that Bunty had rung to ask if she could have a bed for the night and that this request, it was hoped properly, had been granted. M'm. Popsy at the front door with a meat-cleaver at two in the morning. No, all right, but yelled abuse, and more, well on the cards. They were stacking up in the most sinister style – Maureen, Atkinson, Fiona, now Bunty. Perhaps in the end it would have to be off to the Adams Institute after all.

EIGHTEEN

'It's a shame about Chris,' said Howard to Charles. 'I shall miss him.'

'No you won't. Mere conventional expression of regret. Using it of a worthless scoundrel of that calibre robs it of any value it may have had. What you mean is you're afraid somebody worse will come in his place and further lower the tone of the neighbourhood. The trouble with a fellow like that is not so much his stupidity as his appalling lack of style. He imagines he can just walk into London NW1 and carry on as if he was still in Nicosia or wherever it was. So the first deal he makes and everybody suddenly starts getting interested in Stolypin vodka. Mind you, the geezer who flogged it to him must be an idiot too.'

'Of course he is, don't you remember, he approached you at that party in Acton. No, the johnny with the style is young fellow-my-lad who worked for Chris for about five minutes.'

'Oh, the Italian scholar.'

'The expert on the *Purgatorio* to be precise. He'll go far.'

'He already has,' said Charles.

'Please try not to be so bloody obvious. That's a British idea of wit, or English if you insist. Reflex action. An achievement on his part, I agree, to have vanished with such a respectable sum of money after such short preparation and *so utterly*. It was really the Dante that did it.'

'Now you're just showing off.'

'I am showing off not the way you're trying to say. I am allowing to be seen some knowledge of the British or English people I've acquired through living among them. As shown in their attitude to other cultures.'

It was a bright clear sunny morning in the few minutes before the off, before the double doors from the street were thrown back and over the spotless composition floor and among the impeccably squared-off shelves, the videos sorted and spaced, every journal the precise distance from its neighbour so that the identifying signs of all were clearly visible, the greetings cards set out in their categories for every relation and relationship and contingency, including not a few wishing people well in tackling their new responsabilities or congratulating them on having passed there exams – before over that floor and among those shelves and the rest the British (or English) children came with their soiled clothing and snotty fingers, their seniors dropping sweet-wrappers, knocking piles of envelopes off shelves, holding the corner of a magazine back for a couple of seconds only but long enough to render it unsaleable at full price, dislodging and instantly treading on markers or tubes of paint or glue, putting everything they took out to look at back in the wrong place – oh, and fumbling with purses, mislaying lists, thinking about looking for credit card or pen and cheque-book and cheque-card on being told a second or third time the sum required. Howard had more than once said he would like to get everything set up one morning and then simply bloody not open the doors and let them gawp and go on gawping at what lay just out of their reach. Charles could see that was just Howard's fun (he was far too greedy to mean it for one thing) but every other five minutes he also saw what he meant. None of which is to say that there were not parts of the brothers' establishment that few Europeans would have cared to visit.

'It was old Harry Caldecote who was most impressed, of course,' said Howard in pursuance of the Dante topic. 'He is really the most tremendous snob. It's easy to forget that about the British because everybody's known it for so long. Like forgetting that Frenchmen stink of garlic or Jews do you down or Germans kick you to death if they think they can get away with it. Harry doesn't know a word of Italian. But there's no denying it old boy it does have clahss.'

'You mean it *has got* class,' said Charles, whose ear was in some respects better than his brother's. 'Well, there's no great harm in respect for learning.'

'I greatly fear that the esteemed Harry Caldecote Esquire OBE is riding for some kind of fall,' said Howard. 'That pair of hybrids, Bunty and Popsy, for a start. Bad trouble brewing there before very long unless I'm much mistaken. Things should never

186

have been allowed to drift so far, it's . . . undignified, an affront to public decency. I mean, consider how they deal with such matters at home.'

'I have. Several times. I think on the whole I prefer the way they deal with them here.'

'Which is not to deal with them at all. And then there's my lady Fiona. Three months maximum.'

'What are you talking about?'

'Then complete liver failure. Curtains.'

'What do you know about it?'

'Desai was in here the other morning and he got a good look at her close to.'

'Desai,' said Charles contemptuously. 'And what is Desai? A so-called GP. From Leeds or one of those other northern places. Desai. Desai blows pills down horses' throats.'

'We'll see who's right. The only one of those women who's any good is Clare, and she unfortunately happens to be mad. Going round with that bloody great dog, taking it everywhere, and she hates every hair of its head. I heard her say to it, "Oh, if only you had never been born," and it was no joke. And yet she drags it with her wherever she goes. One day I'll take a chance and ask Harry about it.'

'The one of that little tribe I'm sorry for is poor Freddie. Now the way that poor son of a bitch gets treated . . .'

'*That* could never happen at home,' the two said almost in unison.

It was a minute to official opening-time. In the brothers' veins flowed the blood of some havildar of the days of the Raj, for whom things happened when they were set to happen. Howard looked distantly at the few circling, gathering faces in the street outside. 'Oh, they're not a bad lot,' he said with only a little patronage. 'As lazy as they know how to hang together, and the laziest of the whole crowd is Harry. In a dream, goes about in a dream, like so many of them. Dear oh dear, they must be the laziest people God ever made.'

'They don't kill you much,' said Charles.

The heavy bolts came up and down in their sockets. 'No, and that's a lot when you come to think of it, isn't it?' The shutters clashed aside. 'Mind you, now and again perhaps they haven't tried as hard as they might have to keep us alive.'

187

'I reckon they'll see us right,' said Charles.

And after that, naturally, it was 'How are you keeping?' and 'Just came in last night' and 'Been away yet?' and 'Mind how you go.'

NINETEEN

Harry was in his bedroom getting ready to go round and see Maureen. This was a task that normally took him only a few seconds, little more than the donning of a tie and shoes, but as had increasingly started to happen he was slowed down by worrying about the Adams Institute. Inquiries round the Irving, normally a reliable blank-drawer on virtually any question relating to anything before the present century, produced somebody who turned out to have been somewhere similar a couple of hundred miles away for a couple of terms about ten years previously and found it not too bad a place at all, which would have been more encouraging if the somebody had on their short meeting seemed about fifteen per cent less likely to have been a bit of a twit. The air had been marvellous, the chap had remembered, and the riding, on horses presumably, first-rate. The women? Oh, very pleasant and sociable, like the men.

As he fiddled with a rather bold bow-tie at his little dressing-table mirror, Harry began to see how obliged he felt to go and how deeply he wanted not to. The Adams thing meant a real job and one he wanted and if not an end to money troubles a permanent and reliable patch on them. Its only snag consisted of not being here, and when he tried to point to what that would mean being deprived of he felt mostly a vague apologetic embarrassment. His fingers and eyes stopped moving.

One long-ago summer evening that had presumably had to be got through somehow, Freddie, Clare, he and no doubt other boring little pre-adolescent creatures had been playing a round game too flat and uninventive to be called anything he could remember, but whose object, he recalled quite well enough, had been to guess the other fellow's favourite possession or thing most valued, understanding this in the broadest sense to include anything from a favourite walk or view to a pet rabbit. Another

189

memory of the occasion, which clarified and grew more detailed as he stood there now, brought back to him the small, freckle-faced and profoundly undesirable little thing who had opted for the Taj Mahal – here was a first-rate frolic for lying and showing off as well as, of course, for wasting time and attracting attention. A restraint on objects not actually in some sense within one's experience had satisfyingly seen off the Taj Mahal, and tears had been shed, some of them brought on or aggravated, he hoped, by the sly kick in the shins he had managed to deal freckle-face during the subsequent argument and scuffle. (He had forgotten who or what had got the winning vote.)

So far the party had gone no worse than any average children's do, but then it had come to his turn and for the life of him he had been unable to come up with anything he could call any sort of possession or desired object, Fortnum and Mason and much else being variously ruled out. In the end he had tried for the Middlesex cricket eleven, but this had been vetoed when it was found he possessed not a single autograph and could recite the names of only four of its leading players, not including those of its captain and wicket-keeper. After that he was done. The upshot, then, was that whoever might or might not have won this fribbling charade, he had lost, and his routine counter of childishness, inability to be bothered on his part, etc., had got nowhere at all.

Harry wondered why he thought of this, such as it was, at this moment. He was not a man who thought about himself much – took himself as he found himself, so to speak, lived his life by just going on to the next bit. He liked being where he was, which these days boiled down to this house, the surrounding quasi-village, the King's, the Irving, the occasional pal, the occasional Maureen, the occasional library, the occasional trip, a couple of which a year might be abroad. And yet he felt nothing for his house except as the place where he lived, was not fond of or proud of his own personal library, just liked sitting reading and looking things up in it. He felt quite sure it was the same as how Clare felt about the garden – she put time and work into it, did more than wage a purely defensive battle with it but thought and bought and acted ahead, so that it was one of the two or three best kept in the little row (and he quite liked sitting in it), and yet the other evening he had seen from the way she paused on her fork over some dead leaves and looked round that if they should ever pack up and go and live somewhere else she would not even bother to take a farewell look at it.

All right, so what about the people? He was concerned about Bunty, he felt endlessly, boringly, inadequately responsible about Freddie, he was worried about (without really caring about) and would have to do something (or kept telling himself so) about Fiona. As for the Maureens of this world, the state of Adams would have to be a much more peculiar place than it looked if it turned out to have no Maureens in it, even for those of his advanced age. Not much of a set of human reasons for wanting to stay in Shepherd's Hill, was it, Harry? Another memory popped up from nowhere in particular, part of an estimate of his character some officious berk of a schoolmaster had compiled about him and left lying about – lying about in a locked file, actually. He only remembered one phrase – 'very self-contained'. The cheek of the fucking man, he had thought and still thought. As he resumed the apparently interminable task of tying his tie, it occurred to him, very momentarily and unforcefully, that what he needed was a bloody good reason for staying put.

The telephone rang in the hall. The woman's voice that spoke sounded familiar in at least two senses – he recognised it without being able to name it but it was also not the same as before in some way, on top of which it was slightly offhand, or ready to be.

'Is that Harry? Joyce Atkinson here. How are you today?'

'Well, I'm fine, if it matters. How about you?' Surely it was . . .

'It doesn't matter at all how *I* am, but I'm on a teeny-weeny upgrade.'

. . . State Enrolled Nurse Joyce Atkinson with the crackle gone out of her linen. Harry said something – he instantly forgot what, but it had to be something to stop this creature, who presumably really was looking after Fiona in some sense, from ringing off.

'Are you a drinking man, Harry? I imagine in your family you'd have to be.'

'I suppose I am in a way,' he said judicially. 'I wonder if I could have a word with – '

'Well, I wouldn't call myself a drinking woman in the normal course of events, but I don't mind telling you I've broken a little rule of mine this evening and had a whisky.'

'I see. Tell me, how's old Fiona today?'

'Oh . . . Fiona.' The nurse spoke not only in the tones of a professional encomiast but with real personal feeling. 'Now there is a very fine person.'

For the indefinite future Harry put off considering if that statement had ever been truly made about anybody. He had other concerns and was not entirely clear about what they were. 'How is she today?' he repeated feebly.

'She's a good friend to anybody who's prepared to be a good friend to her.'

'What's her, what did you call it, condition? What sort of treatment is she getting? Is there a doctor there I could speak to? Could I speak to her? I've got an urgent message for her from her family.'

Veering back some way towards her official manner, Nurse Joyce said, 'Dr Henriques is engaged with another patient at the moment. Patients are not normally permitted to receive incoming calls.'

'But this isn't a . . . Where exactly are you? I couldn't find that crescent you mentioned on the map.'

'It would be inadvisable for Miss Carr-Stewart to receive a visitor at the moment.'

'But I must see her, I'd like to speak to her but I really have to speak to her in person. It's . . . this official document she has to sign.'

'I can get any message to her more or less immediately.'

'But . . .' Only a feeling of helplessness was helping Harry not to get angry. 'But I've just told you a message is no good. Her personal signature is required to an official document and a seal affixed,' he said, trying much too late to wheel up a counter-battery of legal bullshit. 'An affidavit in the matter of – '

'What do you want to talk to her about anyway?'

'I've just told you, talking to her isn't – '

'What makes you think she's got anything to say to you?'

'It's not a question of – '

'She's a human being like the rest of us, do you realise that? Not a *case*, not a *number*, not a bloody *file*. Anyone would think

192

. . : Well, a fine fucking father you turned out to be, no doubt about that, Harry Caldecote Esquire.'

If there could ever have been truly said to be more of something where something came from, the two at present conversing had run across it. 'Will you just say one word to her?' Harry asked suddenly, louder, higher-pitched, anything that might register as different. 'Tell Fiona that Annie has a message for her and she can get it through me. Have you got that? Annie. I have a message from Annie. A very important message from Annie. Message for Fiona from Annie. From Annie. Please write it down. Annie. Please say it. If you really care for Fiona, tell her Annie – Annie has a message. Oh God.'

When he got the dialling-tone he worked away for some time at telling himself that silence was her only (pissily) dignified way of agreeing to do what he had asked. Then he looked at the half-dozen or so telephone numbers she had given him earlier and thought about trying some of them. Then he heard from the street outside the voice of the minicab that would take him round to Maureen's. Leaving his house by its front steps he heard an instalment of the rolling, jangling noise, as of a giant casting a couple of handfuls of iron poles down some metallic tunnel or channel, that punctuated the day at no system of intervals he had ever been able to discover. He would not have dared to say that he would feel better about it, less impotently outraged on however absurd a scale, if he knew the cause of the distant uproar, but by Christ he would welcome the chance. His thoughts started moving about as slowly as possible along the lines of a lot of life getting like that.

Gordon's in hand he climbed into the minicab. As before, the journey up Fitzherbert Avenue was a real drive, not a crawl, and he only had time to be warned by the driver against the new restaurant in Liege Lane where they gave you tinned grapes with the sole véronique and made-up tomato purée with the spaghetti pot-pourri before being swept round the corner and dropped at Maureen's door. At least approximately there – he was still getting out of the car when he noticed something was different about the house. Yes: the front gate was gone. When he got inside he noticed other changes, pictures leaning against the wall in the passage, a back room apparently quite empty and another with part or all of its carpet up. Maureen herself was different too. Her muttered greeting and peck on the cheek were thoroughly up to standard but she seemed to be giving him even less of her attention than usual. She was more dressed-up, too.

'Well, how are you, my love?'

'No worse than usual.'

'Nothing wrong, is there?'

'Listen, darling, would you mind terribly if we rather sort of got on with things? I've got to go out later.'

'If the schedule's that tight perhaps we'd better not sit about. Only having brought all this gin all his way I must confess I would rather care to moisten my lips with it. Out of the bottle if that'll help.'

'Don't be such an idiot, Harry,' she said, but with some attempt at real apology and taking-back of initial coolness. Uncharacteristically she had hesitated for some moments, but now she got moving in the old style and had the gin-bottle unsealed and two highly respectable drinks poured over ice and a little snogging-area prepared on the sofa with all her usual efficiency.

'Cheers, darling,' she said.

'Marvellous to see you.'

'Look, I do rather wish you'd telephone before you show up like this. I might not have been here.'

'I did, but you were engaged all the time.'

'Having Bernie here for all you knew.'

'I thought I'd take the risk.' He topped up his glass and looked about. 'Having the old place done up? It could do with a lick of paint.'

'Actually I'm moving.'

'Surely not. Not out of London. Not you.'

'House in Regent's Park.'

'You are coming up in the world.'

'Actually I'm not sure I can face it, nattering away with the *surveyor*, and working things out with the *ground landlords*, and the business of the ancient right of *way*, and the rules for when the park is *closed*, and maintenance of the common *gardens* . . .'

But then while she had been going through this rigmarole she had been lowering the venetian blind over the front window and finishing off by twiddling the twiddler. Nothing that might have been taken for the arrival of Bernie happened during the next few minutes. These, even by the non-leisurely tempo common on these occasions, were really quite noticeably few. He offered to fetch more ice as was customary when the present stage was reached, but she ignored this as she restored the blind.

'Darling,' she asked then with the peculiar blend of curiosity and incuriosity that showed a question of some apparent consequence was approaching, 'did you actually enjoy what happened then?'

'Of course,' he said, puzzled, but nothing out of the way. Apparent rather than real consequence was her thing. It went with her being supposed to have a serious side. 'Why, didn't it work for you or what?'

'I want to tell you something,' she said in another voice, another other voice, one he could not remember having heard her ever use before. '*That*, that business has never really appealed to me. I don't actually mind it but if somebody told me I'd have my arms cut off if I did it again not one tear would I shed, not a sausage, me old china.'

Now Harry was astonished. 'But . . . without trying to be funny or offensive or anything you do seem to have got through quite a bit of it in your time.'

'Affection and companionship. Haven't you read about women who screw around to get hold of a bit of affection and companionship and attention? Well, now you've met one in the flesh, mate. The only trouble is it hasn't brought me much of either. It's in and out and away, like you and Bernie and the others, and the nearest to dinner at the Ritz is a couple of gin and tonics in the parlour. You see I don't really appeal to men. I irritate them. The only one who's ever really taken to me is Leonard, and I got too much even for him and when he's been back to see me he's usually only been able to take me in small doses.'

Harry was still astonished. 'Did you work all this out yourself?'

'Leonard explained it to me. But things have changed a certain amount, he said. We're both older. I've slowed down a bit, he thinks. And he's getting rather lonely too. At least he's got to the age when he minds being on his own. So we're going to give it another go. Moving back in together after nineteen years.'

'In Regent's Park.'

'Spot-on, ducks.'

'I hope we'll all still . . . It'll be fun seeing a bit of Leonard again. We'd almost lost touch.'

'You'll be getting back in touch sooner than you think if you go on sitting there. He's due here in about ten minutes.'

'Christ,' said Harry with feeling, and began instinctive preparations to leave.

'Don't be an idiot, darling, stay and have a quickie with him. He'll be delighted to see you.'

'But, but what's he going to think?'

'What do you think he's going to think? You're an old family friend anyway, aren't you, a neighbour? Don't be such a frump.'

'Running a bit of a risk, weren't you, even so, on the timing?'

'Do you imagine Leonard knows what those shutters mean any less well than you do? Or cares more? And . . . darling . . . hasn't it occurred to you that it was rather nice of me not to tell you to forget the whole thing and keep your bloody Gordon's to yourself? And while I think of it, didn't you notice anything different about me from the way I usually look when you pop in with one of your little green bottles?'

'Now you mention it, yes, I did, but nothing much. To be honest.'

'I always thought I'd have made an actress if I'd put my heart into it.'

'Did you ever have a serious try?'

'Or perhaps you just aren't very observant. Now if you possibly can you might totter off and get that fresh ice you so kindly mentioned.'

From out in the kitchen, which had not yet suffered any dismantling, Harry heard a snatch or two of 'Night and Day' quickly drowned by the surge of an engine and crunch of a power-brake that would not have disgraced a NATO strike tank. Doors and voices followed, both pretty loud in their different ways. Leonard. Here was a very small turn in Harry's luck, the chance for quick explanations to be conducted in his absence. He allowed a sufficient time for these, about as long as would be needed for an explanation of the plot of *The Comedy of Errors*, say, with a short note on the role of Pinch. After that, making a noise like a man coming back out of a kitchen carrying a lot of ice, he returned to the sitting-room.

Leonard had changed a good deal over the years. He was still a large handsome man, but he had altogether lost the rather stern rabbinical look Harry remembered from their schooldays, and in recent times had once or twice been mistaken by passers-by for the host of a popular television gift-show. 'Well, this is jolly,' he kept saying, and sounding as if he meant it. 'Sorry I'm a bit early. Though not too early. Well, Harry Caldecote, long time no see. Oh Christ, I can remember him ticking me off at school for using that very phrase. "You're not a bloody American, are you?" he used to say. He was always getting at us for getting expressions and things wrong.'

'He hasn't changed much,' said Maureen.

'I remember one time he actually had the nerve to tick old Prozzie off for using a continental seven.'

'What's *that*?' asked Maureen crossly. It was exactly the sort of thing she most hated hearing about.

'Well, you know, crossed, like a sort of F,' said Leonard, drawing one in the air.

'Ooh, the dirty bugger.'

'The point being, as Harry took about three-quarters of an hour to explain, that on the Continent they make a distinction like this' – he drew again – 'between a large figure one and a capital letter I. So they reckon they need the cross to show the thing isn't a figure one gone a bit skew-whiff. Now we don't make that distinction, so we don't need the cross to show it isn't a – '

'That sort of thing makes me wish I worked doing the washing-up in a station buffet,' said Maureen. 'I'll leave you boys to your class reunion.'

'Shut up, darling, that was just a little flash from the past. You can allow us one of those every ten years, for Christ's sake. Tell me, Harry, what are you doing for dinner?'

'Nothing, actually.'

'Well, you are now. There's a new place off Old Brompton Road some of us thought we might give a whirl. You're invited, nay conscripted. So I suggest we have another quickie here – '

'If we're going out on the town I must powder my nose,' said Maureen, and left the room rather abruptly. As with not a few women there was a limit to how well she liked her men to get on.

197

'You'll have heard all about the dreaded new step, or rather new stab at an old step?' asked Leonard as soon as they were alone.

'Well, some of it.'

'How do you think she's looking, the old girl?'

'Marvellous.'

'She is marvellous, isn't she? Still plenty to say for herself, of course. Ah, and talking of which, while she's out of the way, have you noticed that mannerism of hers where she goes *on* and *on* and *on* about *this*, *that* and the *other*?'

'Yes, I think I have.'

'Well, the really funny part of this whole thing,' and here Leonard came really quite close to bending double, 'what really turned the scale finally and made me take the plunge and ask her to come back, or have me back, was – I know it sounds ridiculous – you know I go in for this fancy electronic junk, well, I was at a sort of posh trade-fair do where a chap was demonstrating a new supersensitive amplifier which is a suppressor as well, in other words it tunes out noises as well as bringing them up, but highly selectively, so that you can have two blokes each a yard away from you and talking at the same volume and hear every word from one and not a bloody peep from the other. See where we're going? Let me top that up for you. In other words you could have a roomful of people nattering away and hear everybody except just one person. Needless to say the thing's about the size of a cocktail onion. Might have been designed especially for the old girl. I couldn't resist it, I picked one up straight away. Next year the Japs'll have one that'll tune out any required section of a symphony orchestra. Mozart's 39th plus or minus clarinets as you prefer. Anyway, I bet you can understand the point.'

Yes, it took a little bit of the embarrassingly sentimental quality out of the marital reunion as it might have struck other people, and made Leonard seem that much more realistic, in charge, having things on his terms. Harry decided it was nice of his old friend to feel vulnerable to charges of sentimentality. It made a good story too to knock off any attempts on the part of old friends to find the situation edifying or charming.

At the bottom of Fitzherbert Avenue a few minutes later Harry, from the depths of Leonard Preveza's gigantic car with its metre-thick doors, glimpsed Freddie and Désirée trudging along the pavement in full paranoia-inducing style, put there on purpose to rebuke the selfish Harry for his indifference to the fortunes of his helpless, indigent brother. Then fuck him and them, he suddenly thought – against many odds he had found a publisher for Freddie's poetical guff, a great altruistic feat in itself, and how much Désirée managed or failed to manage to abstract for her paying-in book seemed a world of concern away. Tomorrow he would write to the Adams Institute requesting more details.

TWENTY

The trouble with less-than-satisfactory ménages, – and in a couple of senses there was no *trouble* at the Freddie–Désirée one at all – is usually held to start in the bedroom. That was certainly the case here, and in the most literal way possible, with bedroom taken in the sense of sleeping chamber. What Freddie liked to lie on was a softish double bed with a blanket over it; what he got was a hardish single bed with a duvet. A hard bed was supposed to be good for his back, or a soft one bad for it. The reason for the duvet was different but he had forgotten it. He liked a thick curtain to keep the daylight out and make for a long sleep in the morning, as long as possible, he sometimes found himself thinking; Désirée liked and got it thinner, which made less difference on her side, away from the window. That meant that Freddie had an hour or two each morning to think things over, and that experience was such that he would readily and regularly have got off his hard little bed that hour or two earlier if he could somehow have come up with a way of doing that without starting the day.

Now and again, in these early-morning self-communings, Freddie got as near as he ever did to working out that while he spent most of his time not feeling very much, when he did feel anything it was likely to be disagreeable or even on occasion painful. When he was some stupidly early age like ten he had been reading something about a soldier's experience in wartime – the Great War, it must have been – and it had said that life at the front, as it was called, was ninety-nine per cent boredom and one per cent fear, and although he had never been one for realising things quickly he had seen straight away that that was a kind of description of his own life. At school, though he had not really known it at the time, he had tried to cover up the fear part by being the silly one, but this had stopped being any good by the time he was about twenty. It was nothing very much, the fear, nothing like any of those phobias they went on about, just enough to make meeting anybody at all not something to look forward to ever, and then he had run into Désirée. Sooner than might have been believed possible she had begun to sort of look after him, take decisions for him, be there when needed, choose his clothes. After a time it had dawned on him that she was set on letting him have more of that than he wanted or than was really good for him or much fun most of the time, and once when he had been in a funny mood after a couple of drinks one Christmas he had said to himself that what he would have been much better off with was six months to a year of Désirée to calm him down and build him up followed by a crafty move on to someone less there all the time than she was, but of course by then it was much too late. And no children. She was quite positive that his nerves would not have been able to put up with them. (Well, just as well for the poor little buggers to stay non-existent.)

Breakfast brought fruit-juices with the fun somehow very cleverly taken out of them, the herbal tea that was better for Freddie than Indian and sweetened with honey similarly deflavoured and *of course*, what else, how could you imagine anything different from home-made muesli that was cheaper as well as also being undemonstrably better for him. It, that is to say breakfast, also on the appropriate days brought *The New Statesman and Society* as well as *The Spectator* and *The Observer* as well as *The Sunday Times*. Désirée was not going to have it said by anybody, in other words presumably by Howard and Charles, that she was the kind of Thatcherite or post-Thatcherite who only, etc. Freddie himself was unaware of any doctrinal difference between the various organs and read the letterpress impartially though seldom for more than a couple of hundred words at a time, its subject seeming to him largely confined to interest rates and people referred to mysteriously as 'live-in lovers'. He found most trouble with the cartoons, which usually consisted merely of serious-looking men smoking pipes or staring through spectacles without any apparent advertence.

On the morning after Harry had glimpsed them taking one of their breaths of fresh air, Désirée said, 'We shall have to start thinking about holidays soon.'

'I thought we'd done all that,' said Freddie. 'Thailand, isn't it? Burma? We spent days on it. Hotels booked and everything.'

'No, no, I'm talking about next year. We'll have to start thinking soon.'

Of all the increasing number of things Freddie hated thinking about, it was holidays. It was not the ordinary airport-lounge exercises and broken-booking wayfarings he minded. That was the part he liked, hoped for, even schemed about – he still remembered getting legitimately lost for nearly a whole morning in Mantua, not a very nice place, but still a place, and having had a coffee and a little look round the shops before Désirée had spotted him from the far side of the entire width of a square and come inexorably snaking across. No, abroad was fine, and no Englishman had ever dreamed more romantically of the alcazars of Granada or the towers of Trebizond than Freddie Caldecote. The snag was that the next seat in the bus to or from the alcazar would inevitably have Désirée in it and the dromedary or whatever it was bound for the tower in question would have her ensconced in or on it looking at her watch. The great Mantua breakout had been a brave but lonely exception, good as a morale-raiser but of no practical use.

Nothing was or ever could be on these trips or anywhere else. For Freddie was *ill*, not actually in a condition of clinical sickness but too close to one to be let out of her sight, in continuous need of special care. The special bed, the special muesli were part of a whole world of special vests, special exercises, special régimes dictated by his prostate. It had been bad luck, that prostate, making his general debility official, public, solid, discussable. He would never now get out of the position of the one who had to be continuously watched over, and watched, by the other. Apart from anything else it was a bit hard because, that aside, Freddie was in pretty fair nick for a man of his age, sound in heart and lungs, regular in bowel performance and indeed of generally vigorous digestion whenever it was not forced to struggle with something specially grown for him in lint or organic manganese. There remained the foot.

'I think we might have a pedicare session tonight,' said Désirée.

'Oh, I don't think we need one of those yet, it can't be more than a few – '

'Darling, it's never the slightest trouble to me, I assure you. I enjoy it. It's such a nice cosy thing to do. And you know you love it yourself.'

Freddie knew no such thing. His feelings about pedicare sessions were mixed, not to say in quiet perpetual turmoil. They were an excellent, perhaps the best, example of the pseudo-treats Désirée was always running up for him. She was the one who got the enjoyment, out of gratified power presumably, from doing something that was supposed to be terrifically kind and self-sacrificial of her and marvellous for him, whereas any enjoyment or benefit he might get was all but swallowed up in humiliation and boredom. (Long inactive intervals, decorated where possible by telephone calls or the occasional providential ring at the door, with him in a state of helplessness, were a great feature of the pseudo-treat.)

Once upon a time, no one could remember when or where, Freddie had been seized by one of those occasional bouts or spasms of nervous energy that occasionally possessed him, grabbed a garden fork and, without a word of explanation, started pronging away at a nearby bed of some kitchen vegetable. By an equally characteristic but evidently unrelated quirk it had only taken him half a dozen thrusts to send a couple of the tines through his own boot and foot. But it was admittedly anybody's bad luck to have got a poisoned toe or two out of the deal. The infection was soon cleared up, but some tenderness and discomfort remained, also the affected area needed keeping an *eye on*, or so Désirée said, bathing it with specially prepared lotion, applying soothing creams afterwards. It seemed natural to apply cosmetic measures to neighbouring toes, clipping nails, getting rid of dry skin and such, and then, overnight as it were, after some careless word or even smile of supposed appreciation, Freddie had found himself committed to a full pedicare session every six weeks or so.

The treacherous, rogue ingredient, what supplied the small but real treat part without which even Désirée could hardly have hoped to mount her project, was that you did feel quite good, comfortable, well seen to and distinguished as to the state of the feet, when the session finally drew to a close and the suede slippers were ceremonially put back on. You felt a cunt, too, but that was an inescapable part of the deal, and it was nothing to

203

how you felt when two of her coffee-shop mates happened (?) to drop in and find them at it. If Freddie had not had a rule against screaming he would have screamed then, but without such rules a fellow in his position might well have found himself going a bit off his rocker. After a pedicare session, and especially after the one with the two mates along, Désirée was quieter for a bit, leaving him alone for ten or fifteen minutes together, as if some deep need of her nature had been satisfied, or, to put the point more in his own style, she had been an old owl that had just polished off an exceptionally juicy mouse.

Every afternoon Freddie had a poetry hour. He spent this on his own in the little green room which opened into and out of the slightly larger orange room where he assumed Désirée sat. Between those green walls he had actually over the past weeks spent perhaps a couple of dozen hours having a fairly serious shot, more serious than he had admitted to anyone else, at writing a poem or succession of poems which as instructed he had passed on to Harry. He had kept no copies of what he had written and at this not very long distance could remember only smatterings of it. What he could remember very well was a reinforcement of his feeling as a boy and a young man that while he loved poetry he had never come across any he really liked. In the same sort of way, he had found with his recent efforts that the conviction, the strong feeling with which he set out on each fresh poem or section seemed each time to have dwindled away long before the end into meaninglessness or claptrap. Nor had the hoped-for escape from Désirée, in creation of new role as poet, in simply doing something she had no hand in, come about. He had been unable not to visualise her all the way, firing up with him at the angry bits, smiling knowingly at the sex. Still, the venture would not have been wasted if it brought in the promised cash (about which he dared not think) and he still had this hour to himself.

From a locked drawer he took out a paperbound book with a label mentioning POEM PART II on a label stuck to the cover. He opened it at a marked inner page, of which the first line read: 'ACROSS 1: Farm animal (6).'

'What do you make of this American business of Harry's?' Désirée asked Freddie later.

'Sounds like a first-rate idea to me,' he said. He could have said, 'Sounds like bloody madness to me' with equal sincerity and equally real feeling, but she was clearly going to tell him about the American business all over again regardless, and he sensed correctly that having shown some small initial approval would cause her some small annoyance.

'He wasn't saying much,' she eventually said, 'but he'll obviously be on the first plane.'

'Well, yes. Top of the tree in his line and all that.'

'Plus,' said Désirée with what she probably thought of as a sly wink, 'no responsibilities any more. Free as the air.'

'Well, he doesn't seem absolutely weighted down with them over here.'

'There's that wretched dipsomaniac creature he has to keep pulling out of doss-houses.'

'No actual legal concern of his, as you frequently remind him.'

'And that son.'

'He seems to be able to steer remarkably clear of him.'

'Think of Harry in America. Only yourself to bother about. No keeping an eye on this, that, and the other. Just fallen into his lap.'

Freddie thought for a moment of saying, purely out of innocent malice, that his brother had earned at any rate some of his success. Then he realised that Désirée had been getting steadily angrier ever since the Harry–America topic had come up. Nobody, certainly not himself, would have called Freddie a keen observer of anything at all, but there were one or two sides of life he had been watching close to for a long time, and the chief one was Désirée. It came home to him now that what he had been watching was indeed a display of anger, anger based on envy, envy of someone soon to be 'free as the air', someone who for whatever reasons had no Freddie Caldecote to look after – and how much of that looking after was necessary or fun or anything else made no difference to this argument. Nothing was ever going to happen to Désirée. All sorts of things might to Harry, now.

It had not occurred to Freddie for what seemed like twenty years to wonder whether he had any feelings about his wife except to wish she could somehow be smaller, quieter, further away, less there all the time, but if he had not rather fallen out of the habit of such ideas he might have said to himself that he felt a bit of sympathy for her. Then everything seemed to swing back to normal, like a fault clearing on a television set, when she said, 'Of course the one person who won't get any consideration at all is Clare.'

'Clare? Well, I suppose he can't . . . Perhaps he could . . .'

'Odd woman, that. I've always thought so.'

If challenged, Freddie would have had to say that he had never come across a woman he would not have described as odd since first noticing that there were two sexes, but he thought he had learnt by now that to hear one woman describe another as 'odd' or 'strange' merely meant that the first was about to propose something derogatory, probably just mildly derogatory, about the second. 'In what way?' he asked, without interest in the answer.

'Well, obviously if Harry accepts this American thing her life takes some sort of turn for the worse, and yet I could have sworn she was delighted he'd been asked, genuinely wants him to go, tells him not to turn down what's evidently a plum of a job. Evidently he was quite taken aback with the idea at first but now he's coming round to it. Doesn't that strike you as odd?'

'Well, if it's as good a job as that . . .'

'Unless . . . it's only just occurred to me – unless she's so keen to stop being his housekeeper she'll take a bit of a drop in comfort and whatever to get away. To get her own freedom.'

'But why should – ?'

'Harry is the dearest, the most attractive, the most affectionate, I think I'd say the most *charming* man I've ever met. And also just about the most ruthless. He's paying, he's giving the orders, she's the housekeeper, she's the doormat.'

'But he's always perfectly decent and polite and what-you-may-call-it in the way he behaves to her and talks to her.'

'That's when we're there. I'm talking about the things a woman sees, how he has friends in for drinks and then says stay on and have a bit of whatever's going, and poor old Clare has to go rushing out to the delicatessen and so on. And the way she has to keep that garden in apple-pie order without him doing a hand's turn himself.'

'She doesn't mind the garden. She was telling me.'

'And that disgusting beast of a dog of his.'

'He was Arnold's dog.'

'You won't change my mind. He's sweet, he's good fun, he's generous, he's all that, but a true gent he's not.'

Freddie was more than ready to leave it there, so he grunted neutrally.

'And as for those pathetic little drunks and dykes and the rest of them, they're just there to make him look good and feel good, take it from me. Window-dressing. Very typical of that kind of man. Right, Caldecote, come on, time for garden drill. Chop-chop.'

The two dispersed. Freddie's brain moved slowly but it had been known to go on digging away after showier instruments had packed up, and while he got out his broom and shovel he went over the new-angle second dose of anti-Harry sentiment he had just sat through. One of the things he came up with was that probable or possible or very short or only rather short (versions varied) affair that Harry and Désirée had had in the long-ago (all authorities agreed on that). He remembered too reading or hearing somewhere something about women never really reconciling themselves to giving up a former attachment. True or not, Désirée would think she felt it. And Harry in America was Harry far away and given up in a sense never before dreamed of. There was an official account of parts of this between Freddie and Désirée, and he might be a fool but he was not going to bring it up now. Not a true gent. That was an unexpected expression. 'Right,' he called. 'Ready for the fray.'

Garden drill was one of the few moments in his day that Freddie comparatively looked forward to. Under its provisions, he cleared the miscellaneous filth and litter and debris that people going home from the pub (not the King's) or the various neighbouring eateries had thrown into the front drive the previous evening. It was always the same kind of muck, tins and packets and what-not, nothing really illegal or horrible because this was a good area, but Freddie had not yet given up all hope of coming across some exotic intruder, a laurel garland, a Fabergé box, a blackamoor's ear, a book. Now and again he did a little caper or dance for no reason he could think of, except something vague about showing a spirit of independence. He was unaware of being watched, with delight and wonder, by the two young Sri Lankan children next door, who timed these appearances as they could have everything else he did, had they cared to do so.

207

Sometimes he sang to himself as well, but that was less good value because he could only remember parts of the tunes and often got the words wrong:

'Old man rhythm (he would bawl with surprising power),
   You can't find him,
I don't mind him
   Round my door.'

For him, music was rather like poetry in that he loved it but seldom ran into any he could have said he really liked.

After ten minutes or thereabouts the drive was as clear as it was going to get, though the stretches of pavement running either side of it were not, and the same sort of thing could have been said of the part round the corner, where people threw things into Désirée's patch, the part of the back garden nearest the wall, where she had once found two ten-pound notes, about which incident Freddie regularly told himself he would go mad at its next mention. Then it was reading-time for the pair of them in their irremovably respective chairs.

Freddie had never been much of a reader of anything. He would have said he quite enjoyed novels, or those dating from before about 1950 when they stopped writing them. Then, recently, he had started to find it hard to concentrate. He could follow the words as well as ever – it was wanting to do so, feeling that he would be better off doing so than not, that in any sense, anywhere in the world, it could matter what was supposed to happen next.

Although he disliked remembering his father in this connection, as in any other, he was constantly forced to recall the old man's habits as a reader – a very serious fellow in this connection with his Jane Austen and his Flaubert, his Trollope and Thackeray, eventually his Aldous Huxley, his Graham Greene – enough. Then once he had watched his father with a new something-or-other on his lap, open a third of the way through and staying there for minutes while nothing else happened, nothing anywhere around them.

'Boring, is it, Dad?'

'No. I'm boring. I can't be bothered. If it was the book that was boring I could get another book, but I can't get another me.'

A moment later it had started being changed into a joke, but it

208

had never been a joke for Freddie even before he had been old enough to take it in properly. Beside his chair now there lay two new paperbacks, one an award-winning political biography he had been looking forward to getting hold of ever since it had first been announced and knew he would never read, the other a compilation of little-known and presumably wondrous facts from the worlds of history, biology and places like that. It was the mildly surprising behaviour of the female bot-fly that he was reading about when the afternoon walk came round. This brought in feet part II, with the special woollen socks she knitted him with no discernible effect except to make them hot and stringy, as if pieces of hard but fine netting were being pressed against them, and the special shock-absorber pads that might be absorbing all manner of shock but made the shoe too tight. Then the walk itself, then tea, then pill-time and, to be glimpsed somewhere beyond it, still some way off but seeming at moments almost luxuriously near, the end of the day.

Pill-time advertised one of Freddie's major territorial victories, a shelf in the bathroom where he held unrestricted, unsupervised sway. It was only made possible because through some now-forgotten ordinance her first downer regularly went down her half an hour before his first went down him. He would scoop up a handful of the purple-and-grey capsules and the little bright yellow jobs and the Gestapo cyanide pills and engulf the lot with a mouthful of Corsodyl, and he could still keep the breakfast muesli down, and fall asleep a lot, and shit from time to time, and pee about when he wanted to, so obviously some of the stuff was doing its job.

'Let's have a nice early night tonight,' said Désirée. This apparently straightforward proposal had several levels of meaning. An early night and no more meant something like what it said, was basically a temporal expression, advertised that there would be no later part to the evening, no social extension or excursion. For Freddie and Désirée did indulge in these now and again, a time or two a week, from something a comparatively large part of mankind would have recognised as social activity, like the dinner with Harry and Clare, to encounters with dreadful aunt-like, colonel-type, would-be-amateur-entertainer-figure-style creatures better guessed-at than described, and much else between. No – a *nice* early night meant not merely the exclusion of anything in the way of company but the inclusion of what it would be only fair, what it is indeed inescapable, to call sexual activity. This too is better, much better, guessed at than described. Nevertheless something must be said.

The proceedings began acceptably enough with a warm nightcap of milk and brandy. Freddie had forgotten the origin of this – something to do with relaxation, no doubt, and now one would never have asked. Whatever else he might miss or get, he had the brandy, and he needed that. What followed, the main event, was always short, just long enough, in fact. Years back, Freddie had loved to make it last, it and what followed it, reaching out for and usually finding an intimacy there that was sometimes missing from the act itself, something he might have described as a cosy little cuddle. But that never happened now – Désirée, who ran the whole show, was off and away, so decisively that in one or two of his less chirpy moments it had crossed his mind that the object of the exercise had less to do with sex in the old-fashioned sense than to serve as boasting-material among her mates, as it once memorably had at Clare's dinner-table, and no doubt had and would elsewhere. If so, the world had certainly turned itself upside-down.

Anyway: to end like the beginning with the beds themselves – they were drawn up as close to each other as possible, and some ingenious work had been done towards joining their top surfaces with some plastic substance, but in whatever position he lay Freddie could feel the division.

TWENTY-ONE

'What are these things Amerindic you'll be expected to take an interest in?' asked Clare.

'Oh, don't. Presumably things to do with Amerinds, taking the adjective as a classy variant on Amerindian. Which is what a few ordinary Americans call Red Indians to make them feel less genocidal about them. Assuagement of guilt and all that. It's a fairly long story.'

'You mean things like mustangs and smoke-signals and tracking and things, I suppose.'

'Plus a spot of scalping,' said Harry. 'No, with no information about it at all in my possession I can assure you there won't be any of that stuff. It'll be pre-Columbian arts and crafts and languages just for a start. A very rich field, native American languages. Did you know that there were more than fifty *entirely* unrelated groups of them north of the Rio Grande alone? Gave the first white man no end of a turn when he found that out, I can tell you.'

'How do you know that?'

'An American told me once when he had me trapped in the Irving. Together with much else besides. Probably on sabbatical from the Adams Institute.'

'Well, you needn't have anything to do with all the languages and things. Not your field, or whatever it's called.'

'Look, dear, I had a friend, an archaeologist of sorts, whose field was four thousand miles away from the college in Peebles where he got his job, and within three months – less – he was in Scottish country dancing up to his armpits, or oxters as I understand they're called up there.'

'Don't be so babyish, Harry, a trivial thing like that. Think of all the fun you'll have writing home about it. It's a joke.'

'It might perhaps be to write about. It won't be at the time.

211

Like getting taken short. You must have noticed that about life. Visualise *actually being at* one of those dinner-parties.' Harry turned a page of Martin van Oudheusden's letter. ' "In this part of the world the people are noted for their sociability." Pfui, if that means what I think it means.'

'You'll soon get over that. You won't find any difficulty in making yourself – not disagreeable, that's not your way – unagreeable enough to the neighbours to clunk their sociability for good and all.'

'Spoken like a true bleeding sister, one whose brother is taking her out to a slap-up dinner into the bargain.'

'Spoken as well as felt like a true sister, instead of just felt and brooded over and blown up into a grievance which then becomes an excuse for buggering off.'

'Being a heavily edited account of the break-up of my marriages.'

'Not that that's the whole story by a long chalk. First-rate dinner, this, I must admit.'

'You know perfectly well that Daisy was quite happy with me until someone richer and better-looking came along with – '

'Who was also more indulgent to her.'

'Let her get away with more impossible behaviour and talk much more rubbish, you mean. When a man has very low intellectual standards, he – '

'He tends not to say "You have absolutely no comprehension of the issues involved in this argument" or "Shut up" to her, especially in public. Women like men who don't say things like that to them.'

'Fuck that, and Gillian was reasonably contented while she thought I was going to be a terrific success and then found I was only going to be a very moderate success if any or was there someone I didn't notice who was taking more notice of *her*?'

'No, I'll go along most of the way with you on that one, I couldn't stand her myself, as you know, but they weren't at all the same, those two. I've never known a man do that business of marrying the same woman twice and you certainly didn't. I could see the point of Daisy after a fashion, but I couldn't make out what was possessing you with Gillian.'

'What? Lust. I couldn't get enough of her. I thought that was generally accepted. Then I found out that as well as my not being enough of a success she wasn't all that keen on lust either. It took a long time for that to sink in because of how she looked. She had the finest . . . But that's more than enough. Why haven't I told you this before?'

'You haven't been going to go away to America before.'

'True.' Harry drained his glass. 'You might also like to hear that they'll be expecting me to do a certain amount of committee work and there's somebody called the General Cashier that everything has to go "through". And' – Harry turned over another page – 'they're developing a new fish cannery in the area that smells very bad when the wind's in the wrong direction. It's a very strange letter. Some of the time he seems to want me to come and the rest it's as if he's trying not all that subtly to keep me away. He sends greetings and encouragements from a certified frightful shit but that might mean anything or nothing.'

'These are all small points really. It's up to you to decide whether you really want to go.'

'Yes, that's the hell of it. Could you manage without me?'

'Of course. We Caldecotes always manage.'

'Freddie Caldecote doesn't manage very well.'

'That's because he's given up trying,' said Clare. 'Or never really started. I don't say we're not all lazy and won't let other people manage for us if we give them the chance. He made it into a way of life.'

'I wonder how bad it really is there.'

'Well, if it's at all as I imagine it it wouldn't do for you or me. But people can have amazingly little in their lives by our sorts of standards and still jog along somehow.'

'Except that poor little Freddie needs a bacon-butty and stamp-collection kind of refuge, you know. I had this idea that was somehow what the poetry might have done for him. I could hardly see it buying it for him, but I thought it might give him something to do or, what, or be. See himself as a poet instead of just an appendage of Désirée. Self-respect. You must have heard about that.'

'She's got her problems too,' said Clare. 'I still loathe her. I'm staying firm on that, but in the same way as Freddie needs her or has to have her she has to have him. They were made for each other in some horrible way that includes him trapping her as well as her him. She's never said anything to me but looking at her sometimes when she's looking at him, I'd swear she'd give anything sometimes to be rid of him. It's like, a cat can get his claws stuck into you, you can't get them out and neither can he.'

'Stuck. A bit worse than it wouldn't do for you or me. In fact it doesn't bear thinking about. So don't think about it – just go on loathing her as before. Remember – nothing says we have to understand and so sympathise with and therefore somehow tolerate everybody. But you've changed the subject, or one of us has. I asked you if you could manage without me.'

'And I said I could. As for throwing my lot in with someone else – two goodish possibilities.'

'That would mean the end of all this. Wouldn't it?'

'All this' was shorthand for the kind of evening they were having and where they were having it, at Odile's, and more besides. Sometimes when it struck Harry that Clare had had a grim or glum day seeing their mother (which he would have contrived to avoid) or something similar he would give her a treat, of the real not pseudo variety. That only happened now and then but managing on her own or mucking in with a pal would mean none at all of it, and not only no Odile's but no taxis, no help in the house, no one to come and stay a few nights, the little bits that increase in importance with age. But of course she would manage.

'But then this is all academic,' said Harry in a sort of cooing voice, beckoning to the sweet-trolley, 'because naturally you won't be managing without me. Without me present in the body, but still part of the scene financially. Of course you'll be getting an allowance from me. I haven't worked out how much because I can't and won't try to work out things like that, and it'll be complicated, though not beyond the wit of some man or other. You can bet I won't be going without anything I really fancy myself, but I'll see you get a decent whack. Of course I will. I ask you, what did you honestly expect?'

'But Harry dear – '

'And don't argue or you don't get any chocolate mousse.'

'But I couldn't just take your money . . .'

'Everybody would think it a perfectly natural thing to do, an inevitable thing to do, and it would actually make me look rather a good chap too. If they heard about it, which they needn't anyway if you have some pissy scruples in the matter, as I suppose I should have foreseen.'

'Harry, I mean it. I couldn't just live off you, which is what it would be. Like a kept woman who wasn't, you know, throwing anything in. Or taking alimony without having been a wife, not that I'd take it even if I had.'

'You'd accept a legacy.'

'If you cared to knock yourself off and leave everything or something to me I suppose I couldn't stop you. And I can see you're thinking of fifty-thousand-dollar diamond tiaras for birthday presents and a hundred-thousand-dollar gold lamé cloak for Christmas and you can forget it. No. It's nice of you, but no. Perhaps I'm a prig or perhaps I read the wrong sort of books when I was a girl, but it'd be too much like taking a salary and not doing any work, or, no, not unlike that enough. But I'm not an idiot either, so if there's a disaster or somebody gets really ill I'll be on the telephone to you right away, but as a regular thing, a dole, a monthly hand-out, it's no.' She half squeezed and half stroked his arm in the manner of one person not well used to touching another, and said, 'Thanks,' and stopped speaking.

'More coffee?'

'Yes please. I've got the feeling there's still quite a bit of mileage to get through before we call this one a day.'

Harry said quickly, 'Do you think I ought to take this job?'

'Well, dear, that depends a little bit on how much you want it, but from all I can see you certainly ought to want it. You'll soon carve your way through the things-Amerindic and the Cashier man, and there'll be Maureens by the score. In fact you'd better be careful not to overdo that side of it. Your biggest real worry is that fish cannery. And . . . listen . . . if you don't take it you'll spend the rest of your life telling yourself you were a fool not to. And I'll be agreeing with you.'

More slowly, or after a longer interval, Harry said, 'Remember this is Truth Night.'

'I'm remembering.'

'What am I like to housekeep for?'

'Bloody awful, dear. No need to wonder where Piers gets *that* side of his character from. Being free of you would be – I don't know, a sort of perpetual holiday. I was discussing you with Désirée one afternoon – yes, that sort of thing does happen, you know – and she had you to an absolute T. She hadn't missed anything. She hadn't even missed those quite genuine bits of sweetness you slip in occasionally. She was so right about you I had to keep remembering not to hit her.'

'What kind of thing?'

'Oh, everything. There's no point in starting.'

'Worse than Arnold?'

'Oh, far worse than Arnold – Arnold used to put things away from time to time. She's no fool, that woman, whatever else she may be.'

'Not much point in starting on that either. Well, in that case . . .'

'Before you go on,' interrupted Clare, 'there's one thing we have to settle once and for all. Or rather a couple of things.'

'Bunty and Fiona.'

'That's right. Now I happen to like Bunty and nobody could like Fiona, but for the present purpose they start and finish equal. I hereby renounce and disclaim any and all responsibility for both those two and for any bits and pieces like Maureen or anyone else I haven't heard about *and*, just in case you might think I'd forgotten about him, young Piers. He's had quite a few dribs and drabs off me over the years by threats of, I don't know what, nameless depravity. I hadn't the pluck to tell him to go ahead and do whatever he fancied, partly because of you, I think. Now I have, I'd lift a finger to save him from the rope but that doesn't apply any more. If any of the others try to come near me I'll call the police. And you know me easily well enough to believe I mean what I say.'

'But what could there possibly be that might involve you in – '

'That's what I'm never going to be in any danger of finding out. If you want to go on having to do with Fiona and Bunty and Piers it'll have to be direct from the Adams Institute. You understand that, and that it's complete, applies to all your concerns here, all debts of all sorts?'

'Yes.'

'And you accept it?'

'Yes.'

'Down to and including all poems of Freddie's, extant or to come.'

They walked the few hundred yards home along the cracked

paving-stones, their shoulders touching occasionally but no nearer each other. Harry had always found it natural to take the arm of any woman he might find himself moving in company with, including aunts and such and especially if he happened to be in any escort-like capacity. But not Clare's. He supposed he and she must have held hands as children but he could not remember it. With their nine years' difference in age it was as if they had never quite learnt to exchange physical affection, or perhaps shared some diffidence. Anyway it was in silence and perhaps a couple of millimetres further apart than usual that they made their way past the classy hand-painted betting-shop, something called just a healing centre, the pullover shop where you were not allowed to try on the pullovers, a very great number of bulging and bursting black sacks and a firm of estate agents apparently aiming for the oil-sheikh section of the market.

On entering the house the two still said nothing and when they reached the sitting-room, instead of separating, Harry perhaps to fetch a drink, Clare for a different kind of drink or a magazine, he towards his padded green armchair with its hinged flap for holding a book (and/or a glass), she it might have been to her high-backed Parker Knoll a little nearer the recess where Arnold's mementoes stood, they arranged themselves in silence and rather theatrically somewhere in the middle, like enemies confronting each other. He thought he saw her arm trembling.

'We'd better sum it up,' he said. 'You could manage all right without me – not luxuriously but all right, though you won't accept any money from me. I'd be a fool not to take this job and would never stop regretting it. You'd be happier without me. I don't really do any good here. That looks like an end of the matter. I go, don't I?'

'I never said I'd be happier without you.' Clare seemed to speak indignantly.

'What was the phrase, like a perpetual holiday?'

'Who wants a perpetual holiday? I don't want a perpetual holiday. A perpetual holiday would be like perpetual prison. I don't want you to go to bloody America. I was going to put all the arguments for your going as fairly as I could and until a few minutes ago I was going to pretend I thought it might be rather fun without you but then I found I hadn't got enough integrity to deliver that particular lie. Because I still think you probably ought to take the job but I'm not going to, what was it, spend the rest of my life telling myself I was a fool not to try to prevent you from going.

'As for that perpetual holiday,' she went on, bursting into tears at this point, 'three weeks in Broadstairs would do nicely and I've already worked out that you could stay with the Prevezas when their new house is ready. What can I say? My life is here with you and you're awful, you're everything I said about you but you're family and I'm used to you, and you know I don't think anybody in the world understands as well as I do how important it is to be used to someone. Of course you know yourself it's not a question of replacing Arnold in any way at all but nobody could replace a child or your best friend or anybody else either and that's not a reason for not having anybody anywhere ever again. And now if you're very kind you'll go out and get yourself a whisky or have a pee or something that takes about two minutes.'

Harry followed both these suggestions and when he came back found Clare looking nearly normal and sounding completely it. 'There's a job in America,' she said in the bored-fascinated style of a television documentary, 'which there are several good reasons why you should take. For reasons of my own I should prefer you not to take it. Will you be doing so?'

'No,' said Harry. 'I had a funny act all ready to do about the fish cannery but now we've got to it I can't do it. I'd decided before we came out this evening, about a minute and a half after opening the letter, in fact, but I decided all over again when you turned down the gold lamé cloak. And aren't I supposed to want someone myself? And of course I'm not going to have you taken away from me whatever it's called.'

He went across the room and put his hand on her bare shoulder near the neck and she put hers on top of his. They looked at each other for a moment, an entirely adequate moment, and with plenty more to say next time were turning away for now when Towser, who had done no more than snuffle and growl tolerantly at their arrival, now put on a top-intensity display of excited hostility soon explained by the ringing of the front-door bell.

'Who is it?' asked Harry.

'Bunty,' said a very troubled voice, one that managed to sound ashamed of itself as well.

Clare looked at Harry without expression. 'Well, if you want to leave her standing on the doorstep that's up to you.'

Bunty's appearance if anything outdid the sound of her. She might have been crying for hours, her face had been hit twice visibly, her skirt was ripped, her shirt possibly slashed, there was blood on her arm, not a lot but not a scratch's worth. She found it hard to say much at a time but she was able to tell them enough of what Popsy had done and said to her.

'Chased you out?'

'Shoved me out. I heard the bolt go in.'

'You walked here?'

'Ran most of the way. Good job I've got good shoes. Sensible shoes. Always believed in sensible shoes.'

'What had you done, according to her?'

'Nothing special. Just gonc on being me. There was a business with a radio.'

'How long's it for, this . . . banishment?'

'For good. Really for good this time. I'm to collect my stuff in the morning.'

All these questions had come from Harry. He decided that others, to do with police, landlord, etc., could keep. Clare said little but went into action with hot water, soap, combs, nightdress, well-known and highly regarded but imperfectly understood stuff like witch hazel. Harry had had the thought that Clare, though he remembered her saying she liked Bunty, might choose to convey her disapproval of the girl's 'orientation' and way of life in a few of those glaringly subtle ways that women were so good at running up on the spot, until he remembered he was not dealing with Gillian or Daisy or Maureen or any of them and remedially called himself an asshole a few times in the intervals of ministering to Bunty. Towser too did his bit, soon settling down, sighing and shifting massively near the foot of the sofa.

'Sorry about this,' said Bunty. 'It's not much use saying so, but I am.'

'I know.'

'I'm so sorry to be a bother to Clare. She can't care for me much.'

'Yes she can. She does.'

'I'll be gone as soon as I can, of course, but I'm afraid you're stuck with me for a day or two. I've got some money – '

'Tomorrow.'

TWENTY-TWO

'Is this your normal way of going on? Or have you had some terrible shock or something?'

'I don't understand,' said Fiona.

'I mean has something terrible happened in your life, like someone you knew just dying or you seeing somebody just this minute knocked down and killed in the street right in front of you? Or is there something else along those sort of lines you reckon I ought to know about?'

'Why should it, why should they? I don't know what you're talking about. Nothing's happened, nothing like that.'

'Oh, so you think it's a perfectly ordinary way of going on, do you,' said her companion, a sharp-featured little man of about twenty-five with restless eyes, 'to invite a perfect stranger you've known it can't be more than twenty minutes into your bed?'

They were lying in it at the time, or rather Fiona was lying on her side with her face towards the wall and the fellow, whose name she never learnt or inquired, sat in what could not have been a very comfortable position with his knees drawn up. Now and then he nudged her as if to make sure she was listening or at least awake. Earlier he had said, 'Struck lucky, haven't I? These sheets can't be more than a couple of days old and the place is looking — well, spotless is hardly the word, but I'm obviously seeing it at its most elegant. Got a mate who comes in, have you?'

'I do it out myself when I'm not . . .'

'Good for you,' he had said. Now he went on, 'Do you do it every day, or just as the fancy strikes you?'

The fancy had indeed struck Fiona when this minicab-driver, evidently new to the firm or the area, had come to pick her up to take her round to Marilyn's. The way he had looked at her on arrival at her front door had put it into her head to ask him if he would like a quick drink before they set off, and he had accepted

221

that and her subsequent offer readily enough, but somewhere along the way, or even right at the start, something had clearly gone wrong. But he had seemed pleased enough to have been doing what he had been doing a couple of minutes before.

'I'm sorry if I wasn't up to expectation,' she said.

'Oh, no apologies, I beg of you, Lady Agatha. Not for that, anyway. But perhaps for being prepared to give away to a total stranger what might be better reserved for people you at least know to speak to. If you follow my meaning,' he added, managing to get a remarkable amount of offensiveness into the last five words.

'You were ready enough to take what was on offer.'

'Oh yes. You offered, darling, I took.'

'Isn't that what they call a bit of a double standard?'

'Yes, it is, isn't it? And here's another bit. A drunken man's pitiful. A drunken woman's contemptible. Now according to my computation you owe me four-fifty for the journey we haven't been taking, but I'll let you off that, just to show there's no ill-feeling.'

Fiona decided to have a drink instead of going to Marilyn's, or rather to have a drink and not go to Marilyn's instead of having a drink and going to Marilyn's. She tried the television and then went over on to a video, one of the ones you were not supposed to have. It showed a kind of circle of black and white people doing things to one another and other people doing different sorts of things all over them. Fiona thought she fell asleep for part of it. When she was fully awake again Sean was in the flat. He was looking furious and he had Brendan with him. Before he said anything he pulled the video out of its compartment under the TV set and stamped on it.

'Filthy muck,' he said, breathing hard. 'Against the law and no wonder. You wouldn't get animals to behave like that. Are there any others of that sort here? Because if there are I promise I'll – '

'One on the window-sill, I think.'

He disposed of that. Then he said, 'This is the finish, my love. Funnily enough it's what I came to tell you anyway. From now on I don't know you. As far as I'm concerned you can go to hell. Well, you're going there anyway, aren't you? A woman like you.'

Fiona got through the rest of the evening without any trouble at all, but when she went to bed everything was different, different from anything she had known before. Her face felt funny, as if its shape was changing. Several times she went to look in the mirror to make sure it had not, but she kept finding it impossible to look her reflection in the eye. She saw patterns forming and moving round her cheeks and forehead, and now and then the skin on them looked odd, like the skin on your fingers when you had been soaking them in warm water for a long time. When Fiona moved to and fro she kept staggering, but again not in what she thought was an ordinary drunk way. When she lay down because she had got too tired to stand up she wanted someone to hold her and tell her she was not going to die. She felt too frightened to shut her eyes and yet she could not keep them open. She could remember very little of what she saw when her eyelids finally closed, just enough to make her try as hard as she could not to let it happen again. She was still lying there shuddering when the light outside made her think she had better try to start the day.

What Fiona was accustomed to take on mornings when she felt exceptionally awful, i.e. every morning, was a drink of some sort, and although she knew in a way that it never made her feel any better, somehow you never thought of that or paid any attention to it. In the same sort of way, although she still felt different from how she had ever felt before, she decided, having considered the matter for a quarter of a minute or so, to take a drink now. A bottle of Cyprus sherry came to hand, easy to get down, not too sweet, and not too strong, or not tasting too strong. When it was all gone, which was after about twenty minutes, there was a shorter pause and then she knew that she was going to faint or die or some other thing was going to happen to her that she knew nothing at all about. She got Sean. She was well beyond thinking what she would have done if he had already left for the site.

'Christ, I told you – '

'Sean, something's gone wrong with me.' She could tell she sounded funny when she spoke. 'Something's happening to me and I don't know what it is.' She went on saying the same sorts of things for quite a time. Then he said, 'Lie down on your front and don't do anything till I come,' and hung up.

223

TWENTY-THREE

'Is it, would it be possible to speak to Mr Harry Caldecote?'

'More than possible. This is he.'

'Would you be kind enough to let me say two things to you?'

'I don't see why not. But kindly make it short because I hope to go out some time before nightfall.'

'Oh, this won't take a moment. This is Nurse Atkinson and I'm sorrier than I can say.'

'Do please speak up, I can hardly hear you.'

'First of all I can't remember all the things I said but I can remember the sort of things they were.'

'Oh.' Only now did Harry realise who was at the other end of the line. 'Oh, don't worry about that. We all say some pretty rough things when we've had a few too many. I should just try to forget all – '

'Oh, but that's only part of it. With Fiona in my care I was in a position of special trust. You see the system here . . .'

After a few seconds of having the system there explained to him Harry started to wish very much for a return to being sworn at. Nor was he told anything, could he get so far as to ask anything, of what he would really have liked to hear about in full detail, of how Fiona had behaved and what else had happened to turn State Enrolled Nurse Atkinson into the bawling wreck who had last spoken to him. But there was no obvious way other than the present one for the poor old thing to get herself to feel a little less awful about how she had behaved. He even let her get some distance into a lament for Fiona's misfortunes, an account of her allegedly overlooked good qualities and suggestions for safe-guarding her future. After all, his only necessary task that morning was the composition of a letter to the authorities at the Adams Institute explaining in suitable terms but as truthfully as possible why he would not be taking up their very kind offer. But

224

when Nurse Joyce had got as far as starting to rebuke him for allowing, even perhaps encouraging, Fiona to embrace the bottle he considered he had given her her money's worth.

'How is the dear girl at present?' she asked on valediction.

'I haven't seen her for a day or two. She's at home at the moment.'

'Do give the sweet thing my love and ask her to try to forgive me.'

But before Harry could turn his thoughts towards America the telephone rang again. A loud foreign strange voice said, 'Mr Caldecote, please.'

'Speaking.'

'This is Howard from the post office, you know? There's been an accident to your niece, is she called Fiona? You'd better come along here right away.'

'Is she badly hurt?'

'You'd better come along here right away. Is your sister there? Right, you'd better bring her along with you. Right away.'

He was gone. Harry shouted to Clare and gabbled some words at her. She was dressed in some indoorsy way he did not stay to take in but she said she would follow in two minutes. He ran out on to the pavement, missed the street light at the cost of a slight stagger, missed a Potandum fork-lift truck, missed, coming out of a side-street, a pair of male West Indians on a tandem bicycle, the one in front perhaps thirty years old, the rear one perhaps three and strapped in, each wearing a gleaming white crash-helmet with two narrow red longitudinal stripes. After that there was not much to see but a crowd of a dozen or more people milling around outside the post office. Except that once you started looking there was plenty to see, starting with a pool of blood on the pavement on the corner. There was plenty to hear too. Harry got a lot of that from the other brother, Charles. If it had come in coherent order and Harry had been able to take it all in, it might have gone something like,

'I didn't see any of this part myself, but what must have happened, a van came down the hill and slowed down at the corner and this girl got the back door open and just then the van took off again like a rocket and turned and this girl came spinning out and crashed her head on the pavement, and Howard recognised her as your niece. He called out but the fellows in the van didn't want to know and quite frankly we were glad to see the back of them. Bog Irish, they were, and believe me Mr Caldecote there's nothing in this world you want to have less to do with than a real dyed-in-the-wool mick.'

One of the reasons why Harry understood parts of this only vaguely and missed other bits altogether was because in the meantime Fiona lay writhing on the pavement in front of them with blood on her head and every muscle of her body either jerking or utterly taut or distorted, grinding her teeth louder than he would have thought possible, her eyes rolled back so that only their whites could be seen in a way he had of course read about but never taken literally before, blood flowing from her mouth where he guessed she had bitten her tongue or the insides of her cheeks. She had fouled herself, but it seemed only with urine, though it was to cross his mind later that there was probably so little solid food in her body that there were no faeces to speak of either. The expression on her face was of agony to the point of death, another phrase he had come across in his reading and considered somewhat overdone.

Little old men and women, young people, all sorts talked to Fiona in distressed tones, told her she was all right, would be all right in a minute, would be looked after, wiped the blood off her head and face, asked her what they could do for her or fetch her. By now Clare was among them.

'Can't they at least sit her up?' someone asked.

'No point in sitting up a person in a fit,' she said.

'That's what it is, eh?' asked the man.

'Well, it's not an attack of the twitches, is it?' she asked him, with just a touch of that primeval contempt, of the basic human type for the variant, perhaps in some way that told of the superiority and seniority of the sex that has always had to do the rough work, the real work, the clearing up of the sick and the shit and the afterbirth and the dead bodies while the men think and create art. 'She's warm enough and that's all we can do for her for the moment. What she needs is an ambulance. Obviously. Has – '

'Our problem,' said Howard, arriving at that moment. 'The ambulance was twenty-five minutes coming for Mr Macallister when he had his coronary and it's a miracle he's still alive. Nobody's fault but there it is. Charles, I'll take Mr Caldecote in the shooting-brake with Fiona in the back with him and we'll buzz straight along to Casualty at the Royal Charitable. Those Irishmen must have – ' At this point he yelled something in a completely different voice, not just a different language, at his wife, or perhaps it was Charles's wife, anyway the prettier one of the two, and she understood all right to judge by the speed with which she made towards the telephone. 'And Mr Caldecote, perhaps your sister would kindly come along with Charles in the Marina. Fiona will be wanting to have a woman there when she's coming round. It's only five minutes. Seven at the outside.'

Howard and Harry got the still struggling, twitching Fiona into the back of the car and Howard took off at speed, flashing his lights and roaring his horn every few seconds. Harry clasped Fiona tightly and kept telling her she was quite safe. He saw that the wound on her head was not terrifyingly large. At one point he noticed Charles's Marina, with Clare in the passenger's seat, swing round a corner after them. Just then he fancied he felt Fiona's shoulders relax slightly and he thought he caught her eye.

'What have I done?' she asked in a blurred voice, clenching and unclenching her fists.

'You've had a nasty fall but you'll be all right.'

'Where are we going?'

'To the hospital. They'll take care of you there.'

'Is my face all right?'

'Well, it could do with a clean-up and a plaster.'

'No, but is it all right? Has anything happened to it?'

Before Harry could understand this question they had arrived, in the forecourt of the Royal Charitable Hospital in five minutes just as Howard had promised. By this time Fiona had started to come round enough to be able, with him on one side and a hospital attendant on the other, to stagger and stumble into a bed on wheels in a corridor that led off the main casualty hall. A doctor, or so Harry assumed the undersized white-coated lad to be, peered closely but briefly at the wound on Fiona's head and nodded. A nurse had joined them. 'We'll give her an X-ray in a moment. I'm afraid we haven't a bed for her in a ward just yet but we'll get her into one as soon as we can. Meanwhile – '

'Aren't you going to, you know, give her anything?' asked Harry.

'It's best if she comes round on her own. She's nearly out of it now. We might give her something later to calm her down. Are you family?'

'Yes.'

'Drink, I take it. Any other drugs you know of? Now she's obviously still very confused. Will one of you stay with her? I have to go now but the nurse will be here. If there's any change she'll come and fetch me or another doctor. Fiona . . . Carr-Stewart. Right. Is this her first, do you know? Well, let's hope it scares the life out of her.'

'Much chance of that?' asked Harry.

'Not really, no, but . . . Never say die, eh? Tell me, just out of curiosity, how old? Thirty-five?'

'As it happens, just about, yes.'

'Ten years off the apparent age is usually about right. More when they're really getting on, of course. My old man was one of them, you know, which is probably why I'm here now.' The doctor shook hands with them both, reassured them most mightily and was gone.

The nurse, a red-headed Irish girl like one out of an old-fashioned musical comedy, had got Harry and Clare a couple of chairs in the vast, clanging, booming hall. Between them the women decided what Fiona would be needing in the way of soap and slippers and such and Clare departed. She was silently followed by Howard and Charles, who had been standing by just out of earshot, almost without moving, since finishing what they had come to do.

Harry bent over Fiona. She looked – how? Profoundly ill, like someone who had been lying in hospital for months without changing for better or worse, or prospect of doing either for an indefinite time.

'What are those bruise marks under her eyes?' asked Harry.

'Stretch marks caused by facial contortions. They'll soon clear up.'

'Is she, what do you call it, out of it now?'

'Well. She understands where she is and what's going on but she's still very confused. Not to be left.'

After another hour or more glancing here and there or at nothing in particular, apparently falling asleep for seconds or a couple of minutes at a time, feeling at her face and many times examining her hands in what might have been puzzlement, restlessly moving her limbs but not it seemed in a painful or distressed way, Fiona gave a pleased but still rather puzzled smile and said, 'Harry,' as if she had unexpectedly run into him in some public place. 'How did I get here?' It was uncomfortable to hear her speak with her swollen lips and tongue.

Harry answered this and other questions, could not answer or even understand others and let the nurse cope with yet others. Several of them came up more than once. If he had not known Fiona better he would have said she was not concentrating very hard, or was simply rather drunk as somebody else might be drunk, no doubt missing a good deal of detail but to be conversed with after a fashion provided no great demands were made.

The nurse looked her over carefully and said, 'Can I leave you for five minutes? She'll be all right but if you think you need help give a real good shout.'

The moment he was alone with Fiona Harry did what he had been thinking of for days to the point of mild obsession and for the past hour or so much harder than that. Without much in the way of either hope or forethought he took her hand and said clearly, 'Fiona, do you remember somebody in your life called Great-Aunt Annie?'

'Yes,' she said at once. 'My mother's aunt who drank herself to death.'

'And your sister Elspeth said she, that's Annie, looked like you, and you saw a photograph of her that made you say the same. Do you remember?'

'Yes,' said Fiona steadily. 'Go on.'

'But your mother disagreed. She said it wasn't a good photograph, not much like Annie, who had a different-shaped face from you. Do you want me to go on?'

'You can't very well stop now, can you?'

'Well, your mother was right. I have that photograph, or another of Annie which proves it.'

'Where? On you now?'

'Well, I don't — '

'Show me.'

So Harry took out the photograph that had been sitting in his wallet ever since he tore it out of the album that day at his mother's. 'You see? Not you, is it? It's Annie. As it says. Not like you.'

'No. No, it isn't.'

'Not you. Not your lineage, not your branch of the family, not somebody who inherited something along with you, not your blood, not your stock. So you're not hemmed in by your ancestry. You can step out of it. It isn't you after all.'

Fiona gave Harry a brilliant smile full in the eyes, and a moment later, as he watched, that smile faded, not into its negation or into belief or any adverse feeling whatever, just faded to nothing, then to the sort of directionless semi-amiability she had been showing a few minutes before. 'Do you want this?' she asked almost conversationally, holding out the photograph of Annie.

Harry took it and put it away. 'I'll keep it for you,' he said. Only now did he consider the harm he might have done or how miraculous was the illumination Fiona had seemed to be capable of for that brief time.

'No change, then,' said the nurse, bustling back.

'It's too soon to tell,' Harry said.

TWENTY-FOUR

One Saturday morning a week or so later Kenneth gave a little party at the King's to celebrate his year in the job. That is to say, he chalked the word on the blackboards where in a cruder age his predecessors had scrawled advertisements of the hot pies and eggs and chips to be found inside. A party in the present sense meant no extension of hours, restrictions on entry or handing out of free drinks, not even one per head as a starter. However there were snacks put out in bowls and saucers along the bar and the tables on both floors. They were not very ample or varied and had mostly come out of tins or packets, though a couple of clearly home-made ham or tongue sandwiches and a lettuce-leaf or so were obviously some token of hospitality or humanity. But the thing bowled forward merrily and certainly noisily enough in an atmosphere of friendliness and increased trade. The holiday spirit was enhanced by the sunny skies outside and the knowledge of a national rail go-slow and a strike of air-traffic controllers at Gatwick Airport.

The cronies and regulars did not much care for this sort of party. They muttered a little enviously to one another about young louts who belonged at the Red Lion down the hill or the Lord Percy packing this place out in the hope of a buckshee lager or two – well, they were welcome to as many mouldy peanuts as they could get down. Gloom was deepened and given an edge by the smartly bound new menus in royal blue and wine-list – a wine-list in a *pub* – Kenneth had put on display, and sarcastically distorted fragments of French and Italian were exchanged in accents of the most wounding sarcasm. 'It's the women, you know,' said the fellow from the butcher's across the road. 'You know, like holidays.'

'Of course it is. But how do you mean?'

'Can you remember the time we used to come in here to get

away from them? Well, they're here now, aren't they? Not to speak of the bloody kids. It's the brewers too, mind. I give it five years. Three.'

But such patches of despondency were very few and scattered.

'You're looking well, Freddie,' said Kenneth. 'Quite your old self. Somebody was telling me you're having a book of poems published. I never knew you were a poet.'

'I expect an awful lot of other people will be saying the same thing. It's really for my own amusement more than anything else.'

'Oh. Expect to make a bit of money out of it, though, do you?'

'Not really. As I say, it's more the satisfaction of writing it.'

'Oh yeah,' said Kenneth in faint distaste. Catching a remark from his other side, he said, 'You're wasting your time, my friend. There's no more point trying to put a point like that than there would be trying to argue with a crime baby. Yes, Harry, my good sir, what can I get you?'

This morning Harry had under his protection three ladies who had in the past done very little carousing together. In fact carousing was not the word at all for Fiona, who had called at his house half an hour earlier with the undeclared intention, which he understood perfectly, of taking him to the pub and showing herself off drinking soft drinks in front of him and the world and generally reminding him of the Great-Aunt-Annie factor, as she had already done by telephone a couple of times earlier that week. So now when asked she said with emphatic casualness that she thought she would stick to apple juice. Few would have said she was looking in the best of health but there was no trace to be seen of the pitiful creature of a few days earlier. None at least to a superficial eye; Harry looked at her and wondered and hoped and wished he could do more than hope.

Clare was not much more of a carouser among the three, but she was drinking a small glass of medium sherry. And Bunty was sipping at a glass of white wine. She had just happened to have been in the house when Fiona called and had of course taken a tremendous amount of talking into joining the party.

'Have you got a spare bed, Clare?' asked Fiona. 'Then we could all move in with you.'

'I'll be gone as soon as I can find somewhere,' said Bunty.

232

'Oh no you won't,' said Clare. 'Not as long as Towser's alive, anyway.'

'Is that that dog-monster I saw just now?'

'He's not a monster,' said Bunty, not managing to keep out of her voice all the resentment she felt at this description. 'He's affectionate and bright and gentle.'

'And always in the bloody way,' said Harry.

'You keep quiet if you know what's good for you,' said Clare. 'Or perhaps you'd like to take turns with Bunty with those runs on Shepherd's Hill.' A moment later she told Bunty, 'I'm serious about wanting you to stay. And I'm not just thinking of Towser. You and I could make those bits of rooms really nice.'

'And I'd love to stay. But I can't.'

'Why not? You're not telling me you're afraid of what that, that Popsy might get up to?'

'You don't know her. You don't know that type.'

'It's all a pose, an act. Tomfoolery. I knew a couple of girls like that at college. If Popsy was a man she'd be roaring about on a motor-bike upsetting street-traders' barrows. She's a hooligan, that's all – I'm sorry, Bunty, I know you've been fond of her and all that, but one has to face – '

'Was fond of her. Still am in a way but getting over her now. But about what she's like, she isn't just a tearaway. What about those notes?'

'What, with those infantile threats? They prove my point. I'll huff and I'll puff and I'll blow your house in? Really.'

'She means it. I'm not talking about a half-brick through the window, I'm talking about petrol through the letter-box. Or something. When she sees her chance.'

'Have you talked to Desmond about this?'

'Well, I have. But I will again. He might look in here later. But I can't really make him understand either.'

'I just want you to know the invitation to you to stay with us stands.'

'But you know what I am? Harry's told you all about what I am?'

'Yes. Well, I don't suppose he knows *all* about it.'

'And you don't mind?'

Trying not to laugh at the earnestness of Bunty's expression, Clare shook her head.

Harry had missed this chiefly because of Désirée, who had had something done to her hair you were meant to say something about and who was wearing a new kind of sunglasses he could not be bothered to consider at all closely and who now said, 'Well well well, so it's good-bye America.'

'So it is. Or not hallo America. Or something. Anyway no America.'

'And we know why, don't we?' she said, starting to snuggle up to him right away, in the bloody pub, early lunchtime. She had never been any sort of drinker but out of ignorance or insensitivity could put down a fast couple of stiffies without realising. She took his hand before he could snatch it away.

'Do we?' he asked, wishing he had readily available some lightweight torturer's instrument like a pair of red-hot pincers.

'Well, the USA may not be to everybody's taste . . .'

A powerful surge of reasoned enthusiasm for all things American swept through Harry, from Bob Dylan to Frank Lloyd Wright. Hamburgers, he thought. 7-Up. Baseball caps. Muzak. Mail-order heirlooms. 'That's as may be.'

'But it was all you wanted, wasn't it, what they offered you?'

'Was it? Norman Mailer,' he added abruptly.

'What? Who?'

'Forget it. In fact if you could very sweetly just manage to forget the whole bleeding – '

'That job was tailor-made for you. Everything you'd always wanted – oh, Clare went through the whole thing with me. And you turned it down. Why?'

'Well, you know, I thought – '

Désirée shook her curiously coiffured head and moved her arm another half-circumference round the one of his she already had hold of, at the same time really quite worryingly trying to push her other hand between his thighs several inches above the knee. He tried to brace himself against bits of pub furniture to keep the sensitive areas pointing away from the rest of the room. What was she doing, or thinking she was doing?

'No, you turned it down for a person,' she said into his face with her pharmacist's breath. 'A very particular person. You couldn't leave Clare. Oh, not the living arrangements or anything. She's all you have, the only one that really counts as far as you're concerned. And you're all she's got. And *that*'s what turned the scale. What have you got to say to that, Harry love?'

Harry just nodded his head to that. He was relieved he had had nothing worse put to him. So far. He had been generally prepared with believable stuff about the dullness of life in provincial America, backed up with a marvellously horrific warning-off cablegram from an acquaintance opportunely placed out there (actually despatched just after the big decision had been taken), but of course only personal explanations, preferably ones into which a touch of piss or worse could enter, would suit Désirée.

And how, as they probably still said at the Adams Institute. Seeming to draw closer yet, Désirée said, 'Of course, she's always been the only woman for you *really* over all these years, hasn't she, never mind all the wives and girl-friends and what-not? There's no mistaking it. I've known it almost as long as I've known the pair of you, which is saying something. It's Clare you *really . . . love.*'

Her meaning was sufficiently plain. Harry was so shocked and confused that he struggled abruptly free of the grotesque quasi-embrace Désirée had got him into, saying wild things about a ricked back and cramp in his leg and wanting to hit Désirée as he had never in his life considered doing to a woman before. Fortunately he had knocked over a half-full glass of wine and the added disarray gave him time to calm down, busying himself with tissues and bar-cloths. He wanted to tell her that even in 1990 a man could love his sister as his sister and she him as her brother and nothing more, but that would never do any good. Feeling nevertheless a vile creep he gave her a small smile or other minor convulsion of the lower part of the face. He tried but could not manage a wink. He had known instantly that no words of any sort would be the slightest use.

She gave him back a special glance or moue or wrinkling of the eyelids or all of the three that he knew he would see again whenever they met, oftener, one of those peculiar small grimaces conveying a whole secret female paragraph. The fact that the secret in this case as in others was all balls was neither here nor there, just as with the amour he and she had/had not had all those years ago, a veteran pseudo-secret getting a bit old for its work and now being handily replaced, even if the new one was a bit of a cheap cut in comparison. All to do with power, of course. Well, she was not going to go spreading the word about this one, and he could already see the approach of the bonus whereby he would henceforth be able to hate Désirée with a clearer conscience than before.

Howard and Charles were up at the other end among the gladiators, getting everything right, not overdoing the style with touches of cashmere and real cotton shirts, not wanting to talk about the way they had got Fiona and the others up to the hospital, saying they simply happened to be around and did what anyone else would have done, accepting drinks but scrupulously buying back, working hard at pretending nothing had really happened at all.

'I think what made the most lasting impression on everybody – ' said the black man from the picture-framer's.

'Oh please,' said Howard.

' – was the way you both kept yourselves in the background afterwards.'

'We're just learning the British way.'

'Your lot'll be taking over running the whole bloody country soon,' said one of the bare-armed yobbos from the antiquarian bookshop, sounding fairly neutral about this prospect.

'Well, with the kind of competition that's on offer from some of the locals,' said Howard as lightly as anybody could have asked for, 'that shouldn't be such an impossibly difficult job.'

Just before the surrounding grins started to fade a little, Charles said very seriously, 'If you ask me, the one who really deserves a pat on the back is Fiona for coming in here this morning and not hiding herself away, as she so easily could have.'

It was possible to underrate Charles's powers of tact. The others at once all went serious with him, and muttered their agreement, and glanced furtively over at where Fiona was sitting, and then became elaborately unconcerned.

'How does Freddie stand Désirée?' Desmond asked Harry. 'I've never begun to understand that, unless she keeps him under drugs all the time. And what does she get out of him? It's not as if he's much fun anyway.'

'Oh, I wouldn't say that. But you haven't come here to talk about Désirée and poor old Freddie.'

'I think you must have worked out a way of reading people's thought-waves by the way they wrinkle their noses. Is she here? Oh yeah, with the – Christ, are those things supposed to help her to see?'

'Before we move on to Bunty,' said Harry, 'how's dearest Philippa?'

'Another cigar for the gentleman. Dearest Philippa is as quiet as a mouse just now. A sort of jungle mouse with bloody great claws and teeth, but nothing to what she was.'

'As, yes, I foretold. Now I go and get Bunty and bring her over, and then I suddenly see an old mate I was at school with.'

'Will she come?'

'You know Desmond, sometimes I think your knowledge of women is limited. She's had you under observation from the moment you showed your face in here and has been holding on to her seat ever since to prevent herself from rushing across the room and flinging herself into your arms. She adores you, you bloody fool. It's only going to bed with you she doesn't fancy.'

'Yeah, so I remember you explaining.'

'You're looking well, Bunty,' Desmond was saying a moment later.

'So are you.'

'I'm afraid you're going to think this most frightfully rude of me,' said Harry, 'but I've just this moment seen an old mate I was at school with come in and I simply must go and have a word with him. Would you both excuse me?'

Desmond got Bunty another glass of white wine and himself a pint of lager. Then he said, 'Still staying with them, are you?'

'For the moment. It's lovely and quiet there. But it can't be for long.'

'Not bloody Popsy again?'

'You should see the note I got from her the other day. She says she'll – '

'Hold it for later. First I want to get something settled with you. This may not be a good time but I don't know when I might get a better. How shall I put it? Do you still believe I completely understand what Harry explained to me about what it would be like for you if you came to bed with me? Got it?'

Bunty looked extremely uncomfortable, but she said, 'Yes. And yes, I still believe it.'

'And do you still believe I'll never try to go to bed with you again?'

'Yes.'

'Promise?'

'Yes. I promise.'

'Then would you agree to an arrangement whereby I come and see you every so often wherever you're living and sometimes I take you out to dinner or something and at the end of it I kiss you on the cheek and depart?'

'Oh, that would be so lovely, Dezzie. But I doubt if it would work, not for very long.'

'Why not?'

'Well, I was sort of discussing things with Harry and Clare, you see, and he said he thought there was a lot of truth in something he'd read in a book somewhere . . .'

'Here we go again. Bloody book. You know, a lot of troubles in this world come from reading books. What did this one say?'

'It went, I think I can remember exactly, friendship is impossible between man and woman because there must be sexual intercourse.'

'It's a pretty funny way of putting it, but I can just about make out what it means. But that's just his opinion, isn't it? I mean, where's his reason and his evidence and the rest of it? Who said it, anyway?'

'James Joyce. Irish writer.'

'Bloody Irishman now. All right. Nobody imagined it would be easy. Any fool would know a friendship like that would be bloody difficult now and then. But as for impossible, we'll see about that. Bloody Irishman.'

Bunty took this in, but a moment later gave a small cry of alarm. 'Look, there's Popsy.'

'Where?'

'There, down the other end. I don't know how long she's been there.'

'Doesn't matter much, does it? There's not a lot she can get up to in here. Or are you afraid she'll be waiting for you outside with an axe?'

'Please don't joke about it, Dezzie.'

'I know it's not a joke to you. Something'll have to be done about old Popsy.'

'There's nothing that can be done.'

'Let me have a think about it and chat to some of my mates.'

From her seat near the alcove, Fiona recognised someone who had just come in – actually two people, but one was somebody she had not seen for years, schooldays almost, Priscilla something, in fact she would not have taken her oath it was not the Hon. Priscilla something, anyway a beaming bespectacled blonde girl with, Fiona remembered, a taste for rather flashy and disreputable young men, so either they had met a bit after all since their schooldays or Priscilla had started early. Or both, of course.

'Surely it's Fiona!'

'Priscilla darling, what ages it's been.'

'Let me introduce my fiancé.'

The fiancé was Piers Caldecote. 'We've met,' he said, as of course they had, though over all the years they had probably not exchanged more than a few hundred words. Nevertheless he conveyed it to her now with a sort of wink that her recent or even less recent difficulties would not be raised during the current conversation. He was smartly dressed in a shirt of unidentifiable material and a suit of which it would have been possible to say with certainty only that it had not been made in an English-speaking country. Fiona wondered how her old friend Priscilla would take to the tea-spilling, ash-scattering side of Piers's nature, until she remembered her fame at school as the most inveterate of all leavers of a tide-mark on the bath, and could foresee them getting along together quite harmoniously.

'I thought I might find the pater here,' said Piers now, 'having happened to be passing and intending to introduce him to his future daughter-in-law, but that can wait a moment longer.'

'Trapped at last, then, Piers,' said Fiona. She had thought in the past that he was probably queer if anything but had not been interested enough in him to decide whether it was for real or just for bits of tactics.

'Yes, I've seen so many promising careers in the kind of business I pursue ruined by unsuitable alliances that I've fought most frightfully shy of any such entanglements in the past. But I've recently become slightly rich, and there was good old Priscilla used to my wicked ways, and I thought sort of now or never. I must say you have a very varied clientele in here. There's that frightful Popsy woman who was a co-lodger of mine in one of my less prosperous periods.'

'Is she one of those ghastly women who would rather be a man?' asked Priscilla.

'That kind of thing. A most disagreeable person I would dearly like to see removed.'

'I've come across her too,' said Fiona. 'What exactly do you mean by removed?'

'She occupies at a nominal rent part of a property I think I could obtain and turn into something quite attractive.'

'This must be rather boring for poor Priscilla,' said Fiona. 'I think we might take her over to meet her future pa-in-law, if we can struggle that far.'

'Sound scheme,' said Piers. 'Would you believe, I met somebody *younger than me* the other day who used that phrase *perfectly seriously*.'

Harry, Clare, Priscilla, even Désirée, Freddie as far as could be expected, behaved suitably. Very soon afterwards Piers was pointing his nose at Fiona and saying, 'There was something you wanted to tell me about this Popsy creature.'

'Yes, I had a disagreement with her. I won't go into what, but alcohol was involved and she insulted me. Now I don't know about you, but I don't take to being insulted.'

'Well, in my line of work one does become rather habituated to it, but I fully understand the objections of others. What exactly have you in mind?'

'My kind of life – I haven't really had any line of work, anyway, I've been brought into contact with some pretty nasty people.'

'So have I. Probably rather different nasty people in general description.'

They looked at each other in the little corner by the bar, sizing each other up.

'Would you like a number to ring?' asked Fiona. 'I mean to somebody who'll – '

'I know just the sort of somebody you mean. And one of that sort of somebody unconnected with me is particularly attractive. And if I ring this one I can get some other person, some third party – what shall I say? Made to feel bad? Nervous?

240

Discouraged? Inclined to leave matters alone that we want left alone? Or simply go a long way away.'

'It'll cost you, as they say.'

'Yes, don't they? Depending on how nervous or discouraged I want the person to be or how far away I want him or her to go. Of course. Actually, to be perfectly open with you, just at the moment I could very much do with a number like that. I suppose you wouldn't happen to have it on you now?'

'I can get it for you today.'

'Fine. Here's my card. Just make sure it's me you're talking to, say it's the number I wanted from you, and perhaps give me a name to ask for. Just by the way – what's your particular interest in the matter?'

'Purely personal. If you wanted to be melodramatic you could call it revenge.'

'Ah, a much and dangerously underrated motive in human affairs these days. Well, how fortunate we should happen to run across each other. I hope I'm not intruding but I gather my old dad has been rather a decent chap where you're concerned.'

'Yes, he has.'

'Perhaps you and I shall be seeing a little more of each other in the future. Now I've gone all respectable with an honourable fiancée and everything he won't be so inclined to steer clear of me. We get on rather well basically but he's got the idea that I'm a dangerous criminal and it's always rather put him off me. Most frightful puritan, as you know. Bit of a snob, too. Now if you'll excuse me I'll just rush over and have a word with Freddie while he's clear of Désirée.'

'Hallo, my dear boy,' said Freddie. He had a very attractive smile even if it did make you think he was a bit mad.

'What can I get you?' asked Piers.

'What did you say?'

'Would you like another drink?'

'What a delightful idea.'

'What would you like?'

'What I had last time.'

'What was that?'

'What I had last time escapes me for the moment, I'm afraid.'

'What about beer?'

241

'*Beer*, yes. You know, my life's very much nicer thanks to you.'

'Make sure it stays that way, Nunks. Don't talk about it to anyone, especially – '

'I know especially who, do you think I'm a fool? You are absolutely sure she can't get her hands on that cash you made for me, are you?'

'It's as safe in the PSB as it would be on the moon. They're forbidden by law to – well, to let any person whatever as much as know you have an account with them. It doesn't bother me in the least but I must have told you twenty times before.'

'Oh, at least that, at least that, but I do so like to hear you say it.'

'Mind you don't give it away by buying a lot of fancy socks and ties.'

'You're joking. It goes into bacon butties and stamps and nothing else. Do you know they've given me the use of a *cubicle* now at Hartmann, Leafe?'

'*No*,' said Piers, his surprise and respect tinged with incredulity.

'Fact. Well. One of these days I really would like you to explain how you made that publishers' money into four and a half times what it had been and getting it to me without anyone knowing, without *Désirée* knowing. Making her think she was going to get all there was. And all the time for every penny she gets out of it I get fourpence ha'penny.'

'Nunkie dear, it wasn't quite like that, and I very much doubt if I could explain it to you in a way that, er, rendered it in all its majesty. Also one or two things have happened in my own life since then that have slightly blurred some of the finer details in my memory.'

'Nice fellows, those, you know, coloured gentlemen just now.'

'I'm sure they were. I must have missed them myself.'

'Not that I care for all of them, between you and me. I gave one of them a most terrific pasting the other day, a woman, this was, lives next door to us and plays her television much too loud, or used to. My God, I didn't half let her have it. Worked, too. Had its effect, I mean. Quiet as a mouse ever since. You know, Piers, I'll tell you a strange thing. She's been kicking up this appalling shindy for years and I hadn't had the guts to do a thing about it before. Then I suddenly found myself going for her and do you know what I was saying to myself? I was telling myself I was a stamp-dealer with a cubicle at Hartmann, Leafe, I was somebody. Or am I talking the most arrant nonsense you ever heard?'

'I follow you perfectly. You've got a stake in Mrs Thatcher's Britain.'

'Yes, I suppose it might be something like that. Very odd, though.'

As they walked back towards the house, stepping aside for the passing traffic, Piers laid his arm round Clare's shoulders.

'I've got a little something for you, Auntie dear. Don't open it now, but when you do you'll find inside a small cheque, made out for the amount you so sweetly lent me some weeks ago with a little bonus thrown in.'

'Oh, Piers, I couldn't possibly – '

'Think of it as interest on the loan. You always get good interest on a ready principal. I thought if I was going to turn honest then you must come very near the start after all your assorted kindnesses. I'm sorry I put on that little sort of act of being queer. All Dad's fault, really.'

'How do you make that out?'

'Well, you see, he'd sooner have a petty criminal or a gambler for a son, or think he had one, than a gay. You're a bit the same – I hinted at all sorts of unspeakable depravities to get some money to put on a horse. Which incidentally finished fifth. I doubt if you would have given it to me if I'd told you what it was for. But Dad's much worse. Colossal puritan about money among other things. In fact he puritanicised himself out of a small fortune just the other day. I'll tell you the story another time. Now surely you don't propose to provide all these people with lunch? Well, Priscilla and my dear old friend Bunty will doubtless give you a hand. And how nice that the old pater isn't going to America after all. What a frightful bore that would have been, to be sure!'

Désirée of course mucked in with the best of them when it came to rustling up a scratch lunch. She would be responsible for the salad. As always she skinned the tomatoes – it only took a few seconds and people often commented on what a difference it made. As might have been expected, Clare's kitchen was rather unadventurous – no cumin, no sesame seeds – but Désirée did her best to make up for that by a good pinch of Madras curry powder in the dressing.

It was odd how even on the safest of ground, like in this house, the little tiny worry about how Freddie might be feeling – safe, comfortable in mind and body – never really left her. She knew nothing of love at first sight beyond what she had heard and read, but her first sight of Freddie, looking even more lost than usual at a party for Iron Curtain poets at Gillian's, had shown her plain as plain someone totally vulnerable, unfitted for life in this modern world, not a child, not a simpleton, not a neurotic in the usual sense, but the somebody she must take care of as best she could for as long as she could – if not make happy, for that was no doubt to ask for too much, then at least protect from all visible harm. That she hoped and believed she had accomplished for the most part so far, and probably it sounded like not a great deal, but she was proud of it.

TWENTY-FIVE

Clare stood at the front window of the house in Shepherd's Hill Road and thought of Arnold. It was not particularly that she felt alone, by herself, with the impromptu lunch-party now dispersed. She could never have been sure, but she fancied that the time of day, the weather, the season were specially conducive to thoughts of him, a brilliant late-afternoon in early summer. At such moments she could not so much see him clearly as remember his look, or rather the expression of his she had been fondest of. She had almost never seen it direct because it would change as soon as he caught her looking back at him – in his way he had been a self-conscious man. That look, with slightly lowered eyelids and slightly parted lips, had been a little cool and a little amused and had said in a way that no one could doubt that of course others were fond of her and might even love her in their way but only he loved and understood her all through and knew everything about her. Most people, she supposed, had never had anything like that in their lives at all, and she knew she should count herself luckier than them whatever happened or might happen to anybody at any stage, but all she could do was miss it and rest in the knowledge that in a few moments the memory would fade until the next time.

Just as these thoughts were passing through her head a freak ray of sunlight, perhaps the reflection of a passing reflection, lit up for less than a second a tiny patch of carpet between the radiators, or rather lit up the one tiny gap where the carpet had not been quite properly fitted up against the wainscoting. In that infinitesimal place for the shortest possible time her eye picked up a distant gleam of luminousness, faint but unmistakably of a peculiar, individual green, that of the little piece of chalcedony that had been embedded as an ornament in that baroque flute of Arnold's, embedded there until the day when the cleaning lady had dropped the instrument on the floor and not noticed the fragment of stone skitter across the carpet and disappear altogether until this moment.

After the necessary taking-up of carpet and floorboards and all manner of other disturbance the minute piece of carved chalcedony was eventually replaced, more firmly now, in its setting and the flute itself restored to the alcove with Arnold's other former possessions. It had always been the outstanding piece in the collection and from now on, as before, Clare would bring it out in response to inquiries and explain that it had been the property, as it bore the likeness, of the distinguished and elegant Giacomo Fraschini, who had many times employed it to delight the court of Frederick the Great at Potsdam more than two hundred years before.